The Devil's Work

By Jack McGugart

Copyright © 2015 by Jack McGugart

First Edition, 2015

ISBN: 978-0-99653-562-5

Published in the United States of America

All scripture is taken from the King James Bible On-Line Version with permission.

The following are recognized Trademarks: AT&T, NCR, JP Morgan, The New York Times, The Wall Street Journal, Kendall Jackson, You Tube, Kroger, Tastykakes, Dunkin Donuts, American Express, James Bond, Macy's, Lamborghini, Ferrari, American Express Travelers Checks, Smith & Wesson, Brooks Brothers, 60 Minutes, New Jersey Transit, Amtrak, Philadelphia Eagles, Seventy Sixers, Philadelphia Flyers, Yuengling, LinkedIn, UPS, Ritz Crackers, The University of Notre Dame, Cheez Whiz, Dallas Cowboys, Chevy Bel Air

Other Acknowledgements: NYU, Home Alone©, Tiffany's©, New Jersey Transit©, Amtrak©, Philadelphia Eagles©, Seventy Sixers©, La Salle University, CDC, World Bank

Dedication Page

This book is dedicated to my wife for her love
and never failing support.

*All that is necessary for the triumph of evil
is that good men do nothing.*
Edmund Burke

TABLE OF CONTENTS

"Though I walk in the valley of darkness I fear no evil,
for you are with me."
Psalm 23

* * *

This put into words the spirit he needed to dwell on as he went forward. He was on a collision course with pure evil, and he knew the only thing that was going to get him through alive was his faith in God.

CHAPTER ONE

He that hath ears to hear, let him hear.

Matthew 11:15

Tommy MacDonald had always enjoyed train rides. Flying was something different all together. Trains were not usually crowded and with few exceptions, there were not assigned seats. He had taken the train from the suburbs to center-city Philadelphia for years and he was always able to get a bench seat for three to himself, or worst case, share it with one other person. The train was only ever packed during rush hour, and with the long hours he worked, he traveled early enough to miss the rush in the morning and returned well after the crowd in the evening. Flights, on the other hand, were most often full; the seats were too small, and invariably, he would end up sitting next to someone who was overweight and encroached on his space. This flight was no exception.

When he first took his window seat, both the middle and the aisle seats were open. He had high hopes for an empty row so he could sprawl and really relax, but an attractive blonde snagged the aisle seat a few minutes later. *At least it wasn't a bad trade off*, he thought to himself. There was still a steady stream of passengers coming down the aisle when he spotted one guy who was stout and unkempt, perspiring from the effort of boarding. His blue wool suit may or may not have been cheap, but the guy was heavy and he had the kind of body shape that even a great tailor couldn't compliment. He hoped, for his and the blonde's sake, this guy was going to sit somewhere else. No such luck—he slumped into the middle seat. This was going to be a long flight.

On the train to and from the suburbs, people kept to themselves. On flights, people wanted to share. Perhaps they were lonely because they were farther away from home or away for longer periods of time. Tommy had a lot to do, and his expectation that the portly gentleman would find the blonde more interesting was instantly fulfilled. It's amazing when the most handsome, well-dressed men are sufficiently insecure for overt flirtation but the portly guy busting at the seams is not at all intimidated.

Tom's routine for any flight was always the same. Pull any paper folders he intended to work on, his tablet, and some reading material from his briefcase. This was once quite the process but with the gradual conversion from stacks of pages to electronic files and laptops to tablets, he no longer needed much space to spread his work items. Today the reading material was a copy of the airline's monthly magazine. It was always good to have some paper reading material to keep occupied until cruising altitude was attained and it was then clear to use electronic devices. Tommy would read during the time it took to board the plane and get to cruising altitude, and again when the flight attendant signaled that all electronic devices had to "be placed in the off position" for descent and landing. He loved that phrase, and could picture in his mind the committee that spent an hour coming up with just the right words to describe what they wanted every passenger to do, covering all the bases and not using any terms that might offend someone. In between takeoff and descent he would usually power through some serious work. This day, his routine unraveled in minutes.

Attractive blondes, he supposed, are often pushed to be somewhat rude to get any solitude. The portly gentleman, after settling in and making both Tom and the blonde physically uncomfortable, quickly set out to make the blonde mentally uneasy. He fanned out his copy of USA Today and was one of those types that had to share the news he found interesting, sparing no details and adding his boisterous commentary. His first shot was sports, and although she had an athletic build, she seemed to show no interest in any of the sports highlights. He then moved on to international affairs, and she started to show not only no interest, but a level of annoyance. He then moved on to finance, at which point she let him know in no uncertain terms that she "had some work to focus on and did not want to be BADGERED all the way from San Diego to Atlanta."

Around the same time they reached cruising altitude, Tom anxiously switched from the exciting article he was reading about the ten best steak restaurants in the country to a prospective client proposal. He had no sooner gotten his client folder opened and tablet fired up when Mr. Portly turned his attention to him. Mr. Portly, aka Pete Robinson, was actually an overall nice guy, and slightly interesting. He was a self-proclaimed geek who worked for Verizon managing a network of servers. Tom maintained some level of focus on the proposal work and politely responded to Pete's news service with perfunctory comments like, "That's interesting," or, "Imagine that," or, "What a world." Like the blonde, Tom was athletic, but not a sports fan, interested in domestic and international affairs, but only in relation to his investments, and while finance was appealing, he didn't think that Pete was in any way an expert.

At that moment, the captain made an announcement that they were moving to a higher altitude in an attempt to avoid expected turbulence, and asked that all passengers stay seated. He added that the food and beverage service would be delayed until the ride was once again smooth. What could be better than turbulence and a talker?

Perhaps because Tom and Pete had achieved a level of tolerance, or because she felt she had probably been too hard on Pete, maybe both, the blonde initiated a conversation with Pete about cell phones. She was a high-end real estate agent and needed the latest and greatest smart phone. Pete unloaded an arsenal of facts on every must-have device and she had a ton of questions. Their conversation provided a reprieve for Tom to figure out the structure for the proposal, complete the outline and the price quote. It would now be just a matter of adding the boilerplate, and his weekend with Claire wouldn't be haunted by the proposal at the top of the to-do list.

Even at a different altitude, the bumpy flight continued. The captain came on the speaker again stating that they were moving to yet another altitude, and of course the food and beverage service would be further delayed. Pete and Carol, aka the blonde, continued their conversation and had moved on from cell phones to a riveting discussion on tablets. Perhaps the way to an attractive blonde's heart was through her electronics . . . *gee whiz, what a big hard drive you have, do you browse here often?*

Despite his growing thirst and hunger this flight was panning out pretty well. He didn't think he would be able to get more than three hours of nearly uninterrupted work done on a flight. Pete and Carol had exhausted their technical gadget discussion, and Pete went back to his paper.

"Hey, Tommy, would you believe that in this economy, the government is considering food rationing?"

"Pete, I wouldn't put anything past the government after what we've seen since the Great Recession," Tom replied.

Pete added, "Yeah, a real bunch of geniuses, come up with a housing plan that ultimately kills the housing industry, puts millions of people out of work, millions on food stamps, doubles the cost of health care, opens the southern border, raise the minimum wage, lets about five million go on disability, and lets people into the country with a deadly virus. Do you think we might run out of food if too many are eating for free, while too few are able to produce enough for the rest?"

"I think you summed it up pretty good, Pete," said Tom.

Carol chimed in, "Not quite. They've done a lot more damage than that, and God knows what they will do next."

"Oh, he knows; Jesus is coming back and boy is he pissed off." Pete huffed definitively and buried his head back into the paper, probably searching for something that would really get Carol's attention.

4

It was obvious that Pete was attracted to her; who wouldn't be—she was built well, quite pretty, dressed impeccably and spoke well. Tom doubted that Pete had gotten this far since high school, if ever, with such an attractive female.

Tom was getting tired, and he was also a coffee addict, so he flagged down a flight attendant as discreetly as he could and asked if it would be at all possible to get a cup of coffee. In her sweetest southern voice the flight attendant answered. "Why, darlin', if I walk down that aisle with a cup of coffee for ya'll, I will not only be violatin' the captain's orders, but everyone else will want somethin' to drink."

Tom was relentless. "Suppose I go to the rest room and on my way back I find a cup of coffee?"

"Well, sir, if you do find a cup of coffee, I am sure ya'll will be thoughtful enough to drink it there and not spill any, despite this just awful turbulence." She winked and said, "Perhaps you will need to visit the restroom in about ten minutes."

He winked back. "You're a daisy."

The next ten minutes seemed like an eternity. He checked his watch at least three times. His mind went back and forth between his work and his plans for the Thanksgiving holiday. His thoughts on work were scattered and bounced from the consulting engagement he had just finished to the proposal he had just prepared for what was hopefully his next engagement—and most importantly, the paycheck that it would generate. He struggled to put work aside, and had an even harder time putting the work he had completed to rest. *Did he deliver real value or just information? Would the final payment come on time? Did he piss off the CMO in the closing meeting that day when he told him something about his operation he didn't want to hear, but needed to hear? Would he be invited back? Tom, stop torturing yourself!*

He would get the proposal out early in the morning after sleeping on it for the night. This was something he always did when he felt he had enough time. Sometimes something important would come to him that he failed to mention and could be critical for getting the business. The most common change, though, was being sure not to overcommit. Much better to under-commit and over-deliver, but most importantly, never, ever, be late. He had learned that the hard way. He was certain that he wouldn't get a decision until late in the year or early next year. Most large company budgets were fairly exhausted by this time of the year. He would likely have the next two months off unless a bluebird flew in the window.

That brought his thoughts back to Thanksgiving weekend and Claire. He loved all holidays, and Thanksgiving had always been his close second to Christmas. In some ways he liked Thanksgiving better, although with his Catholic upbringing, such a thought seemed sacrilegious. He loved the long lazy morning, with a steaming cup of coffee in hand, while watching the parade. He was amused at all the statistics the announcers provided about the floats; how many hours it took to build, helium required to fill it, and how many workers it took to keep it tethered. Equally funny were the famous singers whose lip-synching was so painfully, yet hilariously obvious. Ahhhhh, and the smell of the food being cooked. Nothing like the smell of turkey cooking in the morning and the medley of smells intensifying into the afternoon; sweet potatoes, mashed potatoes, creamed corn, stuffing, string bean casserole. Most dear to him on Thanksgiving was the gathering of family. He would miss family this year.

He had moved to Atlanta because it made more sense for business. His specialty was bank management in general, and credit card processing, in particular. Many of the large banks and credit card processors had offices in Atlanta or just three and a half hours up the road in Charlotte. A major credit card terminal maker and several point of sale system companies were also based in Atlanta. This helped to keep his travel time down and reduced the cost for his clients. When he did need to travel, Atlanta was ideal as home to a world-class international airport and main hub for several airlines. He preferred living in the suburbs, but again, business convenience won out, and he chose to live in a townhouse in the downtown area, or as they called them in his native Philly, a row house. No maintenance, no grass to cut, simple, but fairly spacious, close to clients and the major highways. Probably the best thing about Atlanta was his fortuitous meeting with Claire.

They had been seeing each other exclusively for seven years. Their meeting was by chance, but Tommy supposed most meetings happen that way. He had driven out to the burbs to find a better place to run in the evening. When he got there he needed to go to the bathroom, and quickly. The most convenient and expeditious place was the men's room at a supermarket he was about to pass.

On his way into the store, and in an obvious hurry to get to the men's room, which of course he had been told was in the far corner at the back of the store, he heard a women's voice ask, "What are you doing, laps in the grocery store?"

He almost didn't even bother to look at the source of the question as he replied, "Just going to the men's room," but as he turned his head to look, he stopped dead in his tracks. He hadn't been so awed and attracted by a female in this way since he was a senior in high school. Looking stunned and no doubt stupid, he listened dumbfounded as she spoke in a soft Irish brogue, "Well, if that's what you're about, you better be on with yourself or there will be a call for a cleanup on aisle twelve." His expression mirrored a little boy whose Mom had just told him to go clean up his room, and he quickly moved on. He couldn't finish up quickly enough. He was shy by nature, but adaptable, and certain situations caused him to completely change his stripes. He could become a heat-seeking missile on a mission. He walked across the back of the store, looking up each aisle to see if she was there. As he reached Aisle 1 he thought she must be gone. The optimist within him said she must be turning a corner between one of the aisles. He quickly, but relentlessly ran up Aisle 1 and in doing so realized he was actually doing laps in a grocery store.

When he got to the front he thought, *same approach . . . look down all the aisles, but also scan the checkout lines and out the window in case she has already made her way to the parking lot.* Good God, now he was a 35-year-old acting like a teenage boy.

Breathless and heart pounding, he spotted her in a checkout lane by the head of Aisle 1. *OKAY, play it cool; grab a couple of items and get in line.* There were three people in line; the stunning strawberry blonde, more strawberry than blonde, and two other people, both of whom had more than the permitted 15 items. They glanced at him as he asked politely, but as quickly as possible, if he could go ahead of them since he only had two items; how could they refuse? He moved ahead and stood beside Claire. A good sign, she spoke first. "So, finished all your laps already, have you?"

"Yes, I was quicker than usual." As he looked down at the conveyor belt he said, "Sooo, what are we having for dinner?"

"*I,*" she said with dramatic emphasis, "am having a nice medium-well filet, baked potato, and salad, with a glass of Merlot."

"Wow, what a coincidence, my favorite," Tom grinned. He couldn't tell if that was her final word, and also her signal that she wasn't interested, or if it was because her items had been rung up and she got busy with making the payment. He got even further confused when about three feet away from the checkout stand she turned, clearly knowing he would be looking, and gave him a sweet smile. The items he grabbed—an oversized chocolate bar and a box of garlic-flavored Ritz crackers—didn't take the teenage cashier but a few moments to ring up and he paid with cash to make the process faster, but it dragged on seeming indefinite.

He moved quickly outside and nearly panicked when the lot showed no trace of red hair. Just as he slowed to look up and down before crossing the traffic lane, he heard her voice behind him. She was standing beside the door and he came out so quickly that he didn't see her. "Are you looking for another place to run?"

He started walking back toward her, unsure of what to say. "Well, actually, I was looking to see if I could catch up to you."

"Well you did, congratulations, I guess. I'm an editor at the *Atlanta Daily News* and if you can find my number, feel free to give me a call." Then without hesitation, she strutted to her car.

In many cases his ego would have kicked in and he would have said, *to hell with you*. No ego this time, just a bit of a challenge worth the effort. She wanted to check out his sincerity and see if he was really interested. He quickly got to his car, raced back home, and jumped on his computer. Within 15 minutes and without spending a dime on a background check he had her office number, home number, cell phone, business and personal email, and home address. As an editor for the World News section of a major newspaper, her biography was readily available. Tom smiled as he read the details and picked up the phone to call her house.

"Hello, this is Claire."

"Hi, this is Tom MacDonald, the guy who runs laps in grocery stores. I hope I am not interrupting your dinner."

"The potato has another 30 minutes, and after I put it in the oven I thought I would pour a glass of wine and wait for your call."

"Pretty sure of yourself," he said with a self-amused smile.

"More hopeful than sure, but it seemed that we both wanted to meet outside of the store."

"So, what brought you to the United States?" They talked for another 20 minutes until he reminded her that the potato would be done and she needed to get the steak on the fire. The conversation came easily and when she agreed she better get to dinner, he parlayed this into an opening to ask her to dinner the next night. They were inseparable from that moment.

He glanced at his watch and was relieved. The ten minutes were up. He excused himself to get by Pete and Carol, and started down the aisle with a cat-that-ate-the-canary smile. The smell of the coffee was filling the cabin. The flight attendants had left the service area and were seated in the back of the plane as if they had no idea who had made the coffee, let alone left a cup out with creamers and sugar.

He poured the cup and savored the first swallow. His caffeine-starved body instantly gave up its hold on him and the weak headache vanished. He returned to his seat and put his head back, totally content in the moment. He was ready to resume his Thanksgiving dreaming. His relaxed thought wandering was interrupted by Pete. "It must be dangerous work being a board member for Universe Card." Instantly Tom jerked forward and asked what Pete was getting at. "According to this article, three of their directors have died violent deaths in the last two months," Pete explained. "Can I see your paper for a minute?" asked Tom. As Pete handed over the paper he turned to Carol. "Finally, something in the paper that you guys are actually interested in."

Tom's heart started racing and his thoughts were scattered and confused, racing in different directions as he read the article. He was typically unshakable and calm, but a deep-rooted fear, fear at that level where visceral instinct operates and there is no conscious control of the thought process began to stir as he read. He had to read the article three times before he was able to fully absorb the details. Each time he tried he couldn't get through the article because his mind would uncontrollably go off on a tangent. Could this really be happening? How could it be executed? What could be done to stop it?

Wasim Mirza was now chairman of Universe Card, the largest credit card organization in the world, and a director of Primary Card Processing, known in the industry as PCP. Tom had first crossed paths with Wasim years ago and the immediate suspicion of Wasim, who he thought he might be, and that he would eventually do what Tom now thought he was doing, was reawakened.

Third, Universe Card Director Dies Violent Death

Within the past two months, three members of the Universe Card Board of Directors have met with violent deaths. David P. Cunningham, age 57, former CEO of AT&T, fell from the balcony of his 12th-floor hotel room while in San Francisco for a board committee meeting.

Two other board members also recently died. On Sept. 18, Robert M. Patterson, age 63, former CMO of NCR, was on a hunting trip when he fell down a hill and struck his head on a rock. On October 26, Teresa M. Giuliani, age 49, chief economist for JP Morgan, was brutally raped and murdered while jogging in Central Park, New York, NY.

Attempts to reach and obtain comment from other members of the board and executive officers of the company were unsuccessful. They were either unavailable or refused to comment on the matter. Wasim Mirza, Chairman of the Board and CEO of Universe Card, issued a statement expressing the board's and company's condolences to Cunningham's family and that his loss would be greatly felt by the board, and the business community at large.

The board has been in debate with the US government, the United Nations, and World Bank concerning the use of the payment system as a tool to ration food, water, and gas on a global basis. Members of the board have been divided on the issue and are scheduled to reach a decision on the matter at the January 8 meeting of the Universe Card Board of Directors.

Mr. Cunningham is survived by his wife, three children, and four grandchildren. Mr. Cunningham was a resident of Short Hills, NJ.

Pete must have noticed Tom's emotional state. "Did you know one of those guys?"

"No, I never met any of them," Tom lied.

Pete continued, "Could be a coincidence, but what are the odds?" I mean, you must be talking ten million to one. It's more likely that one of them would have won the lottery." Pete shook his head and said, "Seems more like the work of the devil to me."

Tom turned towards Pete, looked him squarely in the eye and simply said, "Exactly!"

CHAPTER TWO

Remember, therefore, how thou hast received and heard, and hold fast, and repent. If therefore thou shalt not watch, I will come on thee as a thief, and thou shalt not know what hour I will come upon thee.

Revelation 3:3

Pete was all wound up as they prepared to "deplane." He kept beating Tom's ear and doing his best to try to shine for Carol. Tom could tell that Pete was dying to ask her out but was too afraid to try, especially with him within earshot. Guys' egos can't take getting shot down in public.

As they started to walk down the terminal toward baggage claim, Carol said she needed to freshen up in the ladies room and that it had been nice to meet them. Pete extended his business card and seemed shocked when Carol reciprocated. Pete kept talking, but Tom was in a deep fog. They, too, exchanged business cards as they entered the baggage claim area recognizing that their paths were not likely to cross again.

The fog and mental confusion continued. Tom's mind continued to race and in helter-skelter mode. He was so distracted by that article that he didn't even power his cell phone up, let alone look at it while getting off the plane like all the other people trancing through the airport like complete slaves to their electronics. *Oh well, a few minutes won't matter,* he thought.

When he got on the interstate and headed north toward town, he pulled out his cell. He always paused as he opened his phone, expecting to see a missed call or a text message. One text from Claire appeared and he smiled: Call when you get in, can't wait, Love Claire. He called Claire. "Hello, love, how was your flight?"

"It was pretty good. I got done what I needed to despite the chatter from the guy next to me."

"A little light conversation should do you good after a long week to help you wind down."

"I guess, but it didn't quite work out that way," Tom said. Although it was his intent not to bring up the article and his thoughts on it until after Thanksgiving, she immediately recognized that something was bothering him.

"You seem a little down, boyo. What happened?"

"I read an article that was disturbing. I will fill you in completely after Thanksgiving. For now, let's just have a nice holiday together and not let the troubles of the world get in the way, Tom replied sounding more hopeful than he felt.

"I agree, but it must be weighing on you, and I know how you are with problems—you can't rest until you fix them," said Claire, increasingly concerned.

"I will let this rest, I promise, replied Tom."

"You'd better, because I want the best you have for the holiday. Are we still on for dinner tomorrow night?"

"Yes, I made a reservation already, Maggiano's in Buckhead at six."

"Will you be able to get out of work by then?"

"Yes, we are planning on wrapping everything up by two, but we never do. Four hours should be plenty of extra time to make dinner by six. Have a good night. Love you."

"Love you too."

He called his favorite local restaurant and ordered dinner to be delivered.

As soon as he got home he fixed a gin and tonic, turned on his favorite playlist and sat down, planning to review the mail and put together a list of things to do for Wednesday. The mail was mostly bills and account statements. The list of to-dos grew longer as he added paying the bills to the top along with running, taking his clothes to the cleaners, picking up wine for Thanksgiving dinner, and a sub-list of all the items he needed for their picnic lunch on Friday. Tom shot off an e-mail to his longtime friend Andy Newcomb, who invited he and Claire to their traditional Sunday-after-Thanksgiving BBQ, asking him what they should bring. Sending the e-mail reminded him to add to his list: sending out the proposal and a fence-mending e-mail to the CMO whose feathers he had ruffled the day before.

The doorbell rang just moments after he finished reviewing and sorting the mail. The timing was perfect; dinner arrived, and he was absolutely famished, since the food and beverage service was skipped on the flight. After paying the delivery service and plating the food, he sat on the couch and flipped to the late night news. The big story was the continued trouble in the East. Radical rebels were continuing to grow in numbers, ferocity, and gaining territory. The bottom line was that in the war on terror the terrorist were winning. Not a word was mentioned about the executive deaths at Universe Card or the increasingly heated global debate over rationing.

The Swiss & mushroom cheese burger and side salad went well with the glass of Merlot that chased his cocktail while dealing with the mail. He turned off the news and turned on his show tunes playlist. He was hoping that a couple of glasses of wine and some tunes with meaningful lyrics would counterbalance the late-night meal—and sti-fle the ominous concern he felt about the article he read on the plane. Two glasses of wine and about 10 tunes later, he felt the day's exhaustion set in for what should be a solid night's sleep.

But as soon as his head hit the pillow the reeling thoughts began. After an unmerciful rehash of the consulting engagement that had just ended he moved on to the question gnawing behind every attempted diversion. Was this really happening or was he just piecing together a fabric of conspiracy that wasn't really there? For hours he tossed and turned thinking about his impressions of Wasim Mirza, the things Jim

Martin had said about Mirza, world affairs, and the unsettling similarities, whether real or in his mind, with a book in the Bible. The Book of Revelation was believed by many to foretell the end of times.

Jim Martin was the one person who seemed to know Mirza best, and his comments caused him to read Revelation years ago. Tom had to get in touch with Jim. Jim was the only person who might have some clue about whether the scenario now unraveling in his head was real or the product of an overactive imagination. Unable to rest, he leapt up at 3:00 a.m. and added: setting up a meeting with Jim to his list for tomorrow. The cathartic exercise of converting some of his growing alarm to action allowed Tom some rest. He slept till nine thirty.

After a couple of lazy cups of coffee, he changed in his running clothes and took off for a long run. Running helped him clear his mind and sort things out. His rested mind reached a preliminary conclusion that his theory was real and he planned to determine it was correct. The first step was to talk with Claire and Jim and then go from there. Jim knew Mirza well, and was wired at a high level in the world of card payment processing. He was CEO and president of Primary Card Processing, the largest card payment processing company in the world. Tom knew from past experience that Jim was a borderline alcoholic, and if he could get enough drinks into him he could have a slip of the tongue.

Claire had a good view of everything of importance that was going on in the world, and equally important, she had the brand of common sense that his mom had. It was without fuzz or clouds—clear, black or white, right or wrong, free from doubt. There was no room for ambiguity in that pretty, intelligent red head.

Tom had planned on getting up early to knock out everything on his to-do list, and after a troubled night and sleeping in, he now had a lot of time to make up. Most people are unsuccessful in business and in life because they do the easy, fun, nearly mindless things first instead of the important things. Tom wasn't any different than others except that he knew this, and he also knew from experience that by doing the difficult things first it not only produced good results, but also made for a healthier frame of mind.

He prepared a nice, diplomatic e-mail to the CMO. He added the boilerplate and made some minor changes to the prospect proposal that came to him while running, and sent it out. He told them he could start immediately. He hoped and felt sure that wouldn't happen, but it sounded good and created a sense of urgency that might help line up the job for an early start in the new year. He called Jim Martin and got his voicemail. He invited him to dinner on Friday night at a high-end "in-spot" restaurant that he knew Jim would love and have a hard time turning down. He told him he was working on a new engagement and could use some of his insight and guidance. His story was simultaneously a total fabrication and entirely true.

He knocked out all of the items on his list and had just enough time to shower and shave, get dressed, and make it to the restaurant before Claire. Maggiano's was one of his favorites. Growing up in Philly, he experienced the best in Italian food and Maggiano's was one of the few fine Italian restaurants that still had the old-school Italian dishes that he loved. It had the ambiance of restaurants from a time past, with white tablecloths, waiters dressed in tuxedos, and a classic, solid wood bar that was crafted by people who knew how to ornately carve large, rich pieces of wood and finish them with opulent elegance.

He knew Claire would be late, and asked to be seated at a secluded table where they would have some privacy, but still have a good view of the entire restaurant. The latter was a personal hang-up that had no explanation. He preferred to sit with the back wall of any room behind him to have a clear view of everything in front of him. He figured he was either a gunslinger or pirate in a previous life and had some enemies, or maybe he was insecure, or maybe he just liked to see what was going on. Who knows; but at least he would be able to see Claire when she arrived.

He had arrived 10 minutes early although he was sure she would be at least 30 minutes late. World news editors worked late, and she would go to her house in the suburbs before doubling back to the city. Plus, she boarded a horse, Celtic King, at a farm near her house and not a day went by without her stopping to check on him. She loved that horse more than anything or anyone in the world.

Tom sipped his Merlot as he thought about him and Claire. At thirty-seven, she was a bit younger than him. She was born in Cork, Ireland. She was the oldest of seven children, and she acted it. She was sweet and loving, but when the situation called for it her soft demeanor quickly shifted to tough and unyielding. As befits a redhead with long, wavy hair, she had a short fuse, and when the end of the fuse was reached, her temper would go off like a bomb. She had long since lost her Irish brogue, but would turn it on for effect when she felt she needed to make a point with emphasis.

As much as they cared for each other, they both suffered from what he called "lost love syndrome." He was madly in love with his high school sweetheart, but when he went off to college she was swept off her feet by an investment banker where she worked. Claire also had a high school sweetheart that she was forced to leave behind when her father was offered his dream job as editor, in his dream city of New York, at the most renowned newspaper in the world, the *New York Times*. She attended NYU, which is where she picked up a touch of liberalism, and had a second relationship that ended when he graduated. As a result she loved her horse, her parents and she loved Tom, but she never really forgave her parents and had a somewhat arm's-length relationship with her entire family. She could not make a total commitment to Tom, either, but that wasn't a problem. He firmly believed that you get one true love, one trip to the stars and if it doesn't work out, then, that's that.

He ordered a gin and tonic that he nursed while he waited. He reflected on his relationship with Claire. It was odd because it defied their natures and values. They were both religious—Irish Catholics, of course. They both had attended parochial schools for 12 years, both went to Sunday Mass, usually together, and despite Claire's touch of liberalism and dose of political correctness required of all US news media, they were both simple, conservative people with good values. Claire loved folk and country music because of their values and similarity with her Irish musical roots. They were both basic meat-and-potato people with middle-class values; salts of the earth.

He took his last sip of his drink and with his head tilted back he saw her the moment she entered the dining room. He was not alone. You would have thought you were at a tennis match with the way most of the guys in the room turned to look at her, and the women turned to see what the men were looking at, as she was guided by the Maître D' to their table. She was fairly tall at 5'10"; not heavy, not skinny, but had a perfect and very attractive figure. The dress she was wearing accentuated her curves and the color, a deep forest green, contrasted beautifully with her strawberry-blonde hair. He couldn't help but broadly smile and contemplate how great the weekend would be. He rose from his chair to greet her with a hug and a kiss—almost a bit too long and deep for public—and told her how lovely she looked. She blushed as he held her chair while she slid into it.

"It is so good to see you, Claire. I have missed you too much."

"Tommy, I would feel unloved if you missed me less than too much," she answered with a warm smile.

"Did you get the paper and Celtic King put to bed?" Tom inquired.

"Yes, the presses are rolling, and Celtic King should be good till tomorrow afternoon, if not Friday morning."

"Good, then I have you're undivided attention," Tom's smile did not match his serious tone.

"You do; I think the question though is do I have yours? You look like you need a good night's sleep and you have an unmistakable uneasiness in your voice."

"Claire, have you heard anything about the three members of the Universe Card board who have all died violent deaths in the last few weeks," Tom started.

"I did, it was mentioned in one of the stories I reviewed yesterday about the debate over food rationing."

"What are the odds? It's probably more likely you'd win the lottery, which is exactly the problem."

"What problem?" Claire sounded confused.

"The three members were all opposed to using credit card data for the purpose of rationing," Tom said, his voice lowered and he began to slowly lean in.

"So, Tommy, you think someone had them murdered because of their position on the issue?"

"Yes, a policy matter like this is up to the board and I think they were killed to secure a majority vote on the matter."

Claire looked skeptical. "Let's say, for the sake of discussion, that you are right. Other than being a concerned member of the world community, how would such a dastardly deed affect you and your ability to do something about it," she asked.

"I think I know who is behind it and I think the motive goes way beyond rationing of food, water and gas." As Tom spoke, the concern in his voice was almost tangible. "Who do you think is behind it?" Claire asked, with her eyes narrowed.

Tom didn't answer, but with a backward lean glanced to the waiter, who stood patiently, looking for an opportunity to take their order without disturbing their conversation. As soon as their eyes met, the waiter took his cue and with a broad smile told them his name and took their drink orders. Tom asked for a bottle of Claire's favorite, Kendall Jackson, Summation. The waiter, an older black man named Samuel, asked if they wanted any appetizers, and Tom said he was ready to order, but the lady would need a few more minutes.

"Tommy, are you having your usual?" Claire asked casually, lightening the mood.

"Exactly; why fix what isn't broke and tax my feeble brain? And are you getting your usual?"

"I don't have a usual," replied Claire innocently.

"Yes you do, seven out of ten times you get eggplant parmigiana, and three out of ten you get chicken parmigiana."

He smiled as she laughed and said, "Oh my God, I think you're right."

"Are you going to answer my question," Claire asked.

"Yes, but I don't think now is the time or the place, and I want to enjoy the holiday. Let's give it a rest until Friday." This seemed to satisfy her. "Are we still on for a picnic lunch?"

"Yes, I have the day off unless something serious happens, which isn't likely to occur on Thanksgiving. Even the bad actors of the world like a day off and a chance to get some Christmas shopping deals."

They both managed to stay away from the topic they each most wanted to talk about for the rest of the evening and focused on the details for their weekend plans and Christmas. They were going to spend most of their time together until she went back to work on Monday. He neglected to tell her that he would cancel their Friday night dinner plans if he was able to meet with Jim Martin, since he hadn't heard back from Jim, and because mentioning it would lead to further discussion of the taboo topic.

They were nearly finished their entrées when Tom sensed someone was watching him. As he looked across the room, his eyes locked on a pair of dark, piercing eyes staring directly at him, emotionless. It was Wasim Mirza, and he was with Jim Martin. Tom froze as a chill ran up his spine.

They both stared at each other until Samuel arrived at the table to discuss dessert, bringing Tom back to the moment. Claire shook her head no, and as much as he wanted his usual cappuccino, he suddenly just wanted to get out of there as quickly as he could. It wasn't going to happen. Wasim pointed him out to Jim who was now looking at Tom and Claire's table. Tom signed the check and waited for Samuel to return with his credit card. As soon as he and Claire rose from the table, he could see Jim waving to him and beckoning him to his table. Tom took Claire by the hand and said there were some people he had to say hello to.

Jim and Tom shook hands and both expressed how good it was to see the other. Jim said he had gotten his voice mail, but hadn't had a chance to get back to him yet. He didn't think that Friday night would be a problem, and he would get back to him early Friday morning.

While they were going through the amenities, Tom noticed that Wasim was giving Claire a thorough look from top to bottom and bottom to top showing a clear, but detached interest in what he saw. Tom introduced Claire to Jim and Wasim. Jim was very complimentary of Claire, while Wasim coolly and simply said it was nice to make her acquaintance. Jim was about to ask them to join he and Wasim for a drink, but Tom and Claire managed a quick exit when the entrees arrived at the table.

The valet had Tom's car at the front of the restaurant in less than two minutes. Tom held Claire's door, tipped the valet, and hopped in. Neither said a word to the other since they left Jim and Wasim.

"I guess our plans for dinner Friday night are being changed?" said Claire, breaking the silence.

"Yes, if Jim gets back to me and is able to make it. I am really sorry but it is very important."

"So, then, I am to have your undivided attention for the entire weekend except for Friday night and when you aren't thinking about food rationing and murder conspiracy?"

"Well Claire, as always you are a quick study."

"Where do you know Jim from," Claire asked casually.

"I have worked with him on several occasions. He is currently the head of Primary Card Processing. He knows the industry and Wasim very well—Jim's a pretty decent guy."

"Yes, who is this Wasim character? I hate to make snap judgments but he gave me the creeps and I don't think I ever met anyone with a colder or more evil-seeming look."

"Wasim is the chairman of the board of Universe Card," Tom paused. "Claire, he's the guy I suspect had the other board members murdered. I think he's plotting to control food, water and gasoline on the basis of allegiance to the devil."

* * *

Claire asked no further questions. The drive to her place in the suburbs was very quiet. They avoided talking about the subject but both thought about little else. As they got under the covers, he wasn't sure how it would go, if at all, and he wished he hadn't been so glib because of the cloud he had now set directly above in their sky. But as he reached over to hold her she immediately responded, and they made love like lovers should after a long separation. Not quite as good as make-up sex, but overall and on balance, much more satisfying.

Tom fell asleep quickly, and slept solidly until about 3:00 AM. He jolted awake and immediately started churning, thinking about their chance meeting with Jim and Wasim, the things Jim discussed with him years ago and the Book of Revelation. The last time he looked at the clock it was five fifteen.

The next thing he knew, he woke up at eight forty-five to the early smells of Thanksgiving dinner. That made two days in a row that he slept past 7:00 AM. He was becoming a slacker, albeit a tense one. Claire was not only up, but she had showered, had on day-time make-up, and a nice, casual and festive outfit on. Tom was drowsy.

"Oh, thank God the coffee is made," Tom said, eyes half-open.

"You can thank him for providing it but you can thank me for making it," replied Claire. She was at the stove sweating onions and celery for the stuffing in a sea of foamy butter. He brushed and held her hair aside from behind and kissed her neck as she leaned her head back, fully enjoying the moment.

"Do you need help with anything," Tom asked.

"Thanks for offering, but I've got this. I want you to enjoy the day the way a guy should. Go watch your parade, a football game or two, and I will join you when there is a break in the cooking action. Be assured, though, you are required to make the gravy, because you do it best and I am gravy challenged."

"Deal—estimate for dinner time?"

"Around five o'clock if I get this turkey in the oven by ten thirty, which shouldn't be a problem."

Tom's eyes narrowed in on the bird. "That's a pretty big turkey for two."

"It is but my lover likes turkey leftovers, especially day after turkey sandwiches."

"What can I say—you got my number," said Tom with a smile.

Tom turned on the TV, half-watching the parade while he gathered and organized his thoughts. For the past two nights, the same questions rolled around his mind—is this really happening, and if so, how will it go down? He was nearly certain it was real for a few basic reasons.

Firstly, Universe Card was a business focused on making money and even though board members might disagree on how to make money it would have to be pretty serious to kill one, let alone three people, over a money-making disagreement. There was no money to be made by helping governments control the distribution of food. Third, and most importantly, Wasim Mirza was someone who was cold enough to have people killed. Yes, this was real.

Doubt and suspicion surrounding who could be responsible and what the true motive was followed this conclusion, creating even more questions. Based on all the indicators in the world, Tom's first theory was a political group—most likely radicals in the East. His second and much more serious theory was the beginning of end times. For years, especially by many in the West, it was proposed that one of the signs and prerequisites for the end times was the control of food by the devil. One of the most written about and discussed of the all the verses in the Book of Revelation was Revelation 13:17. *And that no man might buy or sell, save he that had the mark, or the name of the beast, or the number of his name.*

Most scholars agree that if you wanted to apply these verses to the means of controlling the necessities of life, you would most likely have to do it using the universal means of buying and selling, which in the modern world means credit and debit cards. To control them, you had to have control of the electronic card processing networks. *Let him that hath understanding count the number of the beast: for it is the number of a man; and his number is Six hundred three score and six.* As outlandish as he thought it might be, Tom leaned toward end times.

As powerful as the radicals had become, it was unlikely they could generate enough influence to gain control of the payments system let alone facilitate its linkage to social media, which Tom decided would be leveraged to distinguish the devil's followers from all the others. Control of the distribution of food, water, gas and probably medicine was beyond complex—it was biblical—and Tom wasn't convinced the extremist could pull it off.

Putting aside a welling sense of fear that grew as he accepted this could signal the end of the world as we know it, Tom focused on the how. If you took control of the payments system for the "purpose of rationing" and you were then able to link it to social media, you would have the power and the information to decide who could buy and sell. Implementing rationing would make gaining control much easier. Once you had control, you could then bend it to your purpose; a simple matter of inserting the programming. If you were going to really control things, though, you would have to link the payments to other vital systems that housed what you needed and wanted to know about people to bend them to your will. Not so simple but doable. Ironically, the devil was in the details.

Tom was so deep in thought spiral he didn't notice that Claire had entered the room. "You seem to be paying more attention to your tablet than you are the parade," she said as she placed a tray on the table that held a glass of orange juice, a small carafe of coffee, scrambled eggs, and toast. He told her he was just making some notes on the parade. "Sure, so you can wow somebody at your next business cocktail party with Macy's Thanksgiving Day Parade trivia. If I know you, which I think I do, you are figuring out how Satan is plotting to take over the world," Claire said with a laugh but Tom could tell there was some worry behind it.

Tom looked at her quizzically. "Did I ever tell you how pretty you look when you know you have caught me red-handed?"

"You needn't change the subject. I plan on watching the parade with you." He put the tablet down, refreshed his coffee and leaned over as she sat down to give him a kiss.

The parade ended. "You must have gotten up pretty early to get such a good head start on dinner and not need any help," said Tom.

"Yes, I got up quite early."

"Even though you put a loving spell on me, I wasn't sleeping well, and decided it would be better to deal with the tasks at hand rather than continue counting sheep," Claire replied.

"Was it something I said," Tom asked.

"Apparently, I decided it had been too long since I read the Books of Daniel and Revelation," said Claire guiltily.

"Were they revealing?"

"Yes they were. Quite revealing. And I feel I will be prepared for our discussion tomorrow," she continued.

"Good, because I am not prepared to discuss that topic today. I have my mind set on you, Thanksgiving dinner and Christmas dreaming."

"In that case, boyo, stop organizing your thoughts and start working on your Christmas shopping list like you said you would."

"Yes ma'am," Tom winked. He finished his breakfast and declared that he was going to go for a quick run, get a shower, and check his e-mail before the Dallas game came on at noon.

Claire got the turkey in the oven, left to check on Celtic King and then came back to work on the side dishes.

While running, Tom laid out a clear plan about those he needed to talk to and what he needed to learn to move forward with his quest. He still had doubts, and he also had a good bit of fear starting to grow within him. If he was right, he was about to dance with the devil.

On the way back from the park, he stopped at the church that he and Claire went to when he was at her place on the weekend. He thought it would be deserted, but to his surprise there were quite a few cars in the parking lot. At first he thought there might be a Mass that morning, but he remembered that Claire said there was only one Mass that day and it was at 9:00 AM. He apparently wasn't the only person who was concerned about the grimness of world affairs and wanted to thank God in person for the blessings they had. He prayed for the strength to do the right thing and to do it right. He only stayed about fifteen minutes because he thought he'd better get back in case Claire needed help with dinner.

"Do you need help or do you have a handle on things," he asked gently.

"The turkey is in the oven, the sides are in process and I visited with Celtic King. Go relax," Claire smiled.

"Okay, I am going to hop in the shower."

Tom got his shower, turned on the traditional football game, and started to call his brothers and sisters. Although he lived far away from his family, he made a point of keeping in touch with all of them. The conversations were lighthearted and heartfelt, and everyone spoke about trying to make a point of having a family reunion within the next year. In between food prep steps, Claire also called her family members. While the conversations were also heartfelt, Claire still had trouble being close to her family. She loved them and they loved her, but she was never able to put aside the trauma of being pulled out of school, away from her boyfriend, and transplanted on the other side of the Atlantic at a critical time in her upbringing.

The afternoon was peaceful, quiet, and full of love and holiday spirit. Tom was almost able to put the possibility of the Antichrist at work on earth out of his mind. He made the gravy and they sat down to a wonderful Thanksgiving feast. "Claire, you are a very good cook, but you out did yourself this time. That was absolutely perfect. I am stuffed and will need to double my run tomorrow."

"I am glad you liked it but you still have dessert to eat.

"I am not sure that I could eat anymore."

"Nonsense, I made your favorite and am preparing *my* favorite after dinner drink to go with it."

"Wow, lemon meringue pie and milk," Tom grinned sarcastically. "No, wise guy, Derby Pie with Irish coffee."

"I feel like a king."

"Why don't you go pick out a good holiday movie for us, while I clean up and prepare dessert?"

He picked out *Home Alone* because it provided the holiday feeling and, more importantly, a load of laughs. They enjoyed the movie, and half way through had their dessert. Claire fell asleep before the movie was over. Tom coaxed her into bed, cleaned up the dishes and decided to get a good night's sleep. Again it started—as soon as he put his head on the pillow the thoughts he suppressed most of the day broke through and he started processing everything all over again. By three in the morning, he had rerun the whole scenario in his head, piece by piece, and was then finally tired enough to fall asleep. They both awoke at seven AM as if the alarm had been set, had their coffee and he began preparing for their picnic lunch.

* * *

As soon as the car doors closed, Claire started asking questions. "What exactly do you think is going on?"

"Let's wait until after lunch," replied Tom.

"I've waited long enough. This is eating you up and I can tell you are not sleeping."

Tom could tell she would not let up. "Okay, you read the Book of Revelation, right?"

"Yes, a bunch of wild statements made by John of Patmos that has several different interpretations. Some say it was about the early persecution of the Christians and meant to give them hope that they would be delivered. They feel that the mark 666 is the number of the name, and the name was Nero. Nero persecuted the Christians. Then there are those who firmly believe that Revelation describes the end of times where the world is ravished by the four horsemen of the Apocalypse, which is the precursor of the takeover by evil, the rise of the Antichrist, and after much tribulation, the Second Coming of Christ. I've seen shows on television that attempt to draw connecting lines between things that are going on in the world today and supposedly what Revelation is predicting.

Then of course there are the TV evangelists who use end time fear to increase their viewership and get more donations," Claire finished.

Tom turned and said, "You're pretty worldly and pragmatic. What do you think?"

"I don't know what to think. The world has certainly been going to hell; morals continue to decay, we have no shortage of disease, drought and famine; several rogue nations now have the bomb and the radicals are spreading like wild fire. But, I am not convinced that what I read in Revelation has anything to do with the end of the world."

They arrived at the park and he carried their picnic basket to a bench that he had picked out the day before while running. It was a beautiful fall day in the Deep South. The spot he picked was by the side of a pond with a mix of sun and shade to be bright, but comfortable. He immediately pulled out a container with an expensive gourmet cheese and thin water crackers and uncorked a bottle of Chardonnay, pouring a glass for each of them. As he raised his glass he said, "Here's kidding about your looks."

Claire started laughing, "That's almost romantic. Hardly original, and I hate to say it but I find it laughable. Tommy, you're not going to propose to me are you?"

"What would you say if I did?"

"Typical Irish-American, he answers a question with a question and manages to be non-committal at the same time."

"Well?"

"You answer my question first."

"I am not going to propose," Tom says fighting a smile.

"Well in that case if you did, I would say no," said Claire with a similar expression.

Claire took a sip of her wine and her grin immediately turned to a serious frown. "I take it you believe that this Wasim creep is the devil and is using his position and the situation with rationing to control access to the basics of life as foretold in Revelation?"

"I think there are two possibilities. I am 99 percent certain he is doing it. What I don't know is if he is doing it because he has ties to the radicals or some political group or if he is the Antichrist or one of his agents," Tom said, too casually for the topic.

"I suppose you have a plan to figure that out?"

"Yes, I do."

Claire went silent, clearly wrapped up in thought for nearly ten minutes. They ate the appetizer and finished their glass of wine. Tom poured Claire another glass of wine and opened a beer for himself. He took out the sandwiches and placed them on the plates, along with a bag of chips. Claire started laughing, "I didn't expect a marriage proposal today, but I was certain you would have lobster rolls, and the only way I would have figured on potato chips was if you put crème fraîche and caviar on them."

"But, Claire, that would have been a complete waste, because you already told me you would say no."

"Boyo, with women and politicians, there is what we say and what we do; the only difference is that with politicians it all comes down to votes and money, and with women it all comes down to emotion." Tom thought for a moment about proposing marriage, but then he thought that she probably meant what she said about saying no.

Claire returned to her serious side and continued her line of questions as if no time had passed. "What is your plan?"

"I am going to talk to some people who should be in the know and see what they know. They will tell me, either directly or indirectly, if they think I am correct or have an overworked sense of imagination."

"And if they confirm your suspicions?"

"Then I will do what I can to stop Wasim," Tom said quietly.

"Tommy, whether you are right or wrong, the idea that you would get involved with something that involves the radicals or the devil, terrifies me. You could be in danger. You could die, if you go up against people like that."

"That thought has crossed my mind," Tom sounded calm despite the stakes.

"Who do you plan on talking to," Claire asked.

"Firstly, Jim Martin. He knows Wasim as much as anyone can, and if there is something going on he either suspects it or knows about it."

"You never told me whether or not you are having dinner with him tonight."

"I am."

"How can you find out what you want to know without letting him know what you are doing and it getting back to Mirza?"

"I will try to be vague and have some sort of legit cover story," Tom improvised.

"Like what?" Claire asked.

"I haven't figured that out yet."

"Then what?" Claire persisted.

"If my read of Jim is affirmative, then I will talk to my friend the archbishop," Tom sounded more confident.

"I thought the Church kept neutral and quiet on these matters," Claire looked less convinced.

"They do, but Archbishop Francis Xavier Gleason has shared some secrets with me before, and I with him, and I trust him completely." "And if he is affirmative?" Claire added, still not sold.

"Then I talk to the other card kingpin who I have access to."

"Is that the guy who heads up World Passport Card?"

"Yes, Nelson Glassman. If this is real, he would know, and more importantly, could be helpful. He has a serious distrust and dislike for Mirza that goes beyond being a competitor."

"Well, at least you are well connected, I only read about these people." Claire sighed and continued, "Tommy, you need to be careful. If you are correct, you are playing with serious fire, hell fire. Let me give you some warnings you need to hear and listen to. None of what you think can be put on a computer; no documents, no e-mail, or any electronic form. None of your conversations can be over a telephone; cell or land line. You must be careful that all your meetings are in discreet places that you choose and that your conversations are not recorded. Do you know what I am saying?"

"Yes, exactly!"

"Now, what can I do to help?"

"Nothing!" Tom blurted, louder than he intended. "In fact, less than nothing. Although you wouldn't marry me, I know that you love me, and I love you more than all the tea in China. So, don't go doing research on this on your computer, because if you are right, they might pick up on what you are doing. I want you out of this completely."

After some thought, Claire resigned. "Okay, but I want updates, even if they are in code."

CHAPTER THREE

Here is wisdom. Let him that hath understanding count the number of the beast: for it is the number of a man; and his number is Six hundred threescore and six.

Revelation 13:18

Like Tom, Jim Martin lived in a townhouse in downtown Atlanta, only his was palatial and he could afford it. Jim was hesitant to meet until Tom said he had made a reservation at Bones in the section where you could light up a cigar after dinner. Jim came from a middle-class family, but he was very shrewd. He was well-educated, organized, dressed impeccably, and was well groomed. At about five foot eleven and 185 pounds he was not an imposing figure. Nevertheless, he had an aura of authority about him. In business he had it "all together." Life seems to demand balance though, and in his personal life he had two weaknesses; women and alcohol. He was on his fourth wife and had an affair every other month. If he had more than two drinks, he was unlikely to have less than ten.

Tom made the reservation for an early time, six thirty, and arrived early so that he could get a secluded table. He wanted a good view of Jim as he entered so that he could make sure he didn't have time to set his phone on record without him seeing him do it.

Jim couldn't turn down an invitation to a restaurant like Bones because it stroked his ego. He loved places where the valets were well-dressed, treated you like a king, and the atmosphere reeked of Old World power and money. Jim thought dining in such restaurants was a reflection in the mirror of his success.

Tom was sitting at the table sipping a gin and tonic, mentally rehearsing his approach to the conversation as he saw Jim enter the dining room. As he suspected, despite the fact that it was a holiday weekend, Jim dressed like he was going to a board meeting, impeccable in every way, and from head to toe was probably wearing attire that cost four thousand dollars.

Tom rose to greet him with a warm handshake. "Jim, it is so good to see you, it's been too long."

"I agree. When you can't remember how long it has been it has been way too long."

"It looks like you are already at least a drink ahead of me," Jim eyed his gin and tonic. Tom immediately, purposefully, and instinctively told him the first of several white lies for the evening. "Actually, I'm two drinks ahead of you."

"Well I will do my best to catch up," Jim promised.

A moment later the server arrived at the table, introduced herself as Scarlett, and asked Jim if he would like to start with a drink. "Well I thought you would never ask, gorgeous." Scarlett was indeed gorgeous, and young enough to be Jim's daughter. In his mind there wasn't a woman he couldn't charm into bed, even if it meant renting a Lamborghini for the night if he thought it would work. "Yes, I would like a martini, light on the vermouth, and shaken not stirred." He tried to imitate a Scottish accent on the last phrase, but it went right over Scarlett's pretty little head. Coming from Richmond, Virginia, he had a bit of a Southern accent that made it difficult to talk like a Brit.

"Would you like to order any appetizers or do you need some time?" Scarlett said sheepishly. Tom asked Jim if he was ready, and Jim nodded yes. Neither had bothered to look at the menu. Jim ordered a shrimp cocktail and Tom French onion soup. Tom immediately said that they would wait to order their entrées; he wanted to drag this out, hoping Jim would get plastered.

They continued with small talk until Jim's drink arrived as if it was a starting signal, he opened the conversation up for business. "So,

Tommy boy, what is the engagement you are working on that you think I can help with?"

Tom had thought it through and while it was a bit bold, he thought it was worth the risk. "I have been retained by the Roman Catholic Church to help them evaluate the possibility of the electronic payment system being hijacked by the extremist to control who can buy food and gas based on their allegiance or lack thereof."

After a moment of silence, Jim looked less surprised than he should by this theory. "Wow, it sounds like they're doing their homework for the third Crusade."

"Maybe, I'm not yet sure," Tom didn't give anything away.

"So, what makes you think I can help you with that?"

"I thought of you because you are pretty much at the pinnacle of the payment system and I remembered our conversations over drinks at the end of the day when we were working together years ago. On numerous occasions you spoke about the possibility of credit and debit cards being the means of the Antichrist to control the purchase of goods. You said you thought it might be analogous to the mark of the beast as described in Revelation. Jim, you brought it up so many times I thought you were fixated on it."

Jim started looking uncomfortable and defensive. He leaned back and folded his arms. This was completely out of character for Jim, who prided himself on always being totally under control. "Tom, if you think back, I wasn't any more fixated by that part of Revelation than a lot of people were at the time. Leading up to 2000 there were all sorts of end times scenarios that were floating around and it made for great cocktail party conversation."

Tom could tell he had pressed too hard too quickly. He could also tell that he had touched a nerve. He backed off a bit and let Jim lead the conversation. Fortunately, Scarlett returned, accompanied by her assistant waiter who placed their appetizers carefully in front of them as she inquired if they needed anything else. Jim ordered another martini and Tom switched to red wine. Jim started hitting on Scarlett again and that helped to lighten the mood a bit.

"Tom, do you think there is a link between the extremist and the devil?"

"At some level; I mean, all evil is connected with the devil, if you believe in the struggle between good and evil and God and the devil."

"Agreed, but you brought up both in the same breath."

"Jim, I don't know if they're connected, or if either of them might be conspiring to gain control of the payment systems. All I know is, like I said, you are in a position to know if something might be going on, certainly know how it might be done, and from past discussions, you seemed to find it interesting."

Jim motioned to Scarlett's assistant to get him another drink as he pondered where to go next. Now that he had some alcohol in him he seemed more relaxed. "Well, I do believe the extremist would try to take over the payment systems with or without the urging or backing of the devil. I also believe in the Second Coming, and being in payment systems, I always felt that the passage in Revelation about the mark of the beast had to do with credit card payments." Tom was glad to see that Jim was really starting to open up.

"Do the extremist have enough power to take over the systems—how would anyone do that?" Tom pushed further.

"Someone would have to have access to the payments system and have the ability to tie into social media platforms and government data bases. To do all of those things you would need to have inside access, know-how, be the greatest hacker on earth or have divine powers," Jim winked, tossing his drink.

"Since two of those alternatives are pretty unlikely, is it possible that someone could get access to the systems from a lower or mid-level or would management have to have some involvement," Tom asked.

"To tell you the truth, I think it would have to be top down and a fairly widespread conspiracy for that to happen," Jim mused.

Scarlett cleared their appetizers and Jim had just about finished his second martini as she asked if they had looked at the menu. "Gorgeous, I've been too distracted by you to look at anything else." Scarlett looked amused but persisted. "Should I give you more time?"

"I know what I want without looking at the menu, how about you Tom?"

"Jim, I know what you want and it's not on the menu, and yes, I am ready to order. I'll have a baked potato, filet medium well, and a side salad with blue cheese dressing."

"That sounds good. I will have the same and being somewhat cannibalistic, I would like my fillet rare." As he looked at Scarlett, Jim added, "My friend is right in saying that what I really want is not on the menu." Scarlett blushed.

Jim ordered another martini after making a big deal about pairing a very expensive bottle of red wine with the entrées. He was playing right into Tom's hand. As usual, once Jim got going, he picked up the pace and loosened up. Tom decided he would indirectly push his luck. Jim had women on his mind and beat him to the punch. "Who was the lovely lady with you at Maggiano's the other night?"

"That was Claire O'Reilly; we have been dating for several years, Tom said, his eyes narrowed slightly.

"Exclusively?" Jim added.

"Yes, quite exclusively."

"Is she the one?" he continued.

"Could be, but I don't think either of us are interested in marriage."

"Is she a career woman," asked Jim.

"Yes, she is an editor at the newspaper here in town."

"Well, she sure looked like she would be a helluva catch, one night or many nights."

"Thanks for the compliments."

"How is your dinner partner from Maggiano's doing?" Tom tried to sound casual.

"Wasim is Wasim, what can I tell you. He is cold as ice and meaner than a wounded badger, but he sure warmed up to your lady."

On that note, Tom decided it was time to get back to business. "It seems it's getting dangerous to be a board member these days," Tom changed topics.

"Yeah, what are the odds losing three board members in such tragic ways over a short period of time?" Jim shook his head looking off into nothing.

"Do you think it was bad luck against the odds or maybe something more serious?"

"Like what?" Jim refocused.

"I don't know. Is the board dealing with anything controversial?"

"Well, it's been reported that the board is debating and in disagreement with the notion of using the card system for rationing, but I still think it would be a real reach though to think that someone would have board members killed and be able to make it all look accidental," said Jim speculatively. Jim was again in a defensive posture and his face looked strained.

Tom again switched gears. "Jim, are you still married or are you in between wives?"

"I am happily married to wife number four. I really think this one might work out." Jim feigned hope.

"I wouldn't know it with the way you are flirting with the waitress."

"Oh come on, you know that's just my way. I don't mean anything by it," said Jim, a portrait of innocence.

"Yeah, I'll bet the first three Mrs. Martins would disagree with you on that. Isn't your flirting why they are ex-wives?"

"No, it was working long hours, too much stress, too much drinking to relieve the stress, and too many consummated flirtations that resulted in three ex-wives."

"So, Jim, what makes you think this one is going to last?" asked Tom with genuine curiosity.

"Because, I am much wealthier than I used to be, and especially because this one is more tolerant than the others." They both laughed heartily.

Scarlett and her assistant arrived with the wine and the entrées. Jim made a big deal out of the wine tasting for the benefit of Scarlett as well as his own ego. He didn't flirt with her though.

"Jim, even if there was a conspiracy, considering what you said, there would have to be some pretty serious changes made to get control of payments, social media, and government systems. You would basically need a system within a system."

"You are correct."

"And that is why you think it would have to be top-down?" Tom continued.

"Correct." affirmed Jim.

"Aren't those systems kept very secured?"

"Yes, but people on the inside have access to the systems, and they do what they're told. There is security controlled access, though, in connection with policy changes."

"Like rationing?"

"Correct, rolling out a policy change requires secured access that comes from the board, and it goes to two people who each hold one half the electronic keys necessary to allow the policy code change to be put into play," said Jim, his face flushed from the drinks.

"Who are those people?" Tom pressed further.

"No one is supposed to know who both of them are. I know who one of them is and Wasim knows the other." Tom's heart was racing as Jim continued to spill.

"You said 'supposed to know.' Does that mean someone does know who both of them are?"

"Maybe, I don't know. I only know one. No one is supposed to ever know the identity of both of them. In addition to the keys, the protocols that each of them carry to allow access are different and complex," Jim said, his glazed eyes looking more distant.

"Jim, wouldn't the sub-system you need to control payments for terroristic reasons look a lot like the sub-system you would need for rationing?" asked Tom.

Jim looked both upset and defensive, yet at the same time amused. He lifted his wine glass and, smiling, he swirled the wine around in the glass as he said, "Well, aren't you clever, Tommy. It seems you have quite a few conspiracy dots connected in your fertile mind."

They spent another hour and a half killing two bottles of wine, decadent chocolate cake for dessert, and smoking some Cuban cigars Tom had smuggled in on his last trip to the Dominican. They mostly reminisced about the times they worked together, and Tom made sure he tied in some memorable moments with Wasim. "I remember the first meeting I was in with him. One of the marketing executives said something that rubbed him the wrong way so he then spent the next half-hour belittling him both on his recent performance and surprisingly, on a personal level. I had witnessed people debate and even argue before in business meetings, but not like that. Most management teams were on their best behavior in front of an outsider and as a consultant I was surprised this happened at all let alone with me in the room. I remember once asking you if he was always like that and how you could put up with it and you said, you get used to it."

"You do, sort of, there is no alternative. As long as you do well and get paid nicely for it, you are kind of trapped," said Jim.

"I remember another time when we were in a meeting on the retail customer database where he went on a tirade about making sure all key customer numbers were cross-referenced with special emphasis on their social security number. Nobody in the room had the hutzpah to ask why."

The whole time they were playing let's remember, Jim managed to evade further discussion of rationing and control of payments. As drunk as he was, he was no longer taking the bait. Jim got totally smashed. Tom didn't press further though. Whether he answered the questions directly or not, he learned everything he needed to know from Jim, save for one thing. It was still unclear if Jim was a willing participant or was being threatened. Either way, it was unlikely Tom could rely on him as an ally. Jim was close to Wasim and there was no hesitation in the explanations he provided.

Jim had gotten a bit sloppy and loud and they were the only customers left in the restaurant. Scarlett brought the check without even asking if they were ready for it or wanted anything else. By now, Scarlett certainly wouldn't ask Jim if he wanted anything else for more than one reason. Jim looked at her as he reached for the check and said he would take that and that she was worthy of a great tip. Scarlett smiled, simply said thank you and made a quick exit. Tom was glad Jim grabbed the check so quickly and didn't offer to pay for any part of it. They had three bottles of expensive wine and Tom only drank three glasses. Jim was going to have one hell of a headache in the morning. Jim barely looked at the check; he quickly signed it, entered the tip amount, and placed his Black Amex card on top of it at the corner of the table. The assistant server seemed to come out of nowhere, grabbed the receipt and credit card, and ran off to close out the check. He was back in a heartbeat with the final receipt. As he neatly folded the receipt and placed it in his wallet, and without looking up, he said very soberly, "Tom, you should be careful as you pursue this. You seem to think it is real, and if you are right you could encounter some nasty people with sinister intentions."

"I will, thanks for the heads up," said Tom with a chill.

They walked out together to the valet stand and both gave their tickets to the attendant. Jim's car arrived first. It was a fire engine-red Ferrari. Tom wondered if he owned it or if he just rented it for the evening to make an impression. "Nice ride, Jim."

"Yeah, it's an attention getter, especially among the gold diggers," Jim grinned, slyly. They shook hands and each told the other what a pleasure it was and that they should get together more often. As Jim hopped into the car he looked at Tom in the eyes and again with great seriousness said, "Watch your back, Tommy." Jim sped out of the parking lot like a seventeen-year-old boy trying to impress the girls outside the movie theater on a Friday night.

As Tom got into his Jeep, he started running the evening's conversation through his mind. Jim had essentially told him he was onto something. He hinted at where the directives might be coming from and how it could be done. Tom was stunned by the information Jim imparted but what was most disturbing were the warnings. He remembered the line from one of his favorite Westerns, where the lead character said in effect that if you pay close attention, a man will share his bad intentions with you. Jim told him that if he pursued this to be careful.

* * *

Edward had been a limo driver in Atlanta for twelve years, and in all those years he had never seen as much traffic on a Friday night. When traffic came to a complete standstill on I-285 he immediately called the number he had been given at Primary Card Processing. "This is Diane Reynolds speaking. How may I help you?"

"Hi, Diane, my name is Edward, and I am scheduled to pick up Mr. Mirza at 5:00 PM sharp. I am calling to let you know that I am going to be late."

"How late do you expect to be Edward," Diane asked, nervously.

"I can't say for sure. I am at a complete standstill on I-285. My GPS is telling me there is an accident three miles ahead and that there are two lanes blocked. It is estimating I will be there at 5:20, but I am not sure."

"Okay, I will let Mr. Mirza know that you will be late," Diane's nerves turned to fear. Edward thought about what he had been told and quickly said, "Don't hang up, Diane. I was told that Mr. Mirza was very demanding and that I had to be on time or early, because being late would not be tolerated. I left twenty minutes early, but my time cushion has been totally absorbed. Perhaps you should call another service and get another car," Edward offered.

"You are right, he is demanding and for that reason we use only one limo service. I will let him know that you left early, but heavy traffic consumed your margin for delay and now you have encountered an accident."

Diane put down the phone, took a deep breath, and selected the guest executive phone. "Mirza!" Wasim answered abruptly. She told him the story and he completely exploded. "This is your fault, damn it. When you select a limousine service you need to pick one that is reliable. I have an important meeting tonight and I don't want to be embarrassed by being late!"

"Mr. Mirza, this is the service we use for all Primary Card Processing executives and they are very reliable. It's just that the traffic in town for the holiday weekend and the black Friday sales is unbelievably heavy," said Diane.

"I don't want to hear excuses. Let me know when he arrives," Wasim snapped. "Yes Sir." Diane, who was Jim Martin's secretary, turned to her co-worker, who despite sitting at a desk ten feet away heard everything. "I don't know how Jim, or anyone could work for him," Diane said. The co-worker just shook her head.

At five twenty-five Edward called again to say he was two blocks away and would be there in five minutes. "Okay, Edward, park at the front plaza, make sure the temperature is comfortable in the car, and then greet Mr. Mirza inside the lobby. I will let him know you will be ready in five minutes." She called Mirza, and after hearing her report, he simply hung up without a word. Thirty seconds later he stormed past her, headed toward the elevator.

The elevator doors were barely opened when he exploded. "When you are hired as an executive driver, you should plan for all contingencies and to be here early. You should be the one waiting, not the customer. My time is valuable." Edward looked at Mirza and said he was sorry. He turned, and led the way to the car where he opened and closed the door after Mirza, holding his breath. Edward had already entered the destination in his GPS and started driving. It was a long, quiet drive. Mirza witnessed now, firsthand, why Edward had been late. It took an hour to go the 10 miles to the to the townhouse complex near the mall.

Edward opened the car door when they finally arrived. As Mirza exited the car Edward issued a final apology. "I am sorry for the delay, Mr. Mirza and hope you have a nice evening." Mirza said nothing. He walked to the door as though Edward didn't exist. He entered his mistress' room number on the keypad and she responded instantly. "Wasim?"

"Yes, this is Wasim." She said nothing, but the buzzer sounded, the door clicked, and he entered the building.

Catherine Anne Brown was not a typical call girl or kept mistress. She had been a professional, mid-level executive at a marketing firm. She wasn't a supermodel, but she was attractive and intelligent, and she liked nice things. They had met at a business-related cocktail party and he asked her out for a date. Mirza would be in town a few days a month and when he was there, he wanted a companion for cocktail parties. He wanted someone who would take care of him, in more ways than one, when the business day ended. He offered to put her up in a nice townhouse, provide her with a car and a monthly check for living expenses and clothes. He wrote the whole deal off as a business expense. The relationship worked extremely well for Catherine. She had all her living expenses paid for and was still able to work as an independent marketing contractor making more money while working fewer hours.

She poured two drinks and set them on the coffee table. Catherine was waiting for him at the door. As soon as the door was closed she wrapped her arms around him, greeting him with a kiss. As she began to release he put his hand on top of her head and applied downward pressure. She did not resist, got down on her knees and commenced the expected foreplay. Mirza made love like a dog in heat. To him, it was all sex that he needed and sex that he got. After all, he was paying all the bills.

When he was done, he told her to open the bedroom window and bring the drinks to the bedroom. She knew the routine, but had to wait for the command. She put on an elegant negligee, opened the window and retrieved the drinks. By the time she returned he had lit a cigarette.

"So, how did your dinner with Mr. Martin go, and your meetings today?" Sex to Mirza was like alcohol to Martin; it stroked his ego and loosened his lips. "The dinner went as planned, as did the meetings."

"You have both the contact names you need and the plans are moving forward?"

"Yes, all we need now is an affirming vote at the board meeting, which is now assured, and the plan will be consummated." He put out his cigarette, rolled over and went to sleep. Catherine returned to the bathroom and showered, trying to wash away the dirty feeling.

CHAPTER FOUR

Fear none of those things which thou shalt suffer: behold, the devil shall cast some of you into prison, that ye may be tried; and ye shall have tribulation ten days: be thou faithful unto death, and I will give thee a crown of life.

Revelation 2:10

Claire was asleep by the time Tom got back to her place. Again, he was unable to sleep most of the night. Although he was certain that what he heard at dinner confirmed his theory, he kept rerunning the situation through his head to make sure he was on the right track with his conclusions and that his plan was solid. It didn't help that Jim's parting words were somewhere between a call for caution and a threat. The last conscious thought he had was when he looked at the clock at 4:22 AM.

Once again he slept way past his normal time and felt like he hadn't rested at all. Claire had left a note by the coffee pot telling him she was about her Saturday routine and that she needed to work most of the afternoon and into the evening. In a way, he was glad, because he needed to set up two meetings, and if he was able to get them set he would then need to make travel arrangements. He also had his Saturday routine to tend to, including picking up some items to take to the BBQ on Sunday. He thought it would be nice to prepare a simple dinner for Claire when she was done work in the evening.

He was starting to feel paranoid, and instead of using e-mail to set up the meetings, he opted to use his cell phone. Both were being monitored by the government, but based on what he knew, e-mail was easier to scan for keywords than cell phone data. Both calls were successful. He was able to set up two meetings with people who could shed a lot of well-informed light on the situation. He would be travelling a fair amount of the time since the meetings had to be set more than one day apart. At least he would be in a part of the country where he could make good use of his time and could crash at his sister's house.

Claire didn't get home until 8:30. He had prepared a light, late evening dinner for them, which she greatly appreciated. She had a hectic day. "It's like all the creeps, murderers, and extremist took Thanksgiving and Black Friday off and decided to make up for lost time today. Three bombs were set off in Israel with over one hundred dead, three more beheadings in Syria, and a street attack on a Jewish couple in Paris. Then, we have to wait until the president finishes his golf game to get a statement."

"Was it worth the wait?"

"No, his address was just the usual boilerplate stuff, condemning the violence, standing beside our allies, and so on and so forth. Nothing but a bag of hot air, they could have just played a tune on a bagpipe instead."

"Did anything good happen today for you," Tom asked.

"So far, just a pleasant ride at the stable."

"I have a line on the tip of my tongue but I am afraid it would be lewd," said Tom.

"You don't have to say it, I got your drift," said Claire with raised eyebrows and a smirk.

"I did some research and found some things you might find interesting about Wasim Mirza. He was born on June 6, 1966," began Claire.

"A lot of people were born on that day, but it doesn't make them all Satan."

"No, but I doubt the others are trying to get control of the payment system."

"What else do you have," Tom asked.

"He has a lot of money, but no one seems to know where it came from."

"Could you define for me how much is a lot?"

"Sure, his net worth is over five hundred million, and there is no way you make that kind of money working for a company."

"Perhaps he invested wisely; anything else?"

"Yes, he made significant contributions to the last election campaign, and it is rumored that the Super Pac he contributed to is the one that leaked unproven, damaging information to the press about the opponent's extra-marital affairs," Claire divulged.

"I know I sound skeptical but this is pretty good stuff," said Tom.

"There's more, I saved the best for last. All three board members who died from those recent 'accidents' were Christians, and they were the *only* Christians on the board. Two of the three have already been replaced, and none of them are Christians."

After a moment of quiet surprise, Tom sighed and asked, "So what do you think this means, Claire?"

"I think you are onto something and again, I think you should be careful, if not just walk away," Claire said softly.

Wanting to change the somber tone of the conversation, Claire straightened up and smiled. "And what has himself been up to that kept you out past my bedtime last night and presumably busy all day today." Tom recounted the entire dinner conversation with Jim, including all the flirting with the waitress, which served to lighten things up.

"Yes, you are definitely onto something and I am getting scared. I think what he said to you was a confirmation and a threat. Tom, I think you should drop this. This guy has had three people killed and will make it four if he has to," Claire begged.

"I am not quitting. In fact, I have set up the meetings with the archbishop, and Glassman at World Passport Card."

"When are you going?"

"I leave Monday."

"Tommy, I love you and respect your abilities, but you are a management consultant. You are not prepared to deal with these people. They will squish you like a grape."

"Maybe, but I have to do what I can. As far as I know, I am the only one who understands what is about to happen. I feel obligated; I can't just walk away now."

"Okay, but why are you going there? Can't you just talk to them on the phone?"

"No, it was you who told me to limit my use of electronic devices and credit cards, and I think you are right. I purposefully didn't use e-mail to contact them because it is harder for the snoopers to get my phone information than my e-mail. I also used my cell phone to make the travel reservations, and I purchased good old-fashioned American Express Traveler's Checks and am carrying a lot of cash. Hopefully, I will fly under the radar of anyone tracking credit card purchases. I will conduct all meetings as discreetly as possible. Which, reminds me, I know you mean well, but please don't do any more research. They can probably see what you are doing and put two and two together. It's bad enough that I have to be involved in this. I don't want any harm to come to you."

I appreciate you trying to protect me but how are you going to protect yourself?" Claire said.

"I have three weapons—your love and support, the Lord's love and support and the support of Smith & Wesson. I bought a gun today." Claire rolled her eyes. "You're talking about being stealthy yet you go out and buy the easiest most obvious thing in this country to track. Plus, you have no idea how to use a gun."

"If I bought it legally that would be true, but if you want to be covert and untraceable, you do what any self-respecting criminal would do, you buy it illegally."

Claire sighed deeply, shaking her head. "Tom, Tom, Tom, I am not even going to ask how you did that. Do you have any idea how to use it?"

"Yes, after making the purchase I went to a gun store where they have a range. I purchased a bunch of ammunition and a concealable holster. I also bought a special metal case with a lock. The case is required for the gun when travelling by air. After spending a couple hundred dollars they were quite happy to provide me with instruction. I did pretty well. I had already done some research online so that I would know what to buy, and I looked at a half dozen videos on-line to learn how to load, shoot and unload. Look, I hope I don't have to use it but these people are murderers."

"Tell me about your meetings," said Claire, grimly.

"My first meeting is with the archbishop of Philadelphia, Francis Xavier Gleason."

"Oh, I know a little about him. He was in charge of the special committee that Pope Francis commissioned in the United States to make sure the high-ups weren't living lavishly and transferring problem priests rather than deal with them directly. He got a lot of attention, because he really rocked the boat. Wasn't he really handsome?"

"Exactly! Frank was always a real heartthrob and it has caused him a lot of concern. He had to rock the boat. His big fear was that his celibacy problem might be exposed by someone who wanted to get even."

"What was his problem with celibacy?"

"His problem, was, is, and probably always will be, that he can't stay celibate. He doesn't go looking for women, but on the other hand, when they throw themselves at him, well, as he puts it, he might be a priest, but he's still human."

"That's a bunch of crap," Claire said flatly. "A handsome married man can have women throw themselves at them and stay true to their vows. A priest should likewise stay true to his vows."

"That's true but I would point out that most married men may be faithful but they are not celibate. They both have vows but celibacy can be difficult for someone who is almost never having sex, has attractive women tempting him, and has to spend Saturday afternoons in the confessional listening to the highlights of other people's sex lives," Tom said.

"Vows are vows. If you aren't going to keep them, then you shouldn't take them. If he can't keep his promise to God, what makes you think you can trust him to discuss something this important?"

"I've known him since high school, and we have always stayed close."

"If you are close, how is it that you have rarely mentioned him to me?"

"Sorry, Claire, I don't have a good answer."

"What is it you think he can help you with?"

"Two things. First, he might know if this situation is on the Catholic Church's radar screen. Second, if it is, he might know if they plan to do something about it."

"If it sounds like they have a plan will you back off?" Tom thought about this for a moment.

"Maybe . . . or maybe I find an ally."

"Or another enemy," said Claire.

"I doubt it. I may well be the only person, other than you, to know that he has had several flings."

"And your other meeting?"

"The Chairman and CEO of World Passport Card, Nelson Glassman. World Passport Card is north of New York. Nelson lives in Connecticut. I had to give him a hint of what I was up to so he'd take the meeting, but as soon as I gave him the gist he seemed eager to meet and suggested a public, but discreet place."

"Well, boyo that sounds promising, I guess. How well do you know him?"

"I know him very well. He was the project manager for the first consulting engagement I ever worked on and I have been fortunate to work with him on something at least every other two years for the last fifteen years."

"Can you trust him?"

"I am not sure, but among those I think I can confide in, he is probably the one who can provide the best insight and assistance, and he may be trustworthy."

"When do you leave?" Claire asked.

"Monday morning," Tom tried to sound calm.

"Tom, please be careful." Tom looked at her with sincerity and love in his eyes, held her hand and kissed her, "I swear I will be careful."

"Tommy, do you need me to do anything for the BBQ tomorrow?"

"No, earlier today I picked up the stuff that Andy asked us to bring."

"Weren't we supposed to make potato salad?"

"Yes, I took care of it."

"I'm impressed," beamed Claire.

"Don't be, I bought it at the grocery store, but I put it in a plastic container as soon as I got back so that you would think I made it from scratch," confessed Tom.

"Do you want to go to early Mass tomorrow," asked Claire.

"You are a mind reader. If we go to eleven o'clock Mass we will feel rushed. Let's go to the nine o'clock."

"I'm tired, do you mind if I get to bed?" Claire yawned.

"No, you worked all day and I have to check my e-mail and make some travel arrangements."

Claire got up from the sofa and gave Tom a long good night kiss. For a minute he reconsidered, but figured Claire was probably pretty tired, and he knew he wouldn't sleep well if he didn't tend to the loose ends.

Tom was shocked when he heard the clock radio start playing at six thirty. It was the first night since he arrived back in town that he had slept through the night. He felt completely refreshed. "Tommy, did you make coffee?"

"Yes, me lady, it should be ready."

They spent the next three-quarters of an hour leisurely waking up, and then decided it was time to get ready for church.

Tom always enjoyed walking into church with Claire. She was stunning, and all the married guys would discreetly check her out; after all, they were with their wives and kids, and were in church. Tom was usually pretty good about paying attention to the readings and participating in the responses, but the gravity of recent events and anxiety for what was coming distracted him. While having morning coffee and quiet time he had slipped into mission mode, and was now fully involved in plotting for his upcoming trip and meetings with the archbishop and Nelson Glassman. He had to remind himself as the pastor began his homily to focus and pay attention to what the priest had to say, not just for his spiritual benefit, but equally important, Claire would often give a pop quiz. She was very attentive, and good at not only gathering the information, but also deciphering the meanings. It was the first week of Advent, and the pastor spoke about the meaning of Advent and the need to prepare for the coming of Christ.

Tom had heard sermons for years during the season of Advent with this theme, but today it seemed more meaningful because the pastor was taking a different, more practical approach. Tom hoped that if Satan was on earth Jesus would be coming as well. The pastor posed a question to the congregation. "What would you do if you knew for sure that this Christmas, Jesus would return to earth this 25th of December? Would you decorate differently? Would you buy fewer presents? Would you go to confession, give more to charity, or go to Mass more often? If there are things you would change because you thought he was really coming, shouldn't you change because he just *might* be coming? And if change is what you need, shouldn't you adjust anyway since we believe he will come again?" The whole congregation looked contemplative, likely realizing all they should change.

When they got to the car, Claire predictably started the conversation. "So, Tommy, what are you going to change just in case Jesus is actually coming back?"

"Claire, I am going to change a bunch of things because I believe this Christmas we really need him back. Plus, I have a feeling that my quest is going to keep me from a lot of my usual commercial Christmas rituals. "How about you?" Tom returned the question.

"The pastor's message really hit home with me. I need to change a lot of things. I haven't been to confession in years, and I've let a lot of my own religious rules take over. I think society in general and most Catholics have reshaped their religion to make it easier and more convenient. I also need to pray for you, Tommy. I think this quest, as you call it, is going to put you in Satan's cross hairs," said Claire.

Well, on that note all I can say is let's get changed and get to the BBQ," Tom replied awkwardly.

Tom met Andy Newcomb only a few years ago. At the time, Andy was the lead programmer for a start-up company. They hit it off right away. Andy was a very down-to-earth kind of guy. He was really smart. He was capable of seeing the big picture and was able to grasp the necessary details to assemble large, complex systems. He also had a great work ethic. He started early in the morning and would usually be the last to leave the office, and if necessary, he would take work home with him. He was the chief technology officer at PCP and worked for Jim Martin. Andy and Jim could not be more different. Andy was married to his high school sweetheart, Barbara. They shared their first kiss, and went to the junior and senior proms together. They had six children. He and Barbara were both Irish Catholics from the south side of Boston. Andy was a big and imposing guy at six feet five, two hundred forty-five pounds, in decent shape, with dark, wavy hair. Andy was becoming an anomaly in the politically correct C-suites of America. He knew his business and wasn't afraid or hesitant to call out the intellectuals and phonies. He had a high school education, but his technical and analytical abilities were very strong. He had written several technical books on coding methodology that had been adopted as the industry standard in the tech world.

Tom and Claire arrived on time and found the entire Newcomb family in their backyard. The grill was fired up and after very warm greetings, Andy started cooking. Barb and Claire set up the picnic table with sides, paper plates and plastic ware, which in the South are called redneck china. The kids played catch and climbed on the swing set. Andy had hot dogs and hamburgers, and Tom bought shrimp and chicken on a stick. Andy cracked two beers and waved to Tom to have a seat by the fire pit while he tended the meats on the grill. "Did you have a good Thanksgiving, Tommy?"

"Oh yeah, plenty to eat and very relaxing," replied Tom.

"You just got back from your last gig of the year didn't you?"

"Yep, just in time for the holidays," smiled Tom.

"Let me guess, you are off for the rest of the year," Andy sounded jealous.

"Well, technically, I'm off until I land my next engagement."

"I guess that's partly why consultants charge so much. You need to cover your downtime," Andy offered.

"Believe it or not, I never factor that into the rate, but I have to be mindful when I am on the clock to make sure I put a portion of what I am making away for downtime and taxes. Not to continue the shop talk but Claire and I had dinner at Maggiano's the other night and ran into your boss and Wasim Mirza, and I had dinner with your Jim on Friday night."

"Oh yeah, I had to spend a good bit of time with each of them this week. Mirza was in town all week so I had to provide a command performance."

"New product," asked Tom. "Not even close. I am working on a project that for some reason or other is near and dear to Mirza's heart."
"Really, I didn't think he had a heart," Tom joked. They both laughed.

"Oh, he has a heart but only in the cold, biological sense."

"What's the project about?"

"Let's talk about it after lunch—it's a bit secretive."

Lunch was great. The kind of old-fashioned barbecue Tom was used to having grown up in the Northeast. Claire even came over to the dark side and tried a hot dog and some potato salad. After lunch, the adults stayed at the table together talking about the world in general while watching the kids play. While Barbara and Claire were cleaning up they took interest in what was on TV so they stayed inside the house.

"Want to help me try out my new corn hole set?" Andy said as he strolled over to boards painted in the Patriots' colors complete with logo decals. "Sure, if you don't mind getting your butt kicked!" said Tom.

"Are you ready to put your money where your mouth is?" Andy flashed a confident grin.

"Sure, that will make it more interesting. Five bucks a game?"

"You're on!"

After settling into the game, Andy got back to business. "So, were you and my boss talking about me or were you trying to sell him on a new project?"

"I was sharing my thoughts with him about a conspiracy theory I have."

"Really, what's that about," asked Andy.

"I believe someone or some group with bad intentions is trying to take control of payment and social media systems, and access government databases for their own purpose."

"Why would anyone do that?" Andy replied.

"To control who can purchase fuel, food and other necessities," Tom explained.

"Well we are building a system capable of that but the purpose is for rationing."

Andy easily beat Tom in the first game. It was almost a shut-out but Tom finally started scoring points just before Andy got up to eleven points. While they switched sides, Andy grabbed two more beers from the cooler and handed one to Tom. "Tommy, I think this barbecue could be costly for you," Andy joked.

"I'm just getting warmed up," said Tom.

"What makes you think someone is trying to take control of payments and social?" Andy asked.

Tom spent the next thirty minutes detailing his conspiracy theory, his suspects, and how they could possibly pull it off. Andy listened intently, and the more he heard, the faster he drank his beer and the worse he played. Tom won the second game, and Andy's performance in the third game was as bad as his had been in the first game.

"Tommy, let's sit and talk a bit." Andy brought his chair over to where Tom was sitting; he clearly wanted to keep distance between them and where the kids were playing. And from the house, in case one or both of the ladies came out.

"Tom, I think you might be onto something," Andy said, hunching toward him in his chair. "Mirza was in town all week and spent almost the entire time beating me up about finalizing the rationing project."

"Wait, you're working on the rationing project?" said Tom in disbelief.

"Working on it, it's my baby, and has been for the past six months. I have half my resources working on it and have three bosses to report to."

"Three bosses?" questioned Tom.

"Yeah, my usual boss, plus Corbett and Mirza. I have a separate meeting with each of them every week, and a conference call with them and Gene Thompson at Giggly."

"What makes you think I might be onto something?"

"A few things although everything I have been asked to do looks like it is for rationing, there are some functions that are based on factors pulling from the social network and government databases as opposed to how you would expect rationing to work. The other is the structure of the project. I mean, we are coding a sub-system that will be used by Universe Card and World Passport Card. Everything that my team constructs gets turned over to Corbett, and I don't really understand why. We do all the processing for Universe Card and World Passport Card as well as the banks, but we never turn over code to them for review or whatever the hell they are doing with it. And then there is Mirza himself. Some of the stuff that he's said sounds closer to what you're saying than rationing. Lastly, all the attention Mirza is giving to the project . . . if this was just for rationing it would be treated like any other maintenance project, but he treats it like its implementation by Christmas is a matter of life or death."

"Andy, you mentioned that some factors don't make sense; can you expand on that?"

"Sure, we're looking at parameters for authorizing and declining transactions by using fields returned from social networks and the factors are generic. If field A is equal to X and Field B is equal to Y authorize, otherwise decline. And there are a lot more factors than A and B and X and Y. And it is really odd that those factors are being hidden."

"Has anything been said that makes you think this is more than rationing?" Tom asked.

"Well, first of all, if it was just rationing and everybody gets a certain share the only thing that should matter is how much each person receives during a certain period of time. Now granted, certain families are bigger than others so they should get more, but that doesn't seem like the social factors we are keying on based upon the way the comparison codes are structured. The code should focus on entity type and number of people or cars per entity, and if exceeded decline. Instead it seems to be collating other factors to authorize or decline. Nothing has been said directly that would cause me to believe the system is to be used for anything other than rationing, but there seems to be a constant theme whenever Mirza goes into a tirade, that is making sure only the right people are being served." Tom sat back sighed and took it all in. Andy continued. "It's been so secretive. Mirza doesn't want anyone to know that we are working on it." Andy said this more to himself than Tom and stared off.

"Anything else," Tom asked and Andy nodded.

"Yeah, let me get us a couple more beers before we get into that though," Andy replied.

The cooler was empty, so he went into the house to reload. When he came out, Barb and Claire were with him, having decided it was time to check on the kids and play some team corn hole matches. Tom and Andy easily beat Claire and Barb in two games, although Andy was still off his game. The discussion they'd had earlier so visibly upset Andy that Barb asked him if everything was alright. He said he was fine, he just wasn't used to losing to anyone at corn hole, let alone a consultant. They changed the teams and it was now Tom and Claire against Andy and Barb. The first match with these teams was pretty close. During the second match, Andy Jr., who was in the house play-ing video games like all thirteen-year-olds, yelled out to his Dad that someone was on the phone for him. Andy told him to take a message, but Andy Jr. said he had told Mr. Mirza that, but he said it was import-ant. Andy was gone for about ten minutes.

During that time, Barb told Tom and Claire that the last month was difficult for Andy. He was being pressured by Mirza, and the closer they got to completion of the project, the worse it was getting. When Andy returned he tried to make a joke of the intrusion. "That SOB never met a detail he didn't like." He tried to seem collected but he was red in the face and his voice was shaky. Tom and Claire easily won the next two matches. Andy was clearly upset, and couldn't focus on the game at all. Tom noticed Barb eyeing Andy with a look of con-cern throughout the match. It was coming up on five thirty, and Barb told Andy that the kids were probably ready for dinner. Andy wanted to keep playing. He said they needed to even the score. Claire and Barb said they would get the table ready for round two while the guys tended the grill.

Andy started to load up the grill, hardly masking his growing anxiety. "Do you know who the key holders are?" Tom asked gently.

"Nobody is supposed to know who they both are. But I know one for sure and I could take a guess as to the other. You know him personally."

"So you might know who both of them are?"

"Yes, and I think your theory of how this works is an oversimplification. The key holders do hold a part of what is needed for access, but they also function as very high-level gatekeepers. We—me and the gatekeepers—need to carefully make sure that the new code is complete and flawless. The procedure for access to the system and for loading the new code is also purposefully very complex."

"Do you know who knows who the key holders are?" Tom asked.

"Yes, Jim Martin knows one and Wasim Mirza the other."

"How do you know that if it's supposed to be a secret?"

"Easy; my boss drinks too much and when he does, things just slip out. We were at a bar after the Christmas party when he told me that he was 'the handler of one of the keepers.' When I asked him what he meant he told me that he had designated a key holder."

"Did he say who it is?" Yes. Tom . . . Jim Martin handles your brother, John."

"Are you serious?" said Tom, bewildered.

"Yes."

"Who do you think the other key holder is?"

Andy hesitated. "If I told you I would have to shoot you," Andy finally replied. It was hard to tell if he was kidding.

"Andy, if you believe that I am right about what's going on, why wouldn't you tell me," asked Tom.

"I am not supposed to tell anyone. Besides, what difference does it make? There isn't anything you can do about it."

"Well, I am going to do what I can and somebody needs to tell the key holders the same thing I am about to tell you."

"What's that?"

"Watch your back," said Tom.

"I am already watching my back and will probably get fired anyway."

"Andy, I'm not talking about getting fired. I am talking about getting killed."

"What the hell are you talking about, killed?" Andy scoffed.

"You heard about the horrible deaths of three board members at Universe Card, right?"

"Yeah, but they were accidents."

"Sure, accidents, accidents that happened to the only Christians on the board, and two of them have already been replaced by non-Christians. They weren't accidents. Someone had them killed, and that someone will kill anyone else who stands in his way."

"Wasim," said Andy soberly. "You think it's Wasim."

"Yes, exactly! You looked like you were going to have a heart attack when you came back out after that call with him. What did he say to you?"

"He called to remind me that we were behind schedule on the project and that I should be working all weekend to get caught up."

"Does he call you at home often?"

"No, he's rarely called before but I work for a different company and report directly to Jim," Andy noted.

"Do you think it would be possible for you to alter the code at some point? You work so close with the code and know the identity of the gatekeepers. If you conduct the final review, couldn't you slip something in," asked Tom.

"During the development process I could insert code, but like I said before, on this project, all of my team's code is being turned over to Corbett for review. If he or his people are scouring the code they would see my changes. Plus, since many of the fields have placeholder names like A, B, X and Y, I would have a hard time coding anything to turn the tables on them. Now at the end, when I go to roll out the code, I *might* be able to, said Andy. "Tommy, what are you planning on doing? I want to help if I can."

"I plan on doing all that I can. I think it best that you just do your job. I will keep in touch with you. We need to keep everything we have discussed completely secret, no phones or e-mail. We should only talk about this in person. Are you going to tell me who you think the other key holder is?"

"Yes, I think it is Sal Asante," said Andy.

"I never heard of him."

"He is the lead network technician at Universe Card."

"What makes you think he's the guy?"

"The way the overall system is structured, you get the highest level of security by securing parts of the network in tandem with software. It makes sense to have the other key holder be someone who has as thorough an understanding of the network used for authorizations as I do of the software. That person is Sal," said Andy.

"Who does he work for?"

"That's the other part that makes sense. He works for George Corbett. He is to Sal as Jim is to me."

"I see. But, George isn't his handler, Wasim is?"

"Yes, but only as a practical matter; Wasim knows that he is the key holder, and if you asked him he would say that he is the handler. His ego and control freakiness requires that he know who the key holder is and that he controls the key holder. He is not half-assed. He is a very complete asshole," finished Andy.

Claire and Barb came out with the sides and Claire said, "Barb, they're at it again. Look at those serious faces. I didn't know corn hole and grilling was such serious business. They look like they are trying to save the world!" Tom looked at Andy and they both laughed, albeit uneasy.

Dinner was great. Both Claire and Tom returned to the light side, passing on the burgers and hot dogs and opting for the chicken and salad. The dinner discussion returned to world affairs, Christmas shopping, and the kids. Andy offered Tom a cigar after dinner, referring to it as birth control, but Tom declined, indicating he had an early start in the morning and had to get home and pack. That was a bit of a white lie. He wanted to spend some time with Claire before heading out, and the scent of cigar on his breath wouldn't help his cause. It took half an hour to say their good-byes, and they all promised to get together over the Christmas and New Year holiday.

On the way back to Claire's house, Tom recapped the conversation between him and Andy. It took a while, but he laid out everything he knew. "Tommy, let this go. It's not your job to save the world," Claire said quietly. They made love with desperation, as if they both felt it might be the last time for a while, if not forever. The good-bye kiss was more of the same. "Tommy, please take care of yourself and come back to me."

"I promise to be careful," Tom said.

* * *

Tom had just finished organizing his clothes for the trip and lay down when the phone rang. He smiled as he reached for it, thinking it was Claire with some final advice. His mood changed when he heard the cold voice of Mirza. "Mr. MacDonald, this is Wasim Mirza. I hope I am not calling at a bad time."

Oh no, Tom thought, everyone I hardly know calls me at 10:30 PM on a Sunday night. "What's on your mind, Mr. Mirza? It is late and I have an early flight," he said instead. His tone was cordial, but more business than friendly, and hardly the tone he would have used with a prospective client.

"I have a project that could benefit from your experience," Mirza's voice hissed on that last word.

"I am sorry, Mr. Mirza, but I am currently involved in an engagement."

"Oh, I am sorry to hear that. I was under the impression, mistakenly it seems, that you were available until at least the first of the year," Wasim said with sinister slowness.

"No, sorry, but I have a project that will keep me quite busy to the end of the year and I have another engagement lined up to start in early January."

"Well, that is most unfortunate for me. Do you mind if I ask who you are working for and the nature of the project?"

"I am sorry, Mr. Mirza, but the firm I am working with has requested complete confidentiality and anonymity."

"I can appreciate that. It is important that the affairs of business be kept secure and confidential. At Universe Card and PCP, we like to keep our business matters to ourselves, and appreciate it when outsiders keep their noses out of our business. Do you know what I mean?" Mirza's tone had sharpened, getting colder and harsher with each word. "I understand and agree completely," Tom replied.

"It was a real pleasure to meet your dinner companion the other night. She is a truly beautiful woman with a great figure. I understand she holds a prestigious position at the newspaper and has a great appreciation for horses."

"You seem very well-informed Mr. Mirza but I am not sure what Claire has to do with our business," Tom struggled to keep his composure.

"Mr. MacDonald, I don't mean to be intrusive. I can understand your instinct to be protective of a loved one. The safety of our friends and those we love is of the utmost importance. We must be mindful in our business matters not to endanger them in any way." Tom's discomfort grew to anger. "Mr. Mirza, I appreciate you thinking of me and I am sorry I am not available for you at this time. If I may be of service to you in the future please don't hesitate to contact me."

"Yes, I will, thank you for taking my call, and please convey my warm regards to Miss O'Reilly."

Warm regards, really, how ironic. As he hung up the phone, a feeling came over him that was like none he had ever experienced before in his life. It was as much physical as it was psychological. The room felt dark, cold, like a damp void and he was engulfed in unease and distress. There was no question about Mirza's message. Stay out of my business or you and your girlfriend will be sorry. Cautionary and threatening, and there was more to it. He felt depressed, weak, and on edge by a sudden feeling there was a presence in the room with him. He looked around, turned on the lights, turned up the heat, and fixed a drink. The feeling subsided after about ten minutes as suddenly as it set in, the room seemingly lighter and more fully warm.

Perhaps Claire was right that he was in over his head. He didn't think he possessed the kind of nerve, whether good or bad, to call someone he hardly knew late at night on the weekend and deliver such a vaguely veiled threat. This was a level of skill—and perhaps evil—that he couldn't match. He told himself the same thing he always did though when he entered situations that were completely new and challenging. *You always learn fast, you always manage to find a way to get the job done. You will do it again.* Tom tried to convince himself he was up for this *but you've never squared off with really nasty people before who are capable of murder. Getting fired is scary, but getting killed is pretty final.*

Now he had a new question to ponder. Mirza wouldn't know that he and Claire were asking questions about him and his companies unless someone told him. There were only three people who were aware of his suspicion; Jim, Claire, and Andy. Jim was the logical choice. He was so close to Mirza. Claire he trusted without question, and Mirza had used her in his threat. He doubted Andy would turn on him, although if they threatened his family, it is understandable that he would protect them. If it was Andy, and they questioned him, that would mean that he and Claire were being followed. That would also be one explanation for Mirza knowing about Claire's love of horses, and possibly where she worked. Again, he questioned if he was up to this if it meant not only risking his life, but Claire's.

He never slept well the night before a trip because of too much anticipation and the need to mentally review the travel checklist over and over. Tonight it was exacerbated by the weight of everything around him. He had an early flight. *This quest could kill me. Exactly!*

CHAPTER FIVE

*And I looked, and behold a pale horse: and his name that sat on him
was Death, and Hell followed with him. And power was given unto
them over the fourth part of the earth, to kill with sword, and with
hunger, and with death, and with the beasts of the earth.*

Revelation 6:8

The flight to Philly was on time, naturally, since he was running
late. No matter how much time you allot for traffic, you can never
leave enough extra time in Atlanta. He wished he had taken a cab, but
since everything had moved online and he was trying as best he could
to stay under the cyber radar, he decided to drive his own car. Most of
the parking lots were full and it took extra time to get a spot. The spot
he did finally get was far from the terminal. Then security was backed
up. He said to himself, *This approach makes no sense. Inconvenience
99.9999% of the people instead of "profiling" the .00001% who are
the problem!*

As soon as he got on the plane, he pulled out his laptop and
sat it on the middle seat. The flight was crowded, but so far it seemed
he had hit the jackpot. He planned on reading Revelation on the
flight in preparation for his meeting with his old friend, Archbishop
Gleason, and had downloaded a copy of Revelation the night before.
While waiting to get to cruising altitude he thought about Archbishop
Gleason and how the discussion would go.

Archbishop Francis X. Gleason, D.D, and Tom had met in high
school. They were friendly, but didn't live in the same neighborhood.
Tom played sports and Frank didn't. They shared a few classes, and
would meet before the bell across the street, sat together at lunch,

and often studied together in the library. They were close, but only at school. Their bond likely stemmed from similar backgrounds. Both came from Irish, Catholic families, and both were very handsome. Frank was pretty enough to be a good-looking girl. Ironically, Tom would often go to daily Mass at the all-boys Catholic high school and Frank never showed. They went to different colleges, but stayed in touch.

After college, Frank decided to become a priest. He was not the stereotypical candidate. He loved Notre Dame football, Italian food, good wine, Irish whiskey and '70s and '80s oldies. He enjoyed a good cigar with his wine, and his real passion was riding and betting on horses. His down to earth nature, unquestionable piety, great looks, and charming personality caused everyone who met him to love him and the effect seemed to increase with age. All of these characteristics served him well and helped in his role as priest, but the one thing that propelled him to be the youngest monsignor, bishop, and now archbishop, in the history of the Church in America, was his air of wisdom. He spoke softly and carefully, thinking and choosing his words well. He always spoke assertively, authoritatively, and was an expert on many subjects. He had common sense. He had girlfriends in high school and in college, and a few flings while in the priesthood. One was with purpose while in the seminary as a test to see if he could actually have sex and then give it up. He took celibacy seriously, both because it was part of the vow, and he didn't want to be a hypocrite. Nevertheless, he had several affairs throughout his career as a priest. He didn't seek out any of them. They came about as a result of gorgeous women flirting with him. He prayed that he could be stronger. He feared someone would find out about his affairs. Fortunately, at least for Frank, there was no benefit for a woman to disclose an affair with a priest.

One vow that Frank kept well was his vow of poverty. He would only accept money from family and friends. His horse and its care were all through the benevolence of the stable owner, and his family and friends were very generous to him. You just had to love Frank.

The plane reached cruising altitude and the captain let everyone know what route he was taking, what scenic views could be had, and that it was now safe to use electronic devices. Tom enthusiastically opened his laptop and fired it up. He had read Revelation before, but this time he was reading for an entirely different perspective. Revelation is a description of a vision had by John, who had been exiled to Patmos. John of Patmos is believed to be John the Apostle, and the author of the Gospel of John. His exile thought to be a result of the religious persecution of Christians under the Emperor Nero.

John explains that a vision is revealed to him by God. There are several schools of thought about what the vision means, and many interpretations of specific elements. Some believe it is centered on the religious persecutions led by Nero against the early Christians. This idea links the spelling of Nero's name with the famous mark of the beast passage in Revelation that says you will know the beast, Satan, by a mark upon him, which is the number 666. Others think that there is no meaning at all, other than the creative writing of an old, exiled man. The most notable and well-known theory claims the book predicts the signs of the end of times. The latter is a bit contrary to a statement in Revelation when God says that you will not know the time of his coming. The writing uses a great deal of symbolism inviting many scholars to interpret meaning. Tom read all the footnotes the last two times he read Revelation, and also watched a documentary on TV that attempted to correlate world affairs and the passages in Revelation to prove that the end times were at hand. He decided that this time he would read it straight through hoping to see beyond the details and better derive true meaning.

John begins by saying that he is directed to write letters to seven churches. Essentially, the Lord is telling John to deliver a message of displeasure from God to the churches that he is displeased with them, and to insist they keep the faith in the future. He talks of their sins and makes it clear that those who do not repent and change their ways will suffer tribulation. For several chapters, a clear line develops between those who follow the Lord without question, those who will be tested, those who pass the test and those who don't. You get the impression certain people are destined to be good and true followers of either God or Satan. Anyone wavering in between is left to choose between good and evil when tested.

Then comes the opening of seven seals. Four of the seals are about the horsemen of the Apocalypse. When each seal is opened, one of the four horsemen is set loose on the earth. The first horse is white and its rider wears a crown and carries a bow. He is a conqueror. The second horseman comes on a red horse and carries a great sword for killing and war. The third horseman is on a black horse and has balancing scales like those held by the Lady of Justice. The fourth and most well-known horseman comes on a pale horse carrying a sword and bringing death to 25 percent of the population. Seal five talks about white robes for the true followers, synonymous with their protection. Seal six results in the unleashing of major geological catastrophes on the earth. Just before the sixth seal is opened true believers would receive a mark on their foreheads from Jesus to protect them. Many interpretations believe that this group are those known to be good, holy, and loyal to God, and they will be raptured and sparred from the tribulation. Seal seven is where all hell actually breaks lose. When the seventh seal is opened, seven trumpets sound and each trumpet heralds a different type of devastation. The first four trumpets bring great destruction to earth and sea. The fifth trumpet results in the devil's arrival on earth. The sixth trumpet signals multiple woes. The first woe is the next round of illness, hunger, and war resulting in death for one-third of the population. Then there is a second woe where two prophets are slain. Finally, when the seventh seal is opened, Jesus and his army of angels are sent to earth.

Tom was starting to get tired from reading Revelation. He rubbed his temples and thought about the way it was written. There are a lot of details. A literal interpretation makes no sense. This is why he was struggling to focus on the general message. The details he did focus on, though, were those that seemed to have a correlation with things that were going on in the world.

He chose a good time to take a break. The flight attendants pulled out the service carts as he finished rubbing his temples and eyes. A coffee break would help him regain the energy and focus he needed to finish reading. He folded the middle seat table down.

The flight attendant asked him what he would like. Without hesitation he responded, "I would kill for a cup of black coffee, a glass of orange juice, and a double order of those fine biscotti cookies." She smiled, thinking that he was mocking the cookies, but he was actually serious. "I really like the cookies."

"Well, sir, you may be the only person in the world who does."

Tom savored his coffee as he looked out the window of the plane. It looked so beautiful from up here, and seated among those who could afford business trips and vacations, it was hard to believe that the world was in such a bad state of affairs. The global economy, with very few exceptions, was in a depression. The United States had a Great Recession because the banks and car companies were more than willing to comply with the government's urging to grant credit to people who couldn't afford to pay it back. In an attempt to stimulate the economy and control interest rates, the government printed money and for quite a while, it seemed to be working. The European Central Bank decided to use the same formula as a means to help with the sagging economies of Greece and Spain. It was contagious; Japan and China also started to use money-based tactics to boost their economy. North America, despite the roadblocks placed by government, used its new drilling technology to produce more petroleum and natural gas products than ever before. Governments in the East responded by further increasing production, which drove prices down and led to a significant number of oil company failures throughout the world.

What appeared to be the cure soon became the poison. Currencies were devalued; business failures cascaded from one related industry to another and one dependent country to another. Concurrent with the financial disaster, every year was seeing an increase in natural disasters. Hurricanes in Central and Southeast America, tornadoes in middle America, tsunamis of biblical proportion in Asia, and record snowfalls in Europe and northern parts of North America. There was a time when each year would bring a slightly different strain of flu to certain parts of the world, but now each year was bringing a serious disease, with each one harder to defend against and contain.

At the same time, a radical group of extremist known as the New Kingdom was formed. The New Kingdom extremist group was originally comprised of numerous extremist groups in the East, banding together to form a powerful and brutal force. Although launched and strongest in the East, the extremist group had expanded around the world. Their principal aim appears to be to annihilate people of Christian and Jewish faith, but their ultimate objective is unknown. Their organization traverses numerous countries and they continue to grow in power and scope, covering more geography each month and growing a massive well equipped army. They are well funded, but the source of their funds is also a mystery. It is believed that they have reached agreements with several countries possessing nuclear bombs to have access to those weapons. Their symbol is a lance that strongly resembles the Holy Lance. The New Kingdom uses the spear as their insignia. Upon close inspection it appears that there is a skull on the insignia and a serpent embedded in its design. The Holy Lance was the lance that was used by the soldier, Longinus, to pierce the side of Jesus, to insure his death as he hung on the cross. According to legend, the spear holds mysterious powers that are evil and hostile. It is also rumored that Hitler was obsessed by the Holy Lance and he may have briefly possessed it near the end of WWII.

Within the last two years, droughts around the world and related crop failures led to shortages of food and water, and food commodities soared in price. Fields of gold, could now be literally equated to the price of wheat. Although hard to connect all the dots, present day affairs seemed a lot like what John of Patmos described. Yet, it all seemed to Tom and others around him like that is a different world. We know it, we read about it, we fear it, but we don't see it.

Refreshed, Tom returned his attention to the Book of Revelation. The third part of Revelation deals with the tribulation, and is the time when the struggle between good and evil occurs. Chapter 13 speaks about the dragon placing the beast on earth in a position of power. "He" causes division between Christians and those who are not Christian. The choice becomes clear, if you want to eat you must follow the beast and accept his mark. The tide starts to turn in Chapter 15, where John writes that seven plagues befall those with the mark of the beast. Chapter 17 is mysterious and intriguing, as John talks about the great whore as a source of sin, deprivation, and deception. Finally, in Chapter 20, Jesus slays the beast and his followers, and reigns on earth without the devil and his followers for one thousand years before Satan is released again.

By the time Tom finished he had a headache. He walked toward the lavatory in the middle of the plane and on the way, asked a flight attendant for a bottle of water, aspirin, and another cup of hot coffee. She apologized for his headache, but due to government regulation they could not dispense medicine. She said she would be happy to bring him the water and coffee, requesting his seat number. The flight attendant proved to be efficient. The instant he sat down she arrived with the water and coffee. The moment she walked away a distinguished-looking man, with the look of a high-level corporate executive, slid into an aisle seat next to Tom. The shine on his wingtip shoes, the intricate face of his watch, and the precision fit of his three-piece suit had an aura of power and money. "Sir, I couldn't help but hear you tell the flight attendant that you have a headache. I am prone to headaches myself when I travel and always carry aspirin just in case." He pulled a small package from his breast pocket and held it toward Tom. "Perhaps these will help; they are completely sealed."

Normally Tom would not take anything from a stranger, but as promised, the package was sealed, looked like a legitimate one-dose package of aspirin, and this man seemed totally professional and sincere.

"Thank you, sir, I greatly appreciate your kindness." He opened the package, took the top off the water bottle and without any hesitation, popped the pills into his mouth and took a long sip of water. Although he appreciated the aspirin, he expected and hoped the man would return to his seat, but no such luck. His eyes aimed toward the laptop in the seat between them.

"I see you are reading the Holy Bible. You don't see that too often. Are you a member of the clergy or just a good Christian?" The gentleman flashed a charismatic smile as he posed his question.

"Well, I am not sure how good a Christian I am, but certainly not good enough to be clergy," Tom said. As much as he wanted quiet time and solitude, he didn't want to be rude to someone who had just gone out of his way to offer him kindness. "How about you, clergy or businessman?"

"Actually, a bit of both. I am a Methodist bishop, but my role is to manage the treasury of the church."

"A single church or all the Methodist churches?" Tom was intrigued.

"At the risk of sounding immodest, all of the Methodist churches," the suit answered.

"That must be a lot of money and a pretty prestigious job."

"It's a pittance compared to my counterpart in the Catholic Church, but yes, it is a serious amount of money and a lot of responsibility."

Tom extended his hand toward the bishop saying, "My name is Tom MacDonald. I work mainly in management consulting with an emphasis on the financial industry and even more of a focus on electronic payments."

The bishop took Tom's hand and they both gripped firmly. "My name is Bishop Michael Walker. Among my brothers and sisters I am referred to as The Treasurer. If you don't mind my asking, do you read the Bible regularly?"

"No, Bishop, I rarely read the Bible, although I know I should. In the few times I have read the Bible I have always read the same section."

"What section is that?" asked the Bishop.

"Revelation."

"Ah, of course, the section of the Bible that these days gets the most press and notoriety, yet it carries so little weight, theologically speaking."

"Bishop, it sounds like you aren't a fan. How do you and the Methodist Church interpret Revelation?"

Laughing at the way Tom posed the question the bishop responded, "Tom, are you Catholic?"

"Yes, how did you guess?"

"Your name, appearance, and the nature of the question are solid clues. To answer your question, the Methodist Church views Revelation the same way the Catholic Church does. We take from it what we believe makes sense, preach it, and because of that we stay away from the interpretations and explanations of the symbols that John speaks of in his vision. We believe the most important message is to be constant in preparation for the Lord's judgment. You will not know when that day will come."

"So you don't think that it in any way foretells the signs of the end times," Tom asked.

"Speaking as a preacher who has to answer to his superiors, no; but as a regular guy, who I really am, I sometimes wonder. I guess since you have read Revelation several times you think it might have something to do with end times?"

"Bishop, I am not sure if it has something to do with end times or just bad times, but yes, I do see parallels between what we see going on in the world today and the vision explained by John. I also think evil is winning. Leaders aren't leading, and we will need some serious help to turn things around."

"What makes you think evil is winning and leaders aren't leading," asked the Bishop.

"I've looked at the numbers and I see the changes in the Church. There are fewer churches, fewer priests and nuns, fewer parochial schools, and fewer people attending Mass. I go to church each week and I notice that the demographics have changed between the past generation and now. My parents' generation is well represented, but if you look around, few seats are filled by young people. Political correctness has gotten so extreme it has paralyzed dialogue. People making up their own religion to suit their need has caused a shift to a fanatically liberal definition of societal norms. Just a few years ago, many now commonplace actions were considered wrong. Christian and Jewish people are under attack worldwide and the violent extremist around the world are growing in number. I've heard my parish priest say he believes the devil is in the Church in reference to the sex scandal among some priests. I hear the pope and the president make speeches, but they aren't acting, just talking—empty words—and the problems are getting worse."

The bishop seemed uncomfortable and changed the subject. "Let me make another guess. As a consultant in electronic payments you are also intrigued by the mark of the beast and the interpretation that it refers to payment accounts and the ability to make purchases."

"Bishop, you hit the nail on the head. As a regular guy, Bishop, what do you think about that?"

"On that subject, Tom, I can't speak as a regular guy; certainly not as a treasurer, just as a preacher."

"The party line, eh!"

"Yes, I hope the aspirin help." With that, Bishop Walker stood up and went back to his seat.

Tom thought about how the conversation ended. No parting handshake, no let's keep in touch, or exchange of business cards, just a complete and fairly abrupt end to the conversation that ironically, the bishop had started.

Tom had long since stopped thinking about Philadelphia as his home, but he still had a fresh, exuberant feeling and a high level of comfort whenever he went back. He looked around for the bishop as he deplaned, but didn't see him. He wasn't eager to continue the conversation or to keep in touch, but there was a curiosity tugging on him in the wake of this somewhat strange encounter. He didn't see him. He couldn't resist buying some soft pretzels as a snack for the train ride to the burbs where his sister lived with her four children and successful attorney husband. He thought about all the old Philly food specials he would have to sample while in town. A cheese steak, of course; Tastykake butterscotch krimpets, scrapple, and sticky buns were all the items on his mental menu. The first leg of the train ride was from the airport to Center City. The second leg would take him north of the city to the Bristol Station. It was now mid-morning and both trains would be pretty empty.

When he arrived at Bristol Station, he could see his sister's car parked on the other side of the tracks. You had to go under a tunnel to get over there. Tom hated the train tunnels. They were always dingy. The walls showed an old coat of light-green paint which once might have been pleasant but was now streaked with brown and green marks running down the walls like small rivers. What lights there were, were usually under-powered, radiating pale shades of yellow beams through cages surrounding the bulbs to protect them from vandals. He noted that he was the only person to depart the train. He walked swiftly to and down the stairs, anxious to see his sister, nieces, and nephews. It had been too long since he saw them last. He made the turn to the section of the tunnel that went under the tracks and froze.

The hair went up on his wrists and back of his neck as a chilling fear came down on him like a torrent of water. Standing at the end of the tunnel between him and a left turn that would lead up the stairs, a shadowed figure lurked just beyond the bleak glow of the light over-head. The tall, broad figure seemed to be wearing a trench coat and hat like his grandfather and all the other men wore back in the forties and fifties —a silhouette of a man from times past. He stood there, not moving, like he was guarding the steps of the tunnel.

Tom gained his composure after about ten seconds but still clinging to his instincts. *This is a real threat.* Tom yelled, "Who are you and what do you want. The man in the trench coat responded, "I am what you fear."

Tom kept his distance but the voice seemed to be all around him. The same cold, damp darkness bled through the tunnel as it did in his hotel room after his unexpected call from Wasim. He felt an overwhelming grief as the darkness grew deeper. *God help me!* He reached inside his coat and pulled out the pistol. He held it to his right side so the bad guy could see it in profile. "I am going through this tunnel one way or the other and I do not fear you!" He raised the gun and pointed toward the menacing figure.

The man slowly turned to go up the steps. The figure paused and released a guttural laugh. "Oh, you fear me."

Tom's head was ringing. He kept the gun pointed in front of him and slowly turned the corner to look up the empty steps. He listened for footsteps above, but hearing nothing, he proceeded cautiously. His sister was parked just to the right of the exit at the top of the stairs and he quickly moved to the passenger side and hopped into the car.

"What the hell is going on—why do you have a gun?"

Tom's eyes darted frantically overly the landscape. "Did you see a guy in a trench coat?"

"I sure did; what a creepy-looking figure. Where did he get on the train?" Tom's heart was pounding. "He wasn't on the train." Did you see what he looked like," Tom asked.

"No, he kept his head down and to the left to shield his face."

"Did you see what he was driving?"

"No, once he passed, I didn't think about him other than he was creepy. He gave me a really weird feeling.

"Like being depressed, in a dark, cold, damp place?"

Yes, how do you know that," she asked.

"I had the same feeling when I encountered that guy in the tunnel."

"You think that that feeling has something to do with that guy?"

"Yes," he said but nothing more. He didn't want to continue. It was stupid to stay with her and the kids. Now he was getting them involved. *You already said too much, you dumb shit!* "I have no idea who he was or why we both got that feeling. It was probably just the way he was dressed, and the station is just damp and dark anyway." Fortunately, Mo, bought this explanation, and didn't go back to questioning him about carrying a gun.

Maureen's house was an old, late-nineteenth century mansion on the Delaware River. It was a complete mess when they bought it, and they had spent a lot of time renovating it to bring it back to its former glory. Mo's husband was an attorney who specialized in divorce cases. After law school he opened his own practice and he lucked into a case that involved a filthy-rich couple who both suspected infidelity. He was hired by the wife and asked to provide a package deal comprised of a private detective to get the proof, file for the divorce, and then handle the settlement, including custody of the kids and amount of alimony. The husband was very well known in the area and thought he was invincible, given his money and position. He pushed back hard, and the wife went public with the information. Suddenly, the husband wanted the wife to be quiet, and Bill set a steep going rate for silence. Word got out, and Bill found himself in the enviable position of being the turnkey attorney for rich, unfaithful couples. The pay was very good and the work steady.

Mo gave Tom a room on the second floor with a private bath and great view of the river. The kids were all at school and the house was quiet. After he got settled, Tom and Mo had coffee and tea and got caught up. After covering all the usual ground that brothers and sisters talk about, Mo got down to serious business. "When are you and Claire going to tie the knot?"

"Mo, you know every time we talk you ask me that question. I never ask you when you and Bill are going to get a divorce."

"That's ridiculous; we know all too well how divorces work out, and two people who really love each other can find a way to overcome any problem. The key word is REALLY love each other. Unfortunately, our culture has evolved to the point where we talk about starter wives, and husbands. Don't be evasive, what's the deal?" Mo was direct.

"I don't know if we ever will get married," Tom said.

"That makes no sense. You make a great couple, very compatible and otherwise you are both practicing Catholics. What does your priest say when you go to confession," she asked.

"I haven't been to confession in years."

"But I bet you go to Church and receive communion every week—just liberal enough to believe that God will find that acceptable."

"I can't argue that point, Tom said. "You win, I will ask Claire to marry me just as soon as I see her again."

"You never change. You've been mocking me since you were thirteen and became the typical Philly wise guy. I love you anyway."

"I know and I love you too. I have some work to do so I am going to retire to my room," Tom said.

"Okay, the kids all have after school activities and will be in around five. Dinner is at six-thirty and hopefully, Bill won't get tied up tonight."

Tom spent the afternoon catching up on his e-mail. He now had three possibilities for new consulting engagements starting in January, and it was important that he keep in contact with the principals to answer questions and make plans on a what-if basis. He wanted to e-mail or call Claire, but they had decided that they should try to keep radio silence except for a phone call a day, which was a minimum normal for them.

The evening was relatively quiet considering the house was full of children between the ages of 10 and 16. Tom made a point of going downstairs to greet the kids as they came home and spend some time with them. Bill made it home just in time for dinner. Sitting at the dinner table reminded him of his early years. He had forgotten how comforting it was to have a simple meal of meatloaf, mashed potatoes, and peas, and the entire family at the table sharing the highlights of the day.

Bill, always the attorney, started the questioning. "So, what brings you to town this time, Tommy boy," his tone jovial.

"I am getting together with my old friend, Archbishop Gleason, tomorrow and then on Thursday I have a business meeting in Connecticut."

Skip, their oldest son seemed impressed. "Uncle Tom, the archbishop is your friend?"

"Exactly; we met in high school and have stayed in touch ever since."

Bill, who was on the church board chimed in. "There is talk that he could be the next pope."

"Could be," shrugged Tom. "The archbishop has a perfect and somewhat rare mix of being regarded as very holy, but very down-to-earth. He has a good sense of the real world," Tom added.

"He's not hard to look at. It's always easier for the pretty people to get ahead," Mo said.

"Oh, Mom, come on, he's a priest," Skip added.

"Tom, Mo says you are going to your meetings by train. You are more than welcome to use one of our cars. It would save you a lot of time," Bill offered graciously.

"Thanks, Bill, but I like taking the train. It allows me to get some work done or read a little and because it's scenic. It is also cheaper, and I try to save my customers' money," said Tom.

"Not me, I'm an attorney. We try to take all of our customers' money." Everybody laughed at this despite its sad truth.

Tom spent the evening with the family, and as he laid his head down he couldn't ignore the truth in Mo's assessment of him and Claire. She was right and on balance, the single, workaholic life wasn't as rewarding as the family life. Perhaps if the world didn't end before the end of the year, his New Year resolutions might include some course changes. He called Claire before bed for a quick goodnight and then he quickly fell asleep and didn't wake until the alarm went off.

* * *

Sal Assante left the office at around nine thirty. He had been working late, setting up network changes that had to be done by Christmas. Sal hated working late. His job was simple, and one aspect of it yielded a nice bonus. But, the holidays were important to him, and he wanted to guarantee this project was completed early so all the inevitable last-minute changes didn't cause him to be late.

He parked in a cheap, convenient lot. As he turned off the main street, he scanned the next two blocks to the parking lot and smiled. *No one in sight.* He hated when panhandlers would confront him. He was slight at 5'4", and he didn't feel confident about fending off muggers. All types of panhandlers, muggers, con artists, dope addicts, and hookers were prevalent in the downtown Atlanta area at night. He hadn't gone ten yards when first he sensed and then heard someone close by. He heard them behind him. He didn't look back, but quickened his pace and the stalker matched the increase. The first of two traffic lights was green, and Sal was relieved that he didn't have to slow down, hoping that the person behind him would turn at the corner. He didn't. Sal was getting nervous.

He decided to cross the street before the cross walk to see if he was really being followed. The long strides of the stalker continued in his path. Sal quickened his pace. As he reached the corner he saw that the traffic light was about to change to red and several cars were coming down the street from the right, the first of which was only a short distance away. His instincts, formed as a street kid in South Philadelphia, kicked in, and he bolted across the street into the parking building. The elevator door didn't immediately open when he pressed the button so he sprinted for the stairwell and up the steps to his car. He never stopped or looked back until he got in. Hands trembling, he locked the doors, turned the key, and pulled out of his spot. He drove down the ramps, and only slowed momentarily to place his key fob by the reader. He pulled out onto the street. Nothing in front of him, and the first light was green. He looked to his left and saw a tall man in a trench coat and fedora style hat. The man's eyes were dark and penetrating, and he looked directly at Sal with a portentous stare. Sal held the wheel tightly. He was scared, a weakening feeling of misery seeped into his thoughts but he managed to maneuver the car despite the strange and debilitating sensation of sadness clouding his reality. His foot slammed the pedal to the floor.

* * *

"I don't give a damn...what other projects . . . you have to support . . . this project . . . is your top priority . . . do . . . you . . . hear me." Wasim sat at his desk with the speakerphone on. As he yelled at Jim Martin and George Corbett, he pounded his fist on the desk after every phrase. "Wasim, you are asking me to put a project at top priority that your board hasn't even voted on yet and may not approve of until the end of the year."

As Jim spoke, Wasim looked like he was going to explode. He slammed his fist on the desk again as if to herald what he was about to say. "I am not asking you, I am telling you! If you value your job you will get this project done before the board meeting," Wasim threatened.

I will do my best to get the project done by January 8, but I can't guarantee it."

Wasim pounded the desk again, his voice lowered as he hissed, "You will complete this project by Christmas Day if you value your position." Then he picked up the phone handset and slammed it down. "George, are you still on the line?"

"Yeah, but I wish I hadn't been on the line."

"George, do you know what the hell is going on? This project doesn't even have board approval and I am being told that if my company doesn't implement by Christmas I lose my job. You're the COO over there; can you give me some guidance on how to deal with this?" said Jim.

George Corbett was COO at Universe Card. He, Wasim, and Jim had worked together for years. George was very much like Jim, except he wasn't at all buttoned-down. He had been Wasim's right-hand man as Wasim and he rose to the top of the card processing industry. He was a serious and skilled manager and he had a great sense of humor; he had to, to work with Wasim and keep his sanity.

"Yeah, if you value your life, let alone your job, you will make sure this project is your top priority and that it's ready to roll well ahead of Christmas."

"You're joking as usual, right, George?"

"Jim, I am not kidding. When you are doing the devil's work, the price of failure is high."

* * *

Tom felt exhilarated as he got off the train at the Market Street Station. He used to travel this route often, and although he didn't miss it, it was exciting to be back in the midst of all the hustle and bustle and experience the familiarity of the train stations in center city. It was mainly business people during rush hour, but since it was almost midday there were also a lot of shoppers and sightseers who were coming into town to shop at the high-end stores and restaurants or visit the historic attractions. As Tom walked the five blocks from the train station to the rectory, he thought about the downtown area of Philadelphia as an absolute wonder. It contained so much history, and was home to grand architecture, both new and old.

The old and great city this morning seemed full of wonder to him. Many buildings dated back to the founding of the country, and museums housed its great riches and chronicled its development from virtually nothing to the greatest nation in the world. It had its down-sides as well, as an old Northeast rust belt city and its ghettos, but this morning all he saw and felt was the exhilaration of being in his old home and meeting with a friend who he trusted and hoped could give him some needed guidance.

He turned a corner and suddenly he could see the majestic Logan Square. His eyes were drawn to the east side of the square where the Cathedral Basilica of Saints Peter and Paul dominated the skyline. The cathedral was the head church of the Roman Catholic Archdiocese of Philadelphia. The cathedral is the largest Catholic Church in the state of Pennsylvania. The building was impressive. It took eighteen years to build because of the cost, and is the largest brownstone structure and one of the most architecturally notable buildings in Philadelphia. The cathedral with its palladium style façade, vaulted dome, ornate main altar, eight side chapels, and a main sanctuary that can hold 2,000 worshipers is an intimidating building. The windows are placed strangely very high up on the walls. When it was built, anti-Catholic sentiment in the city was so high it was feared rioters would smash the windows. Legend is that the builders would throw rocks as high as they could to determine where to place the windows.

Tom looked at his watch to see if he had enough time to stop into the cathedral and say a prayer. He only had enough time left to be on time, and he didn't want to cut his time short with Frank.

The rectory was another brownstone building next to the cathedral. He went to the front door, but there was a sign on the door with an arrow pointing to the left, indicating that visitors should go to the side door. There was an alley about 15 feet wide between the cathedral and the rectory that was paved with cobblestones. He saw a covered entryway about 20 yards down on the right and concluded that must be the entry to the rectory.

Suddenly, he started to feel as though he was sinking, and the alley, already dark from the brownstone shadows, seemed to go darker and damp. He looked around a full 360 degrees but saw nothing.

He rushed to the door and rang the bell. A middle-aged woman came to the door and introduced herself as Kathleen Kelly, assistant to His Eminence. She led him to a large office. Next to the archbishop's desk there was a conference table, where she directed him to be seated. "His Eminence will join you momentarily. He had an unexpected urgent call from Rome this morning and is now running behind schedule. Can I get you something to drink?"

"Yes, Kathleen, coffee would be great."

"Cream or sugar?"

"No thanks, I drink it black."

"Very well."

He sat looking around the room. The ceilings must have been fifteen feet high, and the entire room was done in a dark wood with built-in bookshelves and large, canopied nooks for the statues of Jesus, his mother, Mary, father, Joseph, and the most impressive, a sword-wielding St. Michael the Archangel. Only a few minutes passed before an elderly woman with a decidedly Irish accent entered the room carrying a silver platter upon which was a silver coffee pot, sugar bowl, and creamer. Without a word, she poured a cup for him. "Would you care for cream and sugar?"

"No thank you, ma'am, I drink it black."

"Yes, Kathleen did say that, but me memory isn't what it used to be."

"Neither is mine ma'am, thank you." He thought for a moment that he was in a 1940's movie with the singing priest and the Irish maids.

Tom noticed that his hand trembled slightly as he lifted his cup. He thought about that depressing feeling that struck him again in the alley. He was completely baffled by it. The only time he had anything close to that feeling was when he would wake up in the wee hours of the morning when he was under pressure on a big project and held fears about completing the project on time and with good results. That feeling he had come to understand was self-doubt that can seep into your psyche when you are in a weakened state. He had learned to avoid the feeling by working hard to stay on schedule, getting plenty of rest and exercise. He had also mastered focusing his mind on pleasant things when he woke in the middle of the night. This feeling was different though, and except for last night, he wasn't sleeping well no matter what he tried.

The Archbishop Francis Xavier Gleason entered the room with a flourish. He was dressed in a black wool cassock trimmed in black silk and tailored to flatter his thin, fit figure. He was made even more dashing by a purple silk rabat and silk sash with fringes. He wore a pectoral cross suspended from a chain. Many archbishops wear a purple silk skullcap with crimson lining, but Frank had a full head of wavy, jet-black hair and was vain enough to go without the cap, since it was optional. And of course for the same reasons, he wore an ornate ring of an archbishop bearing Jesus on the cross. He moved quickly and elegantly and for a moment, Tom was reminded of a swashbuckler initiating a sword fight.

Tom, it is so good to see you! It has been much too long since we have talked. First, please tell me about your business and of your lovely lady."

"Frank, it is good to see you as well, and I agree, it has been way too long. Business is good. I have managed to be on almost constant assignment, and over eighty percent of my time this past year has been billable. The work is interesting and the clients have paid on time. I have used the other twenty percent of the time to keep up on the latest developments in the world of finance, and especially card processing. Claire is doing well. She doesn't seem to age, she has a great job, visits and rides her horse daily, and we get along. We're very happy," Tom smiled when he spoke of Claire.

"I would be remiss, my friend, if I didn't tell you that unless you are celibate like me that you are living in sin. Since you think so well of Claire, you should make an honest woman of her and marry her."

"Celibate like you?" said Tom.

"I haven't had an affair in several years. I think aging is serving me well. There hasn't been anyone persisting that was so beautiful I couldn't walk away in a long time. Of course, it doesn't hurt that since

I was promoted, I receive a lot more scrutiny and I am now constantly in the public eye."

"Frank, how long do we have to talk?"

"I know I promised you all the time you need, but something has come up and I am now booked from two o'clock to the end of the day. We have only two hours."

The elderly woman entered with a tray of lunch for them. It was typical Philadelphia lunch consisting of a grilled cheese sandwich, New England clam chowder, a chocolate chip cookie, and iced tea. She spoke not a word as she placed the tray on the end of the table, setting each plate and bowl in front of them. "Will there be anything else, Your Eminence?"

"No, that's perfect, Mrs. Ryan, thank you. You can pick up the tray after our meeting." The Archbishop turned his focus back to Tom. "So, what is it that has caused you to travel to the City of Brotherly Love at the height of prime time Christmas shopping season?"

First, Tom told Frank about the deaths of the Universe Card board members and that he felt it was part of a conspiracy. He then laid out for the archbishop the specifics of his dinner conversation with Jim Martin, relating all the details about how rationing could be used as the pretext for controlling access to life's necessities. He told him about the veiled threat he received on the phone from Wasim Mirza. The archbishop listened to the entire story, and not once did he show any emotion. He ate as Tom talked, and when he finished his lunch he sat back, legs crossed. He sat with the perfect posture you would expect from a young, fit, rising star in the Church. Tom pictured him sitting that way in the confessional on Saturday afternoon. When Tom had related the full depth of his foreboding theory, and the turmoil likely to follow, the archbishop simply looked at him.

"Anything else you want to add?"

"Yes, I have experienced a feeling several times that is hard to explain. The first time was after I got the telephone call from Mirza, the second was when I was confronted by the spooky guy in the train tunnel, and the third time was this morning, in the alley between the cathedral and the rectory."

"Anything else?"

Tom was surprised at Frank's calm reception to his worries. "No, I think that covers it."

"Who have you spoken to about this?"

"A good friend who works at Primary Card Processing and Claire, of course."

"And what did they think about it?"

"Andy seemed to accept what I said, and Claire, after first expressing skepticism, agreed. She also thinks that I should drop my pursuit of the matter, because I am too much of a boy scout and she doesn't think there is much that I can do about it."

"You seem to be certain that this situation is tied to end times and that it can be connected with Revelation. What specific connections do you see?"

"I had read Revelation several times before, and each time I tried to make sense of every detail. I read it again on the plane ride here and I decided to try to capture the main points. As a result, I came to some basic conclusions. John of Patmos's vision encompasses all the wickedness of the world. He is shown images of all of these problems, sins, tribulations, natural disasters, and wars, in an organized and detailed fashion. The array of dire circumstances is so vast it is impossible to correlate everything with what is going on in our world today at one time. Also, it is impossible for someone in the first century to understand and to describe what he is seeing. I am convinced that the only way to make sense of Revelation is to concentrate on the main items and messages apart from what John of Patmos clearly says in a literal context. The overall message is clear that near the end of times, Evil is winning, and God intervenes to save those who remain good. Despite all the tribulation and persecution, Evil will ultimately be defeated." Tom continued, trying to focus on what was most important. "Since we don't have a lot of time I'll try to give you the highlights of my conclusions. I believe that the description of the angels opening the seven seals is the description of the onset of end times. The first seal, the rider on the white horse carrying a bow and crown, the Conqueror, is the rise of the violent extremist. The second seal, the rider on the red horse carrying a great sword for killing and war, is the nuclear bomb capability of unstable societies in the East. The third seal, the rider on the black horse, carrying a scale, is control of the payment system to decide who can buy food and gas. I think the opening of the fourth seal, the rider on a pale horse, carrying a sword and creating hunger, causing death to twenty-five percent of the population, represents all the epidemics, natural disasters, and droughts that we have experienced since the beginning of the third millennium."

The archbishop was listening intently but didn't say a word or show any emotion. "Do you think I am crazy, Frank?"

"No, not at all. Please, continue."

Tom went on. "I think the fifth seal where the angels give white robes to the true believers means the Lord will protect them through this period. When the sixth seal is opened there are epic geological catastrophes, and the true believers receive a mark that, like the white robe, is their protection. I believe this means that the plan to cut off Christians from food and gas goes wrong somehow. Seal seven is an unleashing of all the prior misery combined, signified by the sound of seven trumpets. I take John's message literally for each of the trumpets that sound after the seventh seal is opened. He says the first four trumpets bring great destruction to the earth and the sea. The fifth trumpet of the seventh seal brings the devil himself to earth. The first woe of the sixth trumpet wipes out one-third of the world's population. That has to be the result of a nuclear war. I am not sure what the second woe of the sixth seal is about. It says that two prophets will be slain. That could be the pope in Rome and the head of the Orthodox Christians, since they are the leaders of the two largest Christian populations. The seventh seal seems pretty clear to me. The devil forms his army on earth and Jesus is born again—the second coming." Tom paused. Frank remained silent, still listening intently. "Are you still on board," asked Tom.

"Yes, I am listening and if it helps, I don't think you are at all crazy."

As if to gather the physical strength to continue, Tom took a bite of his sandwich and a sip of his tea. Over an hour into the meeting, his soup looked like it had solidified. "After the seals and trumpets have all been sounded, the struggle between good and evil commences. In Revelation 13, the right-hand man of the devil is placed in a position of power and causes division among Christians. I hate to say it, Frank, but in my view that could only be the pope, or the US president. If you don't follow this powerful guy, then you don't get food or gas. In Revelation 15:7 the tables seem to turn, and those with the mark of the beast are beset by plagues. Revelation 17 is interesting. It talks about the great whore, which I believe is the Internet and the news media that are used by the devil to control and influence what people think and to pervert governments, religious institutions, and businesses. Lastly, and literally, in Revelation 20 Jesus slays the devil and his army. Peace follows on earth for 1,000 years while the devil and his army are locked away in hell."

Tom looked at Frank. "Well, what do you think?" he said simply.

"If you ask me as a leader of the Church I would say that your interpretation is one of the more practical, relatable interpretations that I have heard. The only clear message we can be sure of though is that you will not know the time when Jesus comes again, but we should always be prepared for his coming."

"The party line," said Tom. "That's a lot like what a Methodist bishop said to me on the plane coming here yesterday.

"You told all of that to a Methodist minister?" Frank sounded incredulous.

"No, we spoke in general terms, but when I told him I thought we were in end times he got real quiet. In fact, he abruptly ended the conversation after he initiated it."

"He was a Methodist bishop?"

"Yes, he was a bishop and head of the Methodist Church treasury."

"How was he dressed?" Frank was interested.

"Impeccably, he would have fit in on Wall Street."

"Methodist bishops are fastidious dressers, but they also follow rules like I do. At a minimum, he should have been wearing a purple shirt," Frank said. The archbishop got up and walked to his desk, woke up his computer, quickly typed something in and then said to Tom, "Come over here a minute, please. Did he look like this guy?"

"No, who is that?"

"That is the bishop and treasurer of the Methodist Church. Tom, it is unlikely he was a bishop. More likely, he was following you and trying to find out what you are doing."

Frank motioned Tom to return to the conference table. The archbishop sat in what struck Tom as a regal manner, legs crossed, hands folded in his lap, and head held high. Again, Tom wondered if that was how he sat in the confessional box, but didn't ask. Frank seemed pensive and serious. "Tom, if you think we are in end times, and Revelation is a road map, then you must also believe that these things are pre-ordained. So, what makes you think that you can do anything to change them?"

"I believe that if you are a good person and you see something wrong you should do what you can to fix it. There are some twists and turns in Revelation. Perhaps some of the turnaround is a result of good people doing what they can to stop the devil. If there are people on earth who are doing the devil's work, there needs to be people who do God's work."

"If Mirza can access the keys and the software, why would he wait for board approval?"

"I am not sure he could get the keys. The people who have them are sworn not to give them up and from what I have been told they don't just hold the keys. They're the only ones who know how to apply them," Tom explained.

"Perhaps he's covering his bet," Frank mused.

"To be honest, I don't know."

"Who do you think tipped off Mirza about your interest in all this?"

"Jim Martin," Tom said sternly.

"Are you sure?"

"Yes," replied Tom.

"You're certain it wasn't Andy or Claire?"

"I would bet my life on it."

"Be assured, you are," Frank cautioned. Tom was shaken, not expecting another warning.

"Tom, if I tell you what I really think about all this you have to swear not to repeat it—to anyone." Tom swore and the archbishop went on. "First, as a Notre Dame fan, I prefer Knute Rockne's four horsemen to those of Revelation." Tom smiled, recognizing that Frank was trying to lighten the moment. "Unofficially, I am not sure about the details, but everything you've said seems to generally add up. I agree with Claire, though. You *are* a boy scout and you're in way over your head. Whether it is end of times or these extremist are part of Satan's army, you're dealing with people who are capable of anything. Know this though, Jesus had great faith and drew strength from the simple fact that he represented complete and total goodness. Jesus completed his mission."

"Ah, Frank, that is somewhat reassuring but as you certainly know He was crucified."

Frank continued. "We need to talk about that feeling you described— the sudden onset of augmented darkness—the cold, damp void. It's the presence of evil. Not just bad evil, but satanic evil. People who have suffered through possession have described experiencing something similar just before they were consumed. Priests who have performed exorcisms have told of related accounts. I don't think you are going to be possessed, but you do have to be concerned about this presence. When we are done talking, we will go to the cathedral where we will pray. I will give you a special blessing and a crucifix to help you if it happens again."

"What, no necklace made of garlic," Tom joked anxiously.

"Tom, this is very serious," the archbishop's brow furrowed. "What I am going to do will help you but the strongest weapon, your greatest defense, is believing that Jesus is walking with you, that He wants you to succeed and that no matter what you encounter, he will be there to help you. You must believe this without doubt, hesitation or fear. Put your fate in his hands and then do what you feel you must do."

"I feel like you must see what I see; if you don't think this is crazy. It makes me think your colleagues, the archbishops, cardinals and possibly the pope, see it too. And, if that's the case, then some other people in high places, like the president are probably somewhat aware. Why aren't they doing something? Why aren't they leading?" Tom asked, exasperated.

The archbishop sighed and looked away. His eyes were distant when he answered. "Leaders for the second part of the twentieth century and now into the twenty-first century are politically correct. They have confused views of what is right and what is wrong, and they bow to the thoughtless whims of the masses." He looked back at Tom and continued more excitedly. "This description meets most of the world leaders. Many of them are influenced by what John of Patmos calls the dragon and the beast. You know, most Nazis under Hitler thought they were doing the right thing."

"What do you think we should do next?" Tom asked.

"I will do all that I can from inside the Church. I have spoken out before, both privately and in public. I have no problem doing it again. But while I can speak out, I can't be outspoken. The pope has warned me twice in the past about saying things that might make the congregation fear that the end times are near."

"Really? Did you ask the pope why he wasn't doing anything," Tom asked.

"Yes and he told me that he was doing all that he could."

Frank looked at Tom as if there was nothing more for him to say, and extended his right hand toward Tom with his palm up. "What's your next step?"

"Well, when I came here my objective was to determine if I was losing my mind or if this was actually happening. Since you seem to think I haven't lost it, my next objective is to figure out how to stop it. I am meeting with the head of World Passport Card on Thursday. Hopefully, he is a believer and can help me. I also have a high-up contact at Giggly, and I will see what I can find out from him. I feel like I am searching in the dark though. I am not exactly sure what I am doing. I would rather be acting on what I think I know than just getting confirmation as I try to investigate. I am amazed that with all the power in the world, the pope, the president, , world leaders, that little old Tom MacDonald, management consultant, and card carrying boy scout is the only person prepared to do battle with the devil."

The archbishop glanced at the clock on his desk. As he rose from his chair he reached into his desk and pulled out a small, black felt-covered box. "Come on, Tom. Our time together grows short." They walked together briskly out of the office, down the hallway, and out the door Tom had entered. They crossed the alley, and into the sacristy of the cathedral.

The archbishop put on his vestments as if he was about to say Mass. He led Tom onto the altar of the cathedral.

Tom felt self-conscious. Although there couldn't have been more than a dozen people in the cathedral, all eyes were on him and the archbishop. The archbishop didn't seem to notice. He directed Tom to kneel before the altar. Walking back, the archbishop opened the black box and placed it on the altar. He knelt down and prayed. After a moment he rose, and blessed the contents of the box, and pulled out a fairly large, simple wooden crucifix on a thin rope chain. The archbishop then walked to Tom and placed the crucifix around his neck, blessed him again, and knelt down beside Tom. The archbishop then said several prayers in Latin. He went through a long litany of saints, asking them each to pray for them. Tom instinctively recited the response along with the archbishop after he said each saint's name. The response was simply "Pray for us." When the litany was completed, he said several more prayers in Latin. He led Tom as they recited the Our Father, Hail Mary, and Glory Be. The archbishop rose, gave Tom a final blessing, and motioned for Tom to rise. They walked to the front door of the cathedral. Being that they were now in public, Tom addressed him formally, "Archbishop, was that an exorcism?" said Tom.

"Of sorts. The prayers I said are usually those that would be said at a formal exorcism, commanding Satan to leave you in the name of Jesus and calling for the prayers and protection of Jesus, the Blessed Mother, Michael the Archangel, and the saints."

"You think I need that much help. You think I need a sort of exorcism?"

"You need all the help you can get. Mother Teresa gave me that crucifix when she visited here years ago. Later in her life she received similar prayers. She was suffering from insomnia. The Bishop of Calcutta concluded that Satan was the reason she was having trouble sleeping." He paused and gave Tom, an earnest look. "I will do all that I can to help you, Tom. Keep in touch, and God Bless you." He shook Tom's hand, turned with his usual flourish, and walked back into the cathedral.

* * *

Sal's wife had kept some food warm and was waiting for him when he arrived home. "Sal, what's wrong; you look like you saw a ghost."

"I'm not sure what I saw. Some spooky guy started following me on the street. I had to run to the lot and then to my car at just the right moment to get away. When I pulled out of the parking lot I saw him watch me leave." Sal sounded sick, concerned. He continued, "He just stood there, looking at me with a mean look on his face. I hate to admit it, but it really shook me up. When I was walking down the street I got a funny feeling, you know? Like I knew someone was following me. But it was more than that. I got this strange sensation like it was darker, damp and colder, and I felt like really, really down."

His wife gave him a concerned look. "Well, at least you figured out how to get away from him," she said inhaling loudly.

"I didn't figure anything out, I was just scared and acted out of fear," said Sal.

"I'll get your dinner out of the oven and pour you a beer. Why don't you sit down on the sofa, turn on the TV and relax."

As soon as his wife turned the corner into the kitchen, Sal walked over to the window and pushed the curtain over just enough so that he could see outside. The street was empty, illuminated by the soft glow of the street lamps. Overcome with relief, he thought that it was probably just one of the endless kooks that hang out downtown.

* * *

Tom walked toward the train station with a bounce in his step. It was a relief to him to have someone like Frank confirm he wasn't crazy. He also felt stronger, both spiritually and physically. He took to heart the archbishop's words, and to his soul his blessing. He needed to determine if he was reading this situation correctly, and he not only fulfilled that objective, but he also gained something he didn't realize he needed . . . protection. He had barely eaten any of his lunch since he did most of the talking. He used this as a great excuse to grab a hot dog at the first food cart he encountered, and a soft pretzel from the second cart on the next corner.

As soon as he got to the train station, he checked the schedule and then called his sister to let her know that he was going to be earlier than he had told her. He wanted to call Claire and tell her about the meeting with Frank, but he didn't want to chance a leak, knowing that he was being monitored, and he didn't want to bother her while she was working.

The return train trip was uneventful. He was calm as he entered the tunnel underneath the tracks at the Bristol Station and there wasn't any boogeyman waiting for him there. The evening was a repeat of the night before, and it reinforced his thoughts about family life and what he might be missing.

After the kids were in bed, he sat at the table with Bill and Mo. Bill started the conversation. "So, how was your get-together with the archbishop?"

"It was nice. We had planned to spend the afternoon together, but he had an urgent matter come up and we had to cut off at two o'clock, which is why I was early returning."

"Did the archbishop have anything to say about the wave of violence brought by the extremist and the Church's lack of action," Bill asked.

"It actually did come up," said Tom.

"Does he offer any explanation? The pope is just standing by watching a global slaughter of Christians and Jewish people by the extremist," Bill was heated.

"His bottom line is that the pope and other world leaders lack the intestinal fortitude to mount a meaningful response. He thinks the papacy has long since retreated if not been completely excluded from participation in civil matters," said Tom.

Mo decided to join in the discussion. "Not like the old days. Wasn't your and the archbishop's school mascot the Crusader," asked Mo.

"Yes, it was; funny you mention it. I hadn't thought of that but this all is in itself a crusade." Bill gave Tom and Mo a quizzical look. Bill was raised without religion. He converted to Catholicism to marry Mo. Although he became a serious Christian, he didn't have the benefit of a Catholic school education like Tom and Mo. The Crusades weren't covered in public school. Tom explained to remedy Bill's confusion.

"The First Crusade was a response to the Byzantine Emperor Alexios I Komnenos's request that Western volunteers come to his aid to repel an invasion. The request was made to Pope Urban II. The pope influenced the heads of state in Western Europe and the first Crusade was mounted. They reclaimed the Holy Lands taken in conquests of the Levant, ultimately resulting in the recapture of Jerusalem and freeing Eastern Christians."

"I see. Things are so much different now. Back then the enemy was identifiable and the leaders of the world were clear on what was right and what was wrong. Now in the rise of violent extremist, the enemy is in the shadows, dispersed throughout the world, and even in the East where there are armies, few are willing to attack them. The problem just grows and grows."

Tom responded, "Exactly, plus, the world has a lot of other things to deal with—wrecked currencies and economies, natural disasters, pandemics, droughts."

Mo, as usual, was ready to oversimplify and close the deal. "We need a hero," she said.

"We do indeed, and on that note I think I am going to retire to my room, check on my e-mail and check in on Claire," Tom rose from the table.

"Tell her we send our love, and maybe you ought to think about making an honest woman of her," jested Mo.

"I will tell her you send your love. She is an honest woman."

"You know what I mean."

He hoped when he checked his e-mail that there would be some positive reaction to his last communications with his consulting prospects, but no such luck. He would spend some time tomorrow trying to ignite some interest. As soon as Claire answered the phone, he sensed something was wrong.

"Did you have a nice visit with your old pal?"

"I did. I learned some meaningful things and he gave me something I didn't know I needed."

"Can you tell me any more than that," asked Claire, guarded.

"Yes, but it might sound like the parody of the mafia guys. 'Hey, Louie, did you take care of that thing? Yeah, I took care of that thing, just like you told me. No, Louie, not that thing, the other thing. Oh, that thing, yeah, I took care of that thing, too.' The archbishop listened to my story, which by the way I have now figured out in more detail, and he told me he didn't think I was crazy, and thought there might be truth to my concerns. He also told me to stay the course and put my faith and trust in Jesus. I received his blessing, and he gave me a crucifix that was a very special gift to him from Mother Teresa."

"I wish he could do the same for me," Claire sounded uncomfortable.

"Why, what's happened?"

"I went to visit Celtic King this evening and as I entered the stable I got that creepy feeling. It didn't last long, but it kind of unnerved me."

"Claire, I don't want to alarm you, but you need to be careful. That feeling is something real. It is dangerous. Can you take some time off," Tom asked.

"Are you kidding me? With all that is going on in the world, if I took time off they would tell me to never come back." she replied. Tom wanted to tell her that she was in danger of losing much more than her job but decided against it.

"I will have a few more trips to make in the next couple of weeks. They should be forty-eight hour trips and I want you to go with me. It would be best for both of us," he said instead.

"Okay, boyo, but you will have to give me at least a few days advance notice."

"I promise I will. Claire, you need to promise me something."

"What's that," she asked.

"That you will not go anywhere alone," he said.

"I am not sure I can promise that. I mean, who is going to go to the stable with me?"

"I don't know. Invite a friend, or make sure you go at a time when someone is there tending to the stable or horses."

"All right. I guess I can work that out somehow, I promise. Are you enjoying your visit with Maureen and her family?" Claire changed the subject.

"Yes. In fact, it has been sort of a fringe benefit that I didn't plan on. They have a very nice home. They seem really happy and the kids are all doing great. It's just like the family environment I grew up knowing and loving," said Tom.

"Does it have you thinking about settling down and starting a family," Claire asked.

"Actually, that exact thought has crossed my mind a couple times the past few days. Is that something that might interest you?" Tom sounded hopeful.

"Yes, but to be honest I'm not sure if either of us could change our lifestyle at this point and be happy with the change."

"It would take some effort, but you usually get out of things what you put into them," Tom offered.

"Not to sound like I am making an argument against it, but are you sure you want to bring children into this crazy world?" Claire said in disbelief.

"We have to stay positive and optimistic about the world and do what we can to make it better."

"My charming Boy Scout, on a mission to save the world and believing that he can."

"Do you really think that I am a Boy Scout," asked Tom.

"Oh yeah, you are a Boy Scout out to earn every merit badge you can chasing wind mills. The singing cowboy on the white horse, wearing a white hat, riding after the bad guys into the sunset. All those things wrapped up in one. Maybe when you clean up Dodge we can start a family," joked Claire.

"Ok, I will get right on it."

"What are your plans for tomorrow," Claire asked.

"I hope to get a good run in, see what I can do to get a consulting engagement lined up, and lay out my plans for saving the world in more detail. How about you?"

"I will put in a full day, hopefully find some time for riding, assuming I can secure a chaperone and then have a quiet dinner at home tomorrow night."

"Well, I better let you go. I love you, Claire."

"I love you too. Please be careful," she said sweetly and hung up the phone.

The meeting with the archbishop seemed to help Tom with his sleep. He had no trouble going to sleep despite the early hour. It was unusual for him to put his head on a pillow before ten o'clock, let alone be able to shut off his mind and go to sleep. He awoke at five thirty feeling fully awake and refreshed. He had told Bill he wanted to run in the morning and Bill had given him the keys to his retro muscle car, a mint condition 1962 Chevy Bel Air. The park he wanted to run at was a good dozen miles away, but it was one of his favorites, and with the early start he would be able to get there before rush hour. Tom loved running early in the morning on clear fall days.

All the leaves were off the trees, but the park was beautiful. He chose the running trail that was a 10k and included over a dozen workout stations. Each station had a sign that prescribed the exercise that you were to do using the apparatus at that station; sit ups, pull ups and various other circuit exercises. It took him two hours to cover the course doing every exercise station exactly as described and picking up his running pace as he went along. He felt exhilarated, relaxed, his head clear by the time he was done. It was only eight thirty in the morning. He knew his breakfast plans would undo his head start on the day but there wasn't any way in the world he was going to overcome the urge to visit his favorite bakery. He promised himself that he would only have one cinnamon bun, but he let down his guard at the last minute. At least he didn't order a half-dozen. He picked up a cup of coffee at a drive thru. *Hardly the breakfast of champions but without a doubt the best thing for your soul.*

By noon he had done all that he could to line up a deal for after the holidays. He had some good calls, followed up with e-mail messages, and hoped that they were sincere about getting started. He told his best prospects that he might be taking on a huge deal and that if he did he would not be available for several months. This was all true, but his purpose wasn't to tell the truth as much as it was to get a deal closed.

Bill was at work, and the kids were all at school, so Tom took Mo out for lunch. "What are you up for?" Mo asked as they pulled out of the driveway.

"A good cheese steak, fries covered with cheese and gravy, washed down with an ice cold beer. Preferably served at a real dive bar."

"I know just the place. You can take a guy out of Philly, but you can't take Philly out of the guy. Are you sure you want to offset your workout with such a heavy lunch," asked Mo.

"I already offset my workout with a heavy breakfast. The heavy lunch provides the motivation for a good workout on Friday morning before I head back to Atlanta." They both laughed.

Lunch was great, and they talked about everything from when they were kids to their current lives. "Aren't you going to tell me again that I should ask Claire to marry me?"

"No, this has been too nice an afternoon to spoil it by nagging you. You either will or you won't. I just think it might be good for both of you."

"It might and I have been thinking about it the past couple of days after seeing what a nice life you, Bill and the kids have," Tom said, thoughtfully. "Speaking of the kids we better get going."

CHAPTER SIX

*He that overcometh, the same shall be clothed in white raiment; and
I will not blot out his name out of the book of life but I will confess
his name before my Father, and before his angels.*

Revelation 3:5

Tom stepped out the door at exactly the time that he had
planned, leaving an hour for what should be a thirty-minute trip from
the time the key was turned in the car to the time he sat down on the
train. He had learned from years of travel that not only was Murphy's
Law in effect, but also Flaherty's corollary could come into play. The
latter states that Murphy was an optimist; everything could go wrong.
Besides with cell phones and tablets, you could always sit in a train
station and be productive. He was also thinking that if he was late for
the luncheon meeting he would not soon get a second chance to meet
with Nelson. Nelson was extremely busy. Getting him alone for an hour
or two, hopefully, with his undivided attention, was nearly impossible
and exactly what Tom needed. If anyone knew what was going on and
could help change the course of events, it was Nelson Glassman.

Tom met Nelson when he was performing a new business eval-
uation for retailers that World Passport Card was considering. Nelson
was the leader of the project, and he wanted to use Tom as a sounding
board for the ideas and approaches his team was pursuing. Tom never
met with the team until the very end of the engagement because
Nelson didn't want him to be "contaminated" with their internal
thinking. As a result, most of his meetings with Nelson were breakfast,
lunch, or dinner meetings. This relaxed setting allowed him to get to
know Nelson on a personal basis.

Nelson was a bit of an enigma. For a high-level executive, he never met a detail he didn't like. He also presented the aura of being highly principled, yet he had been married four times. To Tom this represented a conflict, although he recognized that Nelson's inability to maintain a lasting marital relationship probably had a lot to do with his workaholic approach to business matters and attention to detail. He was very handsome. He had Egyptian movie star-type looks, was close to six feet tall with wavy black hair turned to a nice mix of mostly pepper streaked with salt, reflecting his age. Nelson had blurred priorities, often placing a higher premium on loyalty and teamwork over right and wrong. This had given Tom pause and concern when he worked with Nelson and even more so now if he was to be an ally in stopping Wasim.

Tom was going to be jumping through travel hoops all day. The location Nelson chose for the luncheon was nowhere near his sister's place. The ride to the Trenton, New Jersey, train station was uneventful and traffic was light, but parking was another story. He found a lot that looked to have hourly and long-term, but when he tried to pay at the pay booth, the only options offered on the screen were for short-term parking. He asked a chauffeur who was just getting into his limo, after apparently just dropping someone off at the station, and he confirmed that the lot was for short-term parking only. The chauffeur's comment about the signs saying you could also park there long-term was, "What do you expect? It's New Jersey." He didn't mean it to be funny; he was serious. Tom got back in his car and found another parking lot.

All train stations seemed the same. This one was surprising, especially for New Jersey. It was relatively clean and modern, with mostly corporate travelers. There were a few people napping on benches and panhandlers. A man stood at the bottom of a stairwell with a sign that read "Hungry. Anything helps." Tom thought about giving him a dollar but wondered what that money might buy.

The status screen said the train was on time and he had twenty minutes to kill. He passed the time of day dreaming, watching people come and go, avoiding eye contact with the sign man. Tom bought his ticket at an automated machine and paid cash. The train was on time with hardly any passengers. The interior was plush. He loved the fact that there were still workers who dressed nicely in Amtrak uniforms that included ties and railroad hats with black shiny brims. He was also surprised to see that they still took your ticket and punched it with a hole punch. He had been told many years ago that conductors had a unique design on their punch. He wondered how long it would be before automation caught up to this process. He spent most of the ride mentally rehearsing his approach to the conversation with Nelson.

Pulling into Penn Station is eerie; it is cavernous, and full of shadows. There are several lights, but like runway lights, they only serve to light the way. Here and there you can see a crew at work. How could anyone work in what is a cave with monstrous noisy trains running through it, their wheels screeching as they are switched from one track to another? The underground of the station is dark, damp, poorly lit, and filled with bad air. A crew of workers could be seen, all wearing hard hats with lights that made them look like miners.

Tom had less than an hour to find his way up to street level, and either get a cab or hoof it over to Grand Central Station to catch the train for the next leg of the trip. When he got to the main terminal he was confused about which street to exit to as thousands of people scrambled in different directions adding to the confusion. He spotted an information desk and asked for walking directions and whether or not it would be best to walk or jump in a cab. The lady at the desk was devoid of personality, and couldn't have been a poorer fit for the job. She never looked up as he asked his questions and gave him half-interested answers. Her directions were useless and helped him settle on a cab. At least she was able to point him to the cab stand. The line was long, but moved quickly. A cab ride in New York City is a lot like a roller coaster ride at an amusement park. They travel at speeds that seem much too high given all the traffic, and just barely miss the pedestrians, brave or dumb enough, to cross the streets without the benefit of a traffic light. Scariest of all are the delivery guys on bikes. Some are delivering documents and others food, but they dart in and out of traffic like they are playing chicken with the cars and trucks. It suddenly occurred to him that if someone was tailing him they would have a hell of a time keeping up. He was paying cash for his tickets, making train and cab switches, in crowded places, and heavy traffic. *Better to be lucky than good. Exactly!*

New York has everything. Not just a little of everything—it has a lot of everything. As the cab weaved through the narrow lanes, Tom saw flashing stills of faces, all different. They passed swanky hotels with fancy-dressed doormen, a restaurant with Maître D's standing at a podium just inside the door, drug dealers, hookers, Girl Scouts on a field trip, corner food carts and produce markets, dresses and suits being wheeled on carts from one warehouse to another, while cops and ambulances blared their sirens, attempting to navigate swiftly through the traffic. You can see every ingredient in the melting pot of America and the bedrock of its free enterprise system.

Grand Central Station earns its name. It's a core connecting all of New York, New Jersey, and Connecticut. Its architects had expertly crafted a truly grand place. The station is huge, with the main concourse nearly as long and wide as a football field, and the ceiling rises to an incredible height. The exterior has an ancient design that distinguishes it from the surrounding skyscrapers. The main focal points both inside and out are the clocks. The exterior clock sits at the top of the building, surrounded with ornate embellishments and large statues of Hercules, Minerva, and Mercury. The glass on the front of the clock is from Tiffany's; a priceless relic, a crowning jewel. The clock on the interior is atop the information booth. It has four sides. Each face is opal glass surrounded by solid brass. The ticket windows are elaborate brass bars, the floors marble, and the ceiling astronomical, depicting stars and planets in all the constellations. Below the concourse are two levels of unbelievably vast tracks covering almost 50 acres.

Tom purchased his ticket at a ticket window with cash, and looked at the giant train board to determine what track was his. This was a local train, and it looked more like a subway car than the trains used on the main lines that traveled between cities and states. His train was nearly empty. He enjoyed this part. Each stop was a different neighborhood, unique from the last. The stations closest to the big urban cities always looked old, crowded, dirty, spotted with businesses that were equally unkempt. Junk yards, car repair and auto body shops littered the streets accompanied by smelly, sooty industrial and manufacturing plants. Graffiti tagged the walls in the urban areas. These artists chose the stations themselves, the concrete bridge walls, factory sides and even large rocks as their canvass. Tom smiled, remembering one of the most well-known graffiti artists in Philadelphia who marked his art as "Cool Earl." Cool Earl was the art. He would draw his alias in different colors and designs, sometimes eight feet high and wide.

As the train pulled away from the center of the big city, the neighborhoods would improve. The first change was from the poverty areas to the middle class. The row houses gave way to the single homes in styles from the '30s through the '90s of the last century. There were fewer businesses clustered in well-manicured industrial parks. Tom watched as the landscape shifted upscale. He was now well outside of the city and getting closer to Connecticut. The homes were mint in every way, the lots trimmed to perfection. Nelson lived in, Greenwich, in one of the top five highest income zip codes in the country. His neighbors were New York executives and celebrities who lived in monstrous stone mansions and had their yachts anchored somewhere nearby. A Motown superstar and Broadway notable lived just a stone's throw away from Nelson's house.

Nelson's office was in Purchase, New York. He had chosen a lunch spot in Mamaroneck, NY, which was mid-way between his house and office. The automated train announcement said the next stop was Mamaroneck. Before he rose from his seat, Tom noticed the only building on the other side of the tracks, other than homes, was an old train station. He was the only passenger who stepped off the train at this stop. He looked up and down the street and all of the businesses had well-marked signs, but nothing within view was the Club Car Restaurant. As the train pulled away he looked across the tracks again and saw that the old station was the restaurant. *Damn, an underground track crossing. Well, if you are going to dance with the devil, you'd better get used to the tunes. Blow and go!*

The tunnel was deep, long, damp, and smelly, but no boogeyman. It also led directly into the restaurant at the level of the tunnel. Through one door stretched ten feet of hallway. Through another door the dankness of the tunnel was suddenly replaced with the warmth of a beautiful old train station.

The Club Car Restaurant, a beautiful 1880s restoration with a tin ceiling, old pine floors, elegant glass chandeliers, massive windows, wainscoting, brick walls, and stained glass oozed with Old World charm. In an instant he was greeted by a very well-dressed gentleman who was sitting at the bar working on his laptop. "Welcome to the Club Car, sir, one for lunch?"

"Actually, I am meeting someone," replied Tom.

"Well, you are the first to arrive. Would you like to be seated at the bar and have a drink while you wait, or head to your table, sir?"

"I think I would like to be seated," indicated Tom.

"Jason, please show our guest to his table."

"Good day, sir. Please follow me." They walked past the bar to the middle of the restaurant and Jason looked to Tom for approval as he held his hand open to a nearly enclosed booth. "Yes, that will be fine. Thank you, Jason."

"Can I offer you something to drink while you wait for your lunch partner?"

"Yes, a glass of Chardonnay and water with lemon would be perfect." Jason placed two menus on the table and walked to the bar where a well-dressed bartender seemed to magically appear as if he knew an order was about to come in. It was now one thirty, and there was only one other couple in the restaurant. His view of them was partially blocked, but he could pick up enough on their conversation to realize that it was a "first date" between what he guessed was a recent, or soon to be divorcee and an interior designer. The booth they occupied blocked them from view at the front of the restaurant, and you could tell from their voices they had both had more than enough to drink with their lunch.

Minutes later Nelson arrived through the front door. He was greeted by the Maître D'. "Yes, sir, your lunch partner has arrived and has been seated. Please follow me." Tom stood to greet Nelson. Firmly, they shook hands, and with beaming smiles they greeted each other and then sat down. Jason's voice and manner suggested he grew up in the city. He seemed skilled, knowledgeable about food and drink, and understood how to deal with people. He stood at a distance, waiting for a signal. As soon as Tom glanced at him he approached the table. "Sir, can I offer you something to drink?"

"Yes, I would like a Tanqueray and tonic with a twist," ordered Nelson.

"And you, sir, are ready for another?"

"No thanks, Jason, I will nurse this one awhile more," said Tom.

"Gentlemen, please let me know when you have considered menu choices and are ready to order." Jason didn't even look at the couple at the other table. He checked the level of the wine bottles in the chiller, topped their glasses, and moved on without a word. Jason knew that the best way to earn a big tip from a couple having an affair was to leave them alone.

"Tom, it is really good to see you. You look well."

"Thank you, Nelson, and I can sincerely say that you must still be fighting off the women with a bat," grinned Tom.

Nelson laughed, "You're too kind. Tom, I was hoping to have at least an hour and a half to talk, but as is usually the case, I have to go into the office this afternoon to deal with a personnel situation. As a result, we will only have an hour. You said you had something important to speak with me about, and the brief description you gave me was intriguing, so it would be best if we cut short the amenities, place our order, and get on with business."

"Sounds good!" said Tom.

When Jason arrived with Nelson's drink they placed their orders, including a glass of white wine for both of them. Nelson had downed his drink as if it were a glass of water after a five-mile run.

"You heard about the three Universe Card board members, right?" began Tom.

"Yeah, tragic," replied Nelson, shaking his head. "What do you make of the timing? Isn't it crazy that three violent accidental deaths would befall connected people in such a short time?"

"Are you asking me if I think they were accidents?"

"Yes, exactly!" said Tom.

"No. I do not believe they were accidental. I believe they are the result of someone trying to secure a board vote on rationing."

"That's what I think, but only, I think they are going for more than rationing."

"I've thought the same thing," said Nelson.

Tom sensed Nelson didn't want to get too detailed in his assumptions so Tom went ahead. He started by telling Nelson about his meeting with Jim Martin and the phone call he received from Wasim days later.

"Tom, just to clarify, are you saying Wasim is behind this?" questioned Nelson.

"Absolutely, do you disagree?"

"No, I just wanted to confirm," said Nelson.

Tom continued, giving the highlights of his conversation with Andy Newcomb and the archbishop. "I'm not sure about the connection with Revelation. I think that is a bridge too far for me," said Nelson.

"Let me tell you about one other thing that just might change your mind about that." He paused while Jason set their plates on the table and waited until he cleared earshot. Tom told him about the feeling he had after his telephone conversation with Wasim, and the encounter in the train tunnel. He explained that Claire described feeling something similar. Nelson was shaking his head no and smiling as Tom spoke.

"Tom, fear is a funny thing. It can cause a lot of hard to explain emotions, even cause physical changes," Nelson explained.

"I described these feelings to the archbishop. He warned me these sensations are both real and dangerous. He performed a special blessing, prayed with me for my protection and gave me a crucifix." The expression on Nelson's face changed. As if a breather was necessary. They both took a few minutes to focus on their food.

Despite the gravity of the conversation, Tom couldn't help but notice what was going on with the other couple. The guy had an Eastern European accent, although mild, and had to be twenty years younger than the woman. She was inexperienced, but nevertheless was enjoying the attention and going with the flow. The gentleman seemed well versed. Jason had brought another bottle of wine and refreshed their glasses without asking. Except for taking a sip after he filled their glasses, they were seemingly oblivious to his presence. Above the table they had already shared a couple of light kisses and held hands, and although obstructed by the tablecloth, it was pretty clear from the movement of the guy's arm that he was doing some exploration with his non-wine-glass hand, and she was responding favorably. Nelson followed Tom's eyes and smiled. "I think they should get a room."

"Yeah, there are three reasons the prices are high here; the food is good, the décor stunning, and it seems you get a floor show."

"You make a compelling argument for the supernatural, but I'm not sure I can buy into everything you're saying. Nevertheless, I would agree that Wasim is behind it, and his objective is more than just rationing. I also believe that you are spot on about him going after the key keepers, the tie-in with social media, and the board. All of that makes sense. I would still be skeptical of the Revelation part of your story if I were a Christian and not a Jew. Sorry, I think it's a stretch. But as far as the significance of what is going on, it is a distinction without a difference. Wasim is obviously up to no good, in a big way. Do you think he's the devil," asked Nelson.

"Not sure, but whether he's the Antichrist or one of his followers, I believe he is doing the devil's work."

"So, what are you going to do?" asked Nelson.

"All that I can," replied Tom.

"Did you share this with me to see if I could or would confirm your suspicions or did you want something else?"

"Both," said Tom.

"So, what do you want me to do?"

"I want you to help me stop him," said Tom, bluntly.

"What do you think I can do?"

"Well first I want to get your take on something. I think I might know how he's planning to do this. I mean the tie-in with social media, altering the code to perform rationing for his dark purpose."

"I'm fully briefed on how rationing will work and what you have described is exactly how the rationing system will function," said Nelson.

"How do you think he will alter the system," asked Tom.

"Well, he will need the security keys, and someone who is sufficiently familiar with the system code to be able to alter it."

"I believe that would be either Andy Newcomb or George Corbett," added Tom.

"I don't know Andy Newcomb."

"He is a good friend of mine, and I know for a fact that he knows the identity of the key holders and the authorization code very well."

"Do you think he would alter the code for Wasim," asked Nelson.

"I doubt it. I mean, it would have to be at the point of a gun or a threat to his family," replied Tom.

"That leaves George then. George is close to Wasim. He'll do what he's told and has a very technical background," said Nelson.

"Perhaps you can answer a question the archbishop asked that I've struggled to figure out. If Wasim is trying to get the security keys, and does, why would he need board approval?"

"Well he needs to get the code altered. And the people who hold the keys that are making legitimate changes aren't going to do that for him, unless like you said, it is at the point of a gun. Universe Card's board vote controls a significant portion of payment card access, about 80 percent, but to get to 100 percent, there are several others—mainly my board—that need to follow suit. So, if the Universe Card board approves rationing, then the others will fall in line, as they always do. The other 20 percent will route their transactions through PCP. Wasim will have had the code implemented for rationing there and could apply the alterations that serve his real purpose."

"Nelson, can't you get your board to vote against this?" said Tom, realizing the possibility in Nelson's plot.

"On what basis? They don't know Wasim as I do and at this point what we both have is a shared suspicion. We would need proof," said Nelson.

"Assuming we get proof, can you get me access to the board meeting on January 8," asked Tom.

"I can get access, but I am not sure how I could possibly get you into the meeting. Security is beyond tight, and since Wasim has already threatened you, he is not about to grant you access to his board room."

"Looks like we were both pretty hungry," said Tom after a pause.

"Yes, and the food was delicious," said Nelson.

Jason approached the table. "Gentlemen, it looks like you were either quite hungry or you enjoyed your meals."

Nelson seemed familiar with Jason. "We were hungry, and that was delicious," he leaned back—hand on his stomach.

"I'm glad you enjoyed it, because there was no way I was taking anything back to the kitchen. The owner, who is also the chef, was here today and he prepared your lunch," Jason said.

"Well he certainly knows what he is doing—my fish and chips were on a completely different level than any I have had before," complimented Tom.

"Can I interest you in some dessert," asked Jason. There was a simultaneous, "No."

"I do have just enough time for another gin and tonic," Nelson said.

"I think I will switch over to coffee, straight up," ordered Tom.

"So, what's next," asked Nelson.

"I will try to get us some proof. I also have a high-up contact at Giggly, whom I will contact to see what I can learn. I would appreciate it if you could keep your ear to the ground and let me know what, if anything, you hear that may help us," Tom said as Nelson nodded in agreement.

"Also, please think about how you can get us both into the board meeting. If you can't get me in will you carry the ball yourself?"

"I'll see what I can do. I'm willing to do what it takes if I can't get you in there," said Nelson as he retrieved a business card from the breast pocket of his $800 Brooks Brothers classic blue blazer. He wrote something on the back of the card. "This is a secure, personal e-mail address. I suggest you set up an e-mail address that has nothing to do with your name or business affairs, and if possible, use it on a device that has no connection to you by any legal means," Nelson said.

"I need to require that you do not contact me in any other way. I don't want to have an accidental death," said Nelson bleakly.

Jason returned with their drinks and placed the guest check on the table. "Gentlemen, I'll take that whenever you are ready. Thank you for dining with us at the Club Car today," he smiled. As he departed he stopped by the other table and topped off their drinks. As soon as he left their table, the guy reached over, placed his hand to the side of the woman's head and then torridly kissed her. Tom and Nelson looked at each other, smiled, and shook their heads. Nelson picked up the check just as Tom reached for it and said, "Nelson, let me get this."

"No, Tom, from my perspective, this was all about my business and more. I have a responsibility to the stockholders, employees, and cardholders. I can't let the system get hijacked by a mean-spirited egomaniac like Wasim Mirza."

Jason magically appeared the moment Nelson put the book down with his platinum American Express card sticking out the end. Tom looked at him, "American Express, really?"

"Yes, better points than our card; please don't tell anyone." When Jason returned with the check, Nelson entered the tip, signed it, downed his drink, which was still half-full, and stood to leave.

Tom rose from his chair. "Nelson, thanks for getting together with me. It means a lot to have an ally like you."

"Always a pleasure, Tom" said Nelson. "Take care of yourself; you are playing a dangerous game," he added.

Tom sat down and looked at his watch. He had another hour and a half to kill, and he wasn't about to sit on a train platform. He decided to hang out at the restaurant until it was time to go. For the first time, he noticed that Nelson's empty glass had the Club Car logo on it. This would be a great addition to his extensive souvenir collection of match books and logoed glasses from restaurants all over the country. He learned from experience that if you asked to buy a glass that was not regularly for sale, the answer would be no. These glasses had to be ordered in large quantities to keep the cost down. The best thing to do was to swipe one and leave some cash on the table. He wrapped the glass in a napkin, another trick of the thievery trade, and placed it in his briefcase. He pulled a ten-dollar bill from his wallet, folded it, and placed it on the table. He didn't think Jason would return to the table until he was gone, since the check had been paid.

Tom pulled out his laptop, surprised that he was able to connect to the Internet through the restaurant's unsecured Wi-Fi. He laughed as he did this. So many businesses still made a big deal about free Wi-Fi. Nobody has charged for Wi-Fi access in years. He checked his e-mail and sipped his coffee. As if Jason could sense an empty cup, he reappeared in the dining room carrying a pot of coffee in one hand and yet another bottle of white wine in the other. "Sir, can I freshen your coffee for you?"

"By all means Jason, thank you," said Tom appreciatively.

Spotting the cash on the table Jason added, "Sir, your lunch partner took very good care of my tip."

"That's not a tip, Jason. I swiped one of your logoed glasses and wanted to compensate the establishment for it."

"I guess you figured that if you asked to buy it we would say no," asked Jason.

"Exactly!" replied Tom.

"It's not a first, and likely not a last," said Jason. "Do you want another coffee cup or is this one sufficient?"

"I'm not sure. I'll have to check my cash and get back to you," joked Tom. "More wine for the lovers?" he added, jokingly.

"Yes, although I don't know how he will get the job done after drinking this much. He's a better man than me," said Jason with a sardonic expression. Tom laughed.

Tom was feeling more confident, but as he walked out of the restaurant he went out the back door. Jason had told him this door would take him directly to the platform. He felt relieved that he wouldn't have to go through the underground tunnel again. Once on the train, he started running the meeting through his mind —the typical self-debrief. Although he was pleased to have Nelson confirm part of his hypothesis and seemingly have Nelson as an ally, it occurred to him that he didn't gain a lot from the meeting. Nelson remained skeptical about the possible tie to Revelation, and the degree of his offer to help was pretty limited. It required Tom to come up with some proof. Additionally, he didn't seem to be at all confident about turning around his board's position on rationing, nor being able to get Tom into Universe Card's next board meeting. Considering the dates that Andy talked about for his deadline and the board meeting, one of the few promises was that the new year could be very interesting. Wasim wanted a rationing system for Christmas, and the approval of the card associations to allow him to fully employ it.

Tom arrived at Grand Central and hustled to catch the earlier Amtrak so he could get to Mo's place at a more civilized time. He quickly bought his ticket, checked the board, and hustled to the train that was leaving in five minutes. The downside of having an end time scenario running through your head as you push through a busy, unfamiliar train station is that you could easily make a mistake. He boarded the train, found two available seats and slid to the far side feeling relieved. The digital announcement assured him he was on the train to Trenton, but he couldn't hear all the details. He did catch the train that would arrive ahead of schedule.

About ten minutes out of the train station, the conductor asked Tom for his ticket. The man took the ticket and shook his head. "Hey, chief, you are on the wrong train," said the conductor.

"How's that? The board said Trenton . . . the announcement said Trenton."

The conductor pointed to his hat. Tom didn't realize he was actually pointing to the logo on the hat. "I'm sorry, but I don't get it."

The conductor pointed to his hat again and gave him the duh look with his head cocked and a questioning expression. "This is a New Jersey train and you have an Amtrak ticket."

"Ohhhh, I'm sorry. I guess you can't take that ticket?"

"No can do," said the conductor.

"What do we need to do," asked Tom.

"You need to buy a ticket and you need to have cash, because I don't take credit cards."

"No problem, I have cash. What do I owe you?" said Tom.

Twenty-eight dollars and fifty cents, exact change."

"Can I get a refund on the Amtrak ticket?"

"Yeah, but not from me. When you get to the Trenton station, go to the Amtrak agent window and they will take care of you," said the conductor.

"If I didn't have cash, would you throw me off the train," Tom asked innocently.

The conductor kept his snarly look on his face as he answered, "You got it, without slowing down."

Tom's thoughts drifted back and forth among his work, his next steps on this quest, Claire, and looking forward to a pleasant evening with Mo's family as the New Jersey panorama of old industry, new industry, worn-down Newark, and upscale Princeton was presented out of his train window like a movie screen. He was not making good progress on landing one of his prospects for a January consulting engagement. His self-assessment was that he wasn't spending enough time let alone the quality time that was needed. He had learned that the trick was like fishing; to set the hook, with the right bait, at the right time. Quality time is how you learn what bait to use and when to use it. He was too distracted now to do either.

Tom felt compelled to contact the key holders and warn them that they were in danger. His brother, John, would be easy enough since he was going to see him this weekend anyway at his trim the tree party. Sal Asante would be more challenging. He had never heard of Sal, let alone met him. How do you approach someone you have never met before and tell him that he could be in grave danger because he may present a roadblock on Satan's road map for control of mankind?

Tom worried about Claire. He had never made the full commitment to her that she deserved, and now he had involved her in a dangerous situation. Nelson wanted proof, and as much as Tom would like to just go the media and tell his story on *60 Minutes*, he knew in his heart of hearts that Nelson was right. It is one thing to have proof. It is quite another to have suspicion. People might believe a suspicion, but won't act without proof. He did have a high-level contact at Giggly, and it made sense to turn over as many stones as possible. He needed proof and a plan to stop Mirza. *So many people believe based on the things that are going wrong in this crazy world, but I have to gather proof and develop a plan to defeat this evil. What is wrong with the government, church, and business leaders? Isn't this obvious? Dear God, help me!* He needed to keep Claire close and try to lighten things up. A nice weekend focused on Christmas shopping and decorating could do the trick. He had to keep his plans and concerns to himself. Tom wondered if he had been wrong all these years about true love, about spending all of his life around his business affairs. Bill, had a serious business, but he found a way to spend time with Mo and the kids. Tom thought about the difference between the many lonely nights on the road and in his own house compared to the warm, secure, alive feeling he felt the past two days staying with Mo's family. *Asshole! Exactly!*

Funny how fast time moves when you let your mind wander. The recorded announcement came over the PA system and made Tom smile. It sounded like the announcements used in the grand old train stations like Grand Central and 30th Street Station in Philly. A deep, loud, serious, measured tone, droned through the speakers. "The next stop for New Jersey Transit train #327, Trenton, New Jersey, with connections for both New Jersey Transit and Amtrak system trains." They began to slow down, approaching a crawl as they entered the station. The one-hour trip seemed like it took five minutes.

Tom followed the signs to the Amtrak ticket agent counter and was pleasantly surprised. No waiting line and a competent agent who handled his refund efficiently and courteously. *Will wonders never cease, and in New Jersey*, he thought, as he exited the station. He looked up and down the street as the light turned green; how well things had gone on this trip! He gained an ally who confirmed most of his suspicions, and with some proof was willing to help thwart the plan. He saved time and money by getting on the wrong train and he would get to Mo's place in time for dinner.

Just as he was about to step into the street he heard a car engine rev and tires screeched to his left, as if it was in a drag race. He looked in that direction and saw a black town car speeding toward the intersection. He wasn't sure if he thought, *distraction*, or if it was his instincts, guardian angel, or his mother's tug, but some force urged him to look away from the oncoming danger and instead to his right. As he did, he saw a threatening figure in a long black robe and ski mask rushing toward him with a long, curved sword. He yelled something when he was only two steps away and swung the sword toward Tom's neck. Tom couldn't register what he said. Again, he didn't know if St. Michael the Archangel was guiding him, or all the action movies he watched were paying off, but he ducked forward and he could feel the sword clip his hair as it passed overhead. Tom brought his knee forward sharply as he turned and slammed it into the sweet spot of the attacker, breaking his momentum and causing him to fall to the ground in the fetal position with his hand grabbing his crotch. Again, Tom couldn't decipher what he yelled, but this time it seemed more like an expression of agony than anything else. Tom was about to reach for his gun when the attacker surprised him with a quick recovery. The attacker sprung from his fetal posture and deftly pulled a handgun from a pocket in his robe. As the attacker brought the gun toward him, Tom kicked it out of his hand, scaring the hell out of the attacker, himself, and everyone else in sight. The gun went flying a good 20 feet into the street and discharged from the blow of Tom's foot. He had no idea where the bullet went, but he was relieved that he felt no pain. The attacker scrambled to his feet and started running to where the town car waited at the curb. Tom strained to see the license plate, realizing he couldn't see the numbers. The plate was mostly covered in mud and he wasn't exactly thinking straight. As the town car sped away, he was snapped back to reality by the station police surrounding him, asking if he was all right. Moments later, more reality; squad cars with sirens blaring and lights flashing seemed to come from all directions. The Trenton police started talking to the Transit police, telling them all that they saw and knew in less than a couple of minutes. One of the police officers barked orders. "You two, take their statements," pointing to the station police. "Smitty, call in the description of the perp and the getaway vehicle and get the captain and chief of detectives out here ASAP. You two, secure the crime scene and gather witnesses. I don't want anyone within fifty yards leaving until we know what they know and nobody, I mean *nobody*, touches the weapon until the forensic team has surveyed the scene. I'll debrief the victim."

He turned to Tom. "Sir, are you okay?"

"Yes, I am fine," said Tom.

"Are you sure? Sometimes when things like this happen the adrenaline rush is so elevated that people can't feel pain or injury."

"I appreciate the concern, Officer, but I am fine—body and mind. If you asked me a week ago how I would have handled something like this I would have told you that my first move would have been to shit my pants, but for whatever reason, I'm fine," Tom sounded surprised.

"Well, from the accounts I've heard so far you did real good. If you hadn't, you wouldn't be telling the story. If you feel up it to I'd like to go over to that bench," he pointed to a bench about twenty yards left of where they were standing, on the outside wall at the front of the station, "and take your initial statement."

"Sure that'll be fine. Does initial statement mean there will be more statements?"

"Yes. The detective assigned to the case will want your statement, life story, and he would appreciate it if you could quickly solve the case for him." They both smiled and half laughed.

Sergeant Stanley Pulaski was no rookie. He asked Tom to describe what happened and as Tom talked, he typed Tom's statement at the speed of a stenographer into the tablet he had retrieved from his squad car. One of the other officers approached him. "Excuse me, Sarge. The scene is secured, and we have detained twenty-two people. So far they are all deaf, dumb, and blind, but we have told them that as soon as the detective gets here and they regain their senses, they might be allowed to leave."

"Thanks for the update. Let me know when the detectives and captain get here."

"Will do," said the officer.

Tom continued giving his statement. When he was about to tell him that he didn't have time to pull out his gun, he remembered that in the presence of a police officer you are supposed to tell them right away that you are carrying. "Officer Pulaski, I should have told you this at the get-go, but I am carrying a gun."

"No worries, if you have a permit."

"I do," said Tom.

"Okay, pull out the permit slowly and let me see it."

Tom slowly reached into his breast pocket, pulled out his wallet, and showed his license and carry permit. "Am I in any trouble having this gun here?"

"Not at all, Jersey and Georgia have a reciprocity agreement on carry law. Under the circumstance though, I am going to have to hold your weapon until we have finished obtaining your information."

The next three hours were like torture—watching paint dry. The detective, also a sergeant, Willy Hardy, was thorough and methodical. He took Tom to the station and questioned him for three hours. At several points Tom felt like clarifying he was the victim not the attacker. "Mr. MacDonald, can you explain to me how a management consultant happens to be skilled in self-defense?"

"No. I'm not skilled, I just reacted."

"Can you explain to me why a management consultant needs to carry a gun?"

"Yes, but it isn't the management consultant part of me that needs the gun. It's the world, as we saw today, is not very safe, and we need to protect ourselves. Our government sure as hell isn't going to."

"So you carry the gun for personal protection?"

"Yes," said Tom.

"Any idea why this person would attack you?"

"I don't know, my appearance maybe? I'm not exactly threatening. No, I have no idea why I was attacked by that guy."

"Are you sure it was a guy?" asked the detective.

"Pretty sure, most Eastern men aren't that tall and broad shouldered, let alone women, and he seemed to move like a guy would move."

"What are you doing in New Jersey, who did you meet with, what was the purpose . . ." Blah, blah, blah. They questioned Tom about everything. It was annoying, but it was obvious that they had no concrete clues and they felt certain that he must have done something to bring this upon himself. They were right, but he wasn't about to bring that out. At least not now.

He had called Mo and Claire and told them that the train broke down and that he would be late. He said his cell phone battery was dying, so he couldn't talk long. The police were all business, extremely thorough, treated him well, including some awesome pizza and cheese steak from a place in downtown Trenton called DeLorenzo's. But at the end of the day, literally, it was now after midnight, they were clueless. "Mr. MacDonald, thank you for your cooperation. We will be in touch. Where can we drop you?"

CHAPTER SEVEN

And I saw in the right hand of him that sat on the throne a book written within and on the backside, sealed with seven seals.

Revelation 5:1

As soon as Tom got in the patrol car he checked his phone. He had messages from both Claire and Mo, and another number that looked familiar, but wasn't immediately recognized. He knew he had to call Claire. He also knew that if he told her the truth she wouldn't sleep all night. He was hoping he would get her voice mail and he did. "Claire, sorry I wasn't able to call you sooner, but I had some travel trouble and wasn't able to make any calls. I am headed to Mo's place and I am fine. Hope you are too. Love you, Tom." He was relieved that he didn't have to talk to Claire directly.

As he drove down the street toward Mo's house he was hoping to see the house unlit, but no such luck. The main floor was lit up like a Christmas tree. He was six feet from the door when Mo opened the door and said, "Where have you been? We have been freaking out." He waited until he was in the door and saw that Bill was standing only a few feet behind Mo, and then started the story. "I was attacked by a terrorist at the Trenton train station."

"I knew it! Didn't I tell you, Bill? We heard the report on the news at eleven o'clock and right away I knew that it was you. What the hell is going on with you? First you have some henchman tracking you at the train station, you're carrying a gun, and now some terrorist is attacking you."

"Mo, I don't know what's happening—the world is crazy. Apparently I'm a good target for these wackos. Like I told the Trenton cop, he probably attacked me because I was dressed like a Catholic high school boy."

"I'm not buying your story. Bill, maybe you can get something out of him," Mo said.

"Tom, we're worried about you. If you are being targeted for whatever reason, please know we'll do whatever we can to help you."

"Thanks, Bill. I do find myself in the middle of something, but the less you know about it, the better. It was probably bad judgment on my part to stay with you and possibly attract attention to you. You are better off not knowing what I am involved in, and much better off not being involved," said Tom.

"Okay, Tom, but if there is anything we can do, don't hesitate to ask. I have access to private detectives who have some interesting and useful skills," Bill offered.

Mo transformed from the scared sister to the caring sister. "Have you had anything to eat?"

"Yes, more than enough; good pizza and a cheese steak from a place called DeLorenzo's."

Bill chimed in, "Yeah, that's the best pizza and cheese steak place in these parts."

"I could use a glass of wine or sherry to unwind if you have some."

"We sure do, have a seat and I will get a glass for you."

They talked about the attack, but neither Mo nor Bill asked again about the provocation or the nature of Tom's involvement. They also talked about the craziness of world affairs. Mo worried about the world her children would have to face, as it seemed that things had turned upside down. Despite that negative view and concern, though, she once again got after Tom about marrying Claire. "Mo, you just finished telling me that you think the world is crazy and that you're worried about your kids living in it, and now you encourage me to get married. That doesn't make much sense."

"No, maybe it doesn't seem like it does, but it is the right thing to do and anymore I think that's a damn good starting point for decisions, instead of some intellectually rationalized approach for not doing what is right."

"Well I couldn't agree with you more, and on that note, I apologize for keeping you up late and causing you concern. Can you give me a lift to the train station in the morning," asked Tom.

Mo rose from the chair, gave him a big hug and said, "of course, sleep well. See you in the morning."

Tom and Bill shook hands and Bill reiterated his willingness to help.

* * *

Tom awoke refreshed, and decided that he had enough time to get in a good run and attend Mass at nine at St. Mark's, which was only two blocks away from Mo's house.

Despite the good night's rest, Tom was preoccupied that morning. Between work and what he had to do to stop Wasim and God knows who else. He was also looking forward to the weekend. He and Claire were going to spend time together on Saturday and focus on getting their Christmas shopping done. On Sunday, they would help his brother, John, trim his Christmas tree and although it wasn't a good time for the discussion, Tom decided while running that morning that he would talk to his brother about the rationing project and his role as a key holder. He received an e-mail from one of his prospects asking him to come to Charlotte for a meeting next week. He would get Sal Asante's e-mail address from his brother and set up a meeting with him. He also decided that despite the possible danger, he needed to speak to George Corbett, Wasim's right-hand man at Universe Card and Gene Thompson at Giggly. This would be a busy week. He had to make sure that Claire was safe, and gather some concrete proof that could be used to stop Wasim's plan.

He called Claire and again got her voice mail. He was glad that he wouldn't have to rehash what happened to him over the phone. "Hi,

Claire, guess you're busy or in the shower. All is well. I miss you very much and can't wait to see you tonight. Have a good day, love you."

While he was in church that morning, he resolved that he would attend Mass on a daily basis, from now on, whenever permitted by time and place. He, like many Christians, often go to church and pray more in times of trouble. This was certainly a troubled time for Tom, but he clearly understood the sense of peace and strength he got when he went to Mass. He went forward with the feeling that his mom and dad had his back on the left and Jesus and Mary his back on the right. It was both a feeling and a visual that helped him feel confident about what he was doing.

He ran so well that after Mass he stopped by the local bakery and bought a butter cake. He absolutely loved it, and had since he was a little boy. Butter cake was mostly sugar and butter, with just enough flour to allow it to qualify as cake. He did restrict himself to one piece, deciding he would leave the rest at Mo's house for the kids' dessert. He left a confidential note for Bill asking him to send him instructions on obtaining untraceable electronic devices like a phone and laptop computer.

Mo drove him to the train station. They said their good-byes in the car as they pulled into the station, but Mo got out of the car as Tom was retrieving his roll-aboard suitcase and briefcase from the back seat. She gave him a hug and said, "Tommy, I know you are in danger and that you are keeping it hidden to protect us. I appreciate that, but we are your family. Don't hesitate to ask for help. Bill and I will do whatever we can to help you. We love you, Tom," Mo said, a fierce sincerity in her eyes. Tom was a bit taken aback by Mo's show of affection that he was almost speechless, "Thanks, Mo, I love you too. You have a wonderful family and I appreciate the warm hospitality you gave me this past week."

The train to center city was virtually empty from Bristol to the main station downtown, as was the train from downtown to the airport. He couldn't help himself at the airport and had yet again another cheese steak, fries, and a beer for lunch. As he drained his mug he thought that he was going to have to step up his running if he was going to eat this poorly.

The plane, being a midday flight, was half-empty. He had the entire row to himself. It gave him plenty of time to think about the coming week, his meetings, and the weekend with Claire. He spent much of his time putting together his Christmas shopping list. He felt refreshed as he made his way from the plane to his car, and especially when he arrived at home. He checked on his mail and made a list of items to pick up for dinner. He wanted to make the evening pleasant for Claire, recognizing that he was probably driving her crazy by getting involved in something that she felt he was not equipped to handle, and most likely wouldn't be able to make a difference anyway.

Bill sent him information on how to become anonymous with his electronics. He set up his anonymous e-mail address, and also found a local outlet where he could obtain a phone and laptop that would not be tied to him. It amazed him that there was no end to the things you could buy outside the lines. Having lived all his life inside the lines, he never dreamed that there was such a broad range black market, available in plain sight and seemingly uncontrolled and unrestricted. He purchased the phone and food for dinner in less than an hour and got to work as soon as he returned to the house.

He was knocking out one item after another. He sent an e-mail to his brother who promptly responded to his request for Sal Asante's e-mail. He sent an e-mail to Sal, and Sal got right back to him. They would meet on Monday at a café near Sal's office. Sal was agreeable to the meeting, although the tone of his e-mail was apprehensive. He took the same approach with George Corbett. George didn't want to meet with him at first and was evasive, thinking that Tom was trying to sell him on a consulting engagement. Tom assured him that it was not his intent. He just wanted his input on an assignment that he was currently working on concerning the security of the payment system.

He was so busy that he lost track of time, and was shocked when his regular phone buzzed signaling a text message. "I'll be there in thirty minutes." Claire was on her way. Fortunately, the dinner he was preparing wouldn't take long. He planned a simple salad, some pre-packaged pasta and sauce, a nice bottle of wine, and cannoli for dessert. The pasta was a fettuccine, and the sauce a roasted red pepper cream sauce. The cannoli had chocolate on the ends and Claire loved them. He had also picked up a dozen red roses that he carried to the door when the bell rang. Claire looked tired, but smiled broadly as soon as she saw the flowers. They embraced and she said, "I missed you so much and have been so worried about you," Claire whispered, eyes down.

"I missed you too, love." replied Tom.

They kissed passionately and for a minute, Tom thought about skipping dinner and leading Claire to the bedroom, but before he could make a move, Claire said, "I am famished, what's for dinner?" Still embracing, Tom rolled his eyes. "What a mood killer—salad, pasta, and a surprise dessert."

"That's not a mood killer. Flowers and dinner sound like the start of what could be a successful seduction."

"I'll get the salad ready," said Tom.

"Sounds good, I need a few minutes to freshen up."

As Claire entered the dining room, she smiled at the way the table was set. "Tommy, this looks so nice. You could be a keeper."

"I'm working on it, love." He held her chair for her as she took her seat.

"So, tell me all about your trip." She patiently listened as he told her about his meeting with the archbishop. "It was nice of him to pray for you and give you the crucifix. I'm glad that you feel stronger and that you're not getting that presence-of-evil feeling. One thing bothers me, though. Doesn't it strike you as odd that if he shares your belief he and the Church aren't doing anything?"

Tom explained that he asked the same question, and the archbishop's response was that the Church has stayed on the sidelines because that's what they do in this day and age. "I suppose that's true, but it's such a load of crap. They are supposed to represent Jesus on earth, but instead, they represent themselves and hide in their beloved palaces. I hope your meeting with what's his name was more fruitful."

"I'll let you be the judge," replied Tom.

Again Claire listened intently as he filled her in on the meeting with Nelson Glassman. They laughed together several times as Tom sprinkled the recap with the particulars on the couple having an affair.

"How could you keep from telling them to get a room?" said Claire.

"You know, I did wonder several times on the train ride back, exactly what they did the rest of the day. I wondered if it was just a flirty lunch or if they wrapped up the deal in a nearby hotel room."

Claire was again skeptical when he finished his summary of the meeting. "Tommy, I am not sure why you feel good about that meeting. It's nice and comforting to know that people think like us, but unless they are going to do something to help, it's just a bunch of hot air. If Nelson really cares about his customers and stockholders and he thinks that Wasim is a bad guy with bad intentions, he should do something himself instead of just encouraging you to get proof."

"Yes, you're right, but again, I think that is part of the way the world has become. It's why evil spreads while good shrinks. People know something is wrong, but they don't stand up, speak up and fight. Instead they take the easy way out," said Tom.

"What kind of travel trouble did you encounter that caused you to get delayed on your return trip?" asked Claire. He looked down at the table like a schoolboy about to make a guilty confession for throwing the stone that broke the window. "Well, it was a little more than travel trouble. I was attacked. The guy was huge—he was wielding a sword and wearing a mask."

"Oh my God! When I saw that report come out I thought, Dear God, please don't let it be my Tommy who was attacked, but then I got your message and was relieved. It was reported as a random terrorist attack. Do you agree?"

"Hell no, I think it was on Wasim's orders. It had all the earmarks of a hit disguised as a terrorist attack. The getaway car was a town car and the attacker, although dressed like a terrorist, seemed too tall and broadly built to be an Eastern type. And, he was carrying a gun. I think the sword, although very real, was part of the disguise. I mean, if you are carrying a gun, you use the gun. No, it was a targeted hit made to look like a terrorist attack," Tom said decidedly.

"What did the police think," asked Claire.

"I think they believed it was a terrorist attack. They seemed more interested in why someone would attack me and how a management consultant was able to fight off an attacker, than they were about the motivation behind it. The guy was wearing gloves and there wasn't a license plate to ID so I doubt they will get a lead."

"Tommy, I'm begging you, please give this up. No one is going to help you, and the people you are up against seem hell-bent on shutting you down."

"Claire, we've been through this before. I'm not quitting. I have to do what I feel I must do." said Tom.

"Is there anything else that himself is keeping to himself about his trip?" Claire asked.

"Yes, in fact, there is. I really enjoyed staying with my sister and her family. It was nice to see the kids come home from school, share the highlights and low points of their day, everyone sitting around the dinner table, the good night rituals, and the happy chaos of everyone getting ready for work and school in the morning. It reminded me of my family when I was growing up, and it kind of made me think that we might be missing something in life," Tom said.

They stared at each other without saying anything, and Claire reached across the table and held Tom's hand. "That's sweet, and I know what you mean. Is there something you want to say to me," Claire asked.

"Yes. Are you ready for dessert?" said Tom. They both laughed and Tom got the dessert for them.

"Ah cannoli. You do indeed know the way to a woman's heart."

"That's my story," said Tom. "How was your life while I was out of town," he asked.

"Oh, nothing unusual, except that I haven't been out to the stable since I promised you I wouldn't go alone and couldn't think of anyone who could go there with me. Work has been very busy. It seems like global affairs and the troubles of the world are getting worse each day."

"How about tomorrow morning, I go for a run early and then go out to the stable with you while you visit with Celtic King, go to lunch, and then shop till we drop?"

"That sounds good to me. If we are going to get an early start we better get to bed."

"Sounds good to me." They made love slowly and with great tenderness. The time spent apart, Claire's concern for Tom, his desire for a family life, and the danger of the situation, all combined to heighten their love.

* * *

Tom was up before the crack of dawn, had a cup of coffee, and he was out the door and into his run before six thirty. He was careful not to disturb Claire as he prepared to go out. His mind was clear, and after such a nice evening he felt completely rested, content, and confident. He wanted to get his to-do items out of the way and spend the day shopping and dining with Claire.

He was running along the river as the sun came up and he took in the beauty of the morning. Reflecting on how content he felt, it was hard to reconcile his feelings with, as Claire said, "the increasing troubles of the world." He went to Mass at eight and prayed for his and Claire's safety, the wisdom to know God's will, and the strength to go forward.

When he got back to the house, his timing was perfect. Claire was up, dressed, and had breakfast prepared. He got a quick shower and they headed out to the stable. When they arrived, one of the grooms told Claire that they had missed her the past week, and also that a strange guy had been hanging around the stable. They hadn't been able to speak with him because he kept his distance, but they notified the police and were warning the owners. Claire was so excited to see her horse, and she pampered him like a child before heading out to the pasture.

Tom was thinking intently about what the groom said about the strange guy hanging out at the stable the past week. Someone with bad intentions would most likely follow Claire to the stable instead of wasting a lot of time hanging out there, right? Unless, it was his intent to hurt her horse or . . . he quickly called to the groom and asked him to get to Claire and check her tack.

The groom, Angel, wasted no time. He mounted the nearest horse bareback and sped out of the stable and into the nearby field where Claire was warming up with Celtic King. "Miss Claire! Miss Claire! Wait for me! Your amigo wants me to check your tack!"

Claire brought Celtic King to a halt and dismounted. Angel dismounted and examined her saddle and straps. After a couple of minutes he could see Angel pointing something out to Claire and they both started walking the horses back to the stable. Concerned about what Angel found, Tom walked toward them. Angel spoke first. "Mr. Tom, how did you know?"

"Know what?"

"That King's front cinch and flank cinch were both cut halfway through. They would have probably broken at full gallop," said Angel.

Claire was visibly upset and shaking. Tom tried to lighten the moment and move on. "Do you have another saddle Claire," he asked.

"No. That's the only saddle I own," she said.

"Angel, do you have a saddle that Miss Claire can borrow until we get her a new one," asked Tom.

"Yes. We have a saddle she can use. We always need a saddle for one reason or another and Miss Claire can use it."

"Are you alright to ride, Claire," Tom asked.

"Yes." I'll get the saddle for you Miss Claire," Angel said.

While Claire continued her ride, Tom spoke to Angel.

"Do you have security cameras here?" Tom asked.

"Oh no, sir, we don't have any fancy stuff like that."

"Would it be all right if I set up a camera near Celtic King's stall?"

"Sure, that be fine. Do you think someone cut the saddle on purpose?"

"Yes. Maybe it was that strange guy you saw hanging around the stalls this week. I'll be out within a few days to set up the camera."

"Okay, Mr. Tom. Let me know if there is anything I can do to help."

"Thanks, Angel."

Claire finished her ride and then pampered Celtic King more than normal, as if it was him that they were out to hurt. Tom kept his distance, respecting Claire's relationship with her horse. She loved that horse, and the time she spent with him was precious. She loved the way Celtic King carried himself and she loved the freedom of riding. For Claire, this was her release from a pressure-filled job that seemed to never end. The news was always happening, and it was always more bad than good. When she was with her horse the troubles of the world were left behind. When Celtic King was cooled down, combed out, given plenty of treats and extra oats, she said her good-bye and walked to Tom's car. He could tell by her walk that she had enjoyed her time, but she was visibly troubled.

As they pulled out of the lot she finally spoke. "Tom, I want you to give this up. If they will try to kill me, there is no question that they will kill you. This was not a matter of a worn-out saddle. The saddle is less than a year old. There was a strange guy hanging around the

135

stable and my saddle cinches were cut. They were out to hurt me, perhaps kill me, and either way their intent was to warn you. Tom, for God's sake, take the warning seriously. This isn't your fight, and it is a fight you can't win."

"Claire, I am really sorry. I can't stop what I am doing. I promise I will not let anything bad happen to either of us," said Tom.

"I know you mean well but that's a promise you can't keep. If they can kill three prominent members of the same board and make it look like an accident they can do the same to you and me. They've already tried once with both of us. Is that not enough warning?" Claire said, at a loss.

* * *

"This is Wasim."

"Wasim, this is the President. Do you have a few minutes to talk?"

"Yes, Mr. President."

"How are you doing?"

"I am well, and you?"

"Couldn't be better. Everything is coming together for us nicely. I'm calling for an update on your progress with the rationing initiative," asked the President.

"We are on track, sir. The board is now aligned, and the programming is proceeding on schedule."

"We've talked about the two prongs necessary to carry this out and the back-up in case there are issues. Have you positioned your people to be able to make this happen one way or another," the President inquired.

"Yes, I have identified the people who hold the keys and we will obtain the information we need from them at all cost. I will have the payment systems end completed and all the necessary codes by Christmas."

"Are you certain there will be no further trouble with the board," asked the President.

"Yes. All existing board members have confirmed their vote, as has my nominee."

"Is there any chance you can move up the board meeting," asked the President.

"Is that necessary?"

"It would be helpful."

"Are you experiencing any difficulties or do you foresee any obstacles?" the President wanted to know.

"There is a man who seems to understand our purpose. He's been snooping around, but we are taking actions to neutralize him. How are things on your end," Wasim asked.

"They could be better. It is unlikely that Congress will pass the rationing bill anytime soon. I will most likely have to enact the program with an executive order. As soon as we have a good crisis I will seize the opportunity," said the President.

"And with the bigger picture?" asked Wasim.

"There will be a financial crisis by year end that will enable us to act on our plan for a single currency. At the same time form the New Order and government," said the President.

"With all due respect, Mr. President, you make that sound rather easy," Wasim doubted.

"Wasim, it is easy. The people are so dumb and the world so wired. You could touch off a stock market crash with a Tweet just by hijacking a well-known TV analyst or billionaire's Twitter account and sending out a message saying, 'Sell.' Most of the major countries' economies and currencies are already in bad shape. It won't take much to put them over the edge," the President said arrogantly.

"And you don't anticipate any resistance?" Wasim calculated.

"I expect two groups to resist—the extremist rebelling in the East and the Catholic Church," the President replied. "It's ironic that the extremist are all about power, not religion, and with the Catholic Church, the pushback is all about religion and not power. They will both have to be subdued. One requires that we cut off their money and the other, unfortunately, their heads. Stay the course, Wasim, and let me know if you need any help," said the President darkly.

"I will, Mr. President." The call ended.

* * *

The rest of the ride home was quiet and the silence followed them into the house. Tom and Claire freshened up and were ready to move on by noon as planned. Tom wasn't sure what to say, and figured he better wait for Claire to make the first move. It seemed like she was doing the same thing, or she was waiting for Tom to see the light and decide to drop this pursuit of good against evil. Tom took advantage of the quiet time to think about some plans he needed to make. Instead of going for convenience, he chose one of Claire's favorite restaurants for lunch. He was about to add new saddle to the gift list but decided to just order it right away. It was his fault that this happened, and it would be best for their relationship if he took responsibility for it and made it right.

Parking was always difficult at Leon's because it was so popular, so he dropped her off at the door and then went to find a parking spot nearby. He didn't tell Claire where they were going for lunch, and the plan was starting to work. They pulled up to Leon's. "As usual, I will drop you off and go park the car."

As she opened the door, she smiled at him and said, "You don't fight fair."

"All is fair in love and war, and at the moment I am not sure which I am involved in."

She smiled again and simply said, "Love."

When he walked into the restaurant, Claire was already seated at a table and waved to him with a big smile. She had ordered for both of them, knowing without question that he loved the beef brisket dish and his favorite pale ale. "You know me well."

"I do indeed and despite your very thick head you have a good heart. The combination may not serve you well."

"Maybe, maybe not, but from now on I will be certain that it serves you well."

The lunch was pleasant, with the entire conversation centered on their shopping plans for the afternoon. They would go to the outdoor mall near her house. They would stay together when shopping for relatives, and separate between four thirty and six thirty while they shopped for each other. "Claire, when we are shopping separately, I want you to keep your phone handy and ready to text me if you encounter any problems. Text me immediately if you have any suspicions, or have any strange feelings."

"Yes Da, as long as you promise to do the same." I do," Tom agreed.

They drove out to the mall. Tom would usually drop Claire off at the door and then park the car, but he wanted to keep an eye on her. He found a spot somewhat close to the main entrance and they walked together, holding hands. As they entered the mall, Tom looked at Claire. "Where to my fearless shopping leader?"

"Macy's," she said with an excited smile.

"Will that work for you?"

"It will indeed," Tom gave a warm smile back.

Claire had a long list, but it was completely organized. Tom's list was short. He had already done most of his shopping online. "Claire, why don't we shop for everything on your list, and I'll just grab what I need when we're in a department store." Tom explained he knocked out a lot online.

"You cheater," smirked Claire.

"That would be one way of looking at it. I prefer calling it an effective use of time and resources. The good news is I will be able to spend most of our shopping time with you." Tom hated malls, but today was different. He felt a need to stay close to Claire and make sure she was safe. As they worked their way through the list they talked about their relatives and recalled happy moments from Christmases past, and noting why they thought each gift would be the perfect gift.

"Well, boyo, it's four twenty-four and the relative list is complete." said Claire.

"How's that for efficient use of time and resources?" she continued.

"Very good. You are organized, and a joy to be with. From all the guys that have been checking you out this afternoon, I would have to say I am lucky to be with you."

"You are indeed," Claire blushed.

"Let's make a car run and lighten our load before the next round of shopping," Tom suggested.

They returned to the mall sans four large shopping bags. "Okay, let's meet back here at six thirty. If either of us completes our mission before then, we text, and reset our plan," said Tom.

"Sounds good!" Claire said.

Tom didn't tell Claire, but he had already finished shopping for her. He just didn't want her to be alone after the incident this morning. There wasn't any way she was going to let him tag along with her while she was shopping for him, so he planned to follow her from a distance. It felt wrong. He had to laugh when he thought that he was acting like a peeping Tom, but he wasn't about to leave her alone.

Claire finished her shopping around six twenty and sent Tom a text saying she was ready to go if he was. He said he'd meet her at the main entrance. As he watched her shop he made sure no one was following her. He felt less guilty since she seemed oblivious to him. He walked slowly, watching behind columns if she stopped. All the while not realizing he was being followed and watched.

Claire gave Tom a big hug when they met up as if he had just returned from an extended overseas business trip. She eyed Tom's empty hands. "Is himself going to give me coal for Christmas? I guess I haven't been a good girl," she joked.

"To the contrary, you have been a very good girl. I just didn't find anything I liked. All the clothing seemed to be made for women with less than perfect figures, and every accessory and form of makeup seemed unnecessary for your pure beauty."

"Tommy me boy, surely you kissed the Blarney stone and were given the gift of purest BS." They laughed together and hugged once more.

"I am famished. What's the plan," Claire asked.

"We have reservations for seven at your favorite Italian restaurant, outside the city—Provino's."

"More BS, they don't take reservations," Claire said.

"It is true that they generally don't take reservations, however, I did call and asked them, if at all possible, to hold the secluded romantic booth in the back for us so that we could have some privacy for passionate activities."

"You didn't!" beamed Claire.

"I did ask for the table in the back that we like but didn't say anything about passionate kissing as much as that was on my mind."

"I love you but you are truly the inspiration for the phrase, piece of work," Claire said as she laughed.

Provino's reminded Tom of some of the old, Italian restaurants in the Northeast. The décor was dark. The tables were spaced well apart for privacy, unlike a lot of the newer restaurants. The lighting was subdued, and there were private, dimly lit wood booths on the perimeter and much of the interior of the floor.

"Good evening. My name is Tom MacDonald. I called earlier today requesting that you hold a particular table for me."

"Oh yes, you are right on time and just in time. We are beginning to fill up, but we have reserved your table." Sue Anne, who had taken position next to the hostess, said, "I will show you and your lady to your table."

They made their way to a cozy booth in the back. Their server arrived immediately. "Good evening, my name is Mary Anne and I will be taking care of you tonight. Would you like to hear our specials?"

"Well, we have been here many times before and we will probably order—excuse me—I will probably order my favorite, but I guess it wouldn't hurt to consider the specials," said Tom.

To Tom's surprise and delight, one of the specials was one of his favorites from a restaurant in Philly, Veal Mandolese. "Well, Mary Anne, it must be your presentation, but I will skip my regular and go with the special."

Claire chimed in, "Me too, that sounds really good."

As soon as Mary Anne completed taking their order and walked off, Tom said, "Did you notice that the hostess used the word *reserved*?"

"Yes, but she was referring to the table, not an actual reservation."

Tom shook his head side to side and scrunched his lips together. "No, I believe that if something is reserved for you at your request, and especially if it is a table at a restaurant at a specific time, whether the restaurant generally does or doesn't take reservations, it is considered a reservation."

"Begging your pardon, but it's just a request, if the policy of the restaurant is not to take reservations, and she implied that if they were filling up, and we weren't here, that this table would have been given to someone else."

"Did you also notice how the hostess referred to you," Tom asked Claire.

"Yes, and she was 1,000 percent correct. I am your lady, albeit unofficially."

"I think we should clarify that. Officially you are my lady, but not yet legally."

Mary Anne arrived with their wine and salads and couldn't help but pick up on the conversation. "Here are your official starters. They will be legally yours after you pay your check." They all laughed.

The conversation continued to follow the same lighthearted tone. They talked about their gift purchases, the festive decorations, seeing the children in line waiting to talk to Santa Claus, and laughed at the people who were stressed and hurried about their shopping. It was like they were teenagers. For the moment, the near tragedy of the morning was forgotten.

Mary Anne came with the check and as she placed it gently on the table said, "It has been my pleasure to serve you, please come again. I will pick this up when you are ready."

Before she could get away Tom said, "Mary Anne, our compliments to the chef. The veal was superb and outdone only by your service." Mary Anne blushed and thanked him. Claire looked at Tom. "You know if you leave anything less than a 25 percent tip it will confirm that you are just plain full of it." Tom left 20 percent. "Well I might be full of it but I'm 5 percent richer." Claire shook her head. "Finish your wine, boyo."

They left the restaurant arm in arm, feeling festive, and happy. As they walked toward the car, Tom caught a glimpse of a car that had been parked at the end of the row of cars, pointed toward the lane they were crossing, moving forward quickly. The car's lights were off and it hit full speed quickly. The tires squealed producing a small cloud of smoke at the rear of the car. Tom stooped down, placing his shoulder at Claire's waist and his arms around her legs. He picked her up while moving toward the nearest car. When he was a few feet away from the car, he leapt forward, flinging Claire ahead of him onto the hood of the car, and not a moment too soon. The oncoming car's bumper sideswiped the bumper just missing Tom and Claire. Tom nearly fell off the hood. He hung on and scrambled to his feet, trying to get a good look at the car. He failed to get the tag number. The car was moving too fast.

Claire was lying on the hood of the car in a fetal position, motionless. He leaned over her, and brushed her hair from her face. "Claire, are you okay," he whispered softly.

Tears welled up in her eyes. "I'm OK," she said. "But we can't keep running like this."

A half-dozen people saw what had happened, and gathered around Tom and Claire. An older man approached Tom. In a fatherly way he put his hand on Tom's shoulder. "Are you and your lady all right?" he asked.

"Yes, sir, we are probably a little bruised and don't feel it yet, but we are fine."

"You know, son, that didn't look like an accident to me," the old man said. "I think you need to be real careful. You might want to call the police."

For the second time in a day, the ride to Claire's house was silent. As they entered, Claire finally spoke. "I am going to freshen up and put on some comfortable pajamas. I'll be about ten minutes."

Tom quickly started a fire and poured two glasses of Merlot. Normally, she would cuddle up on the sofa next to him, but the message was clear. She sat on the sofa in talking distance. "Tom, I know you feel what you are doing is important, but is it important enough to you that we both get killed?"

"Claire, there's no right answer to that question for me. The last thing in the world I want is for any harm to come to you. On the other hand, I feel that our lives and many others are at stake. I feel compelled to keep pressing on until this is over. Claire, I would like for you to move in with me or me to move in with you. It's your call. Unless I have to go out of town, I want to accompany you everywhere. I will drive you to and from work, take you shopping, to the stables, and anywhere else you need to go. Fortunately, I have the time now to look after you, and I love your company anyway."

Claire was touched. "I love your company, too, but I am really scared and upset. These people are playing for keeps and we are not in their league," Claire said meekly.

I know this sounds trite, but we are in their league, and if good people don't stand up against evil, then evil will surely win," said Tom.

"You need to get help with this thing," she responded.

"I'm trying. It's not easy since I have to watch what I say and who I say it to. I do have the Lord with me. I can't explain it but I feel confident about being able to stop this and take care of us."

"Your reaction was impressive this evening, although I am not used to you throwing me around like a rag doll," Claire said.

"Sorry about that; it was just gut instinct. Are you okay," Tom asked.

"I have a few bruises but nothing serious," replied Claire.

"Anything I need to kiss and make better?"

"Yes, but not tonight," she said.

"Do what you must, but if you are going to move in with me, you need to share in the cooking and cleaning. I'm not your grandfather's-type lady, and I won't be referred to as the woman of the house." She moved over and snuggled next to him. They both stared at the fire and drank their wine. When the glasses were empty and the flame was off the logs and turning to embers, Tom woke her from her cat nap and whispered it was time for bed. As much as he wanted to make love with Claire, and thought that she would probably be responsive, he thought it best to let her just go to sleep. It had been a long day.

As he laid his head on the pillow he thought about the events of the day. It had been a roller coaster ride. The day had started down and then turned around and was full of Christmas spirit and the kind of love he hadn't felt in a long time, and then it came down from the stars like a rocket that had lost its power. He was starting to question his theory about getting only one trip to the stars. He was in love with Claire—madly in love. He vowed to God and himself that if he made it through this he would spend the rest of forever with Claire. His last conscious thought was just 15 days until Christmas.

CHAPTER EIGHT

*And I saw when the Lamb opened one of the seals, and I heard, as it
were the noise of thunder, one of the four
beasts saying, Come and see.
And I saw, and behold a white horse: and he that sat on
him had a bow; and a crown was given unto him: and he went forth
conquering, and to conquer.*

Revelation 6:1-2

John and Tom MacDonald were brothers, but unless you were told you would never know. They were different in virtually every way.

Tom was chronologically six years older. He aged emotionally much faster than John, furthering the gap. Tom was a risk-taker. He was constantly busy, expanding, and trying to reach the next level in every aspect of his life. Tom was also extremely well-organized and totally anal retentive in every way, but he liked to keep things simple.

John was a perfectionist, and preferred that the world revolve around him. He didn't do a lot, but everything he did was done very well. He was extremely neat, pressed and tucked in at all times. He was a great cook. John, like Tom, grew up in the Philadelphia area, and his heart was still there. He loved everything about Philly. He remained a devoted, loyal fan of the Eagles, Sixers, and especially the Flyers. He had to have the best cable sports package so he would never miss a game. Every game had to include an appetizer comprised of soft pretzels with mustard, a cheese steak, and Tastykakes for dessert. Each course, even dessert, was washed down with Yuengling. If it were a special game, he might have the pretzels and rolls sent overnight and pick up Cheez Whiz for the sandwich.

Their biggest difference was the way they carried themselves. Tom tended to be bold and outgoing while John was very timid and stayed within his own little world. John was also into movies and a card-carrying sci-fi fan with serious Trekkie credentials.

John met his wife, Diana, while they were in college. Diana was a perfect match for John. She was very bright, easygoing, and reasonably attractive. They dated for two years in college and another six years after they graduated. Tom had never asked them why they didn't have children. He assumed John wanted to keep his well-ordered life under control, and knew that children wouldn't fit that mold.

John worked at Primary Card Processing. Tom helped him get the job and then helped him relocate to Atlanta. He worked directly for Tom's friend, Andy Newcomb. John was a high-level network technician. He was a perfect fit for the job because it involved a lot of detailed files containing data elements that had to be organized and maintained with absolute perfection. One mishap here or there and suddenly a bank—or multiple banks—customer's transactions could be negatively affected. John never made mistakes.

Their differences made getting close a challenge. They were brothers, and either would do anything for the other, but they weren't hanging out every weekend. Both wished it were otherwise, but some things, like oil and water, just don't mix well. The exception was John's annual trim-the-tree Christmas party. Their parents, Thomas and Katherine MacDonald, had always made Christmas special for their children. Mo and Bill carried on the traditions exactly the way their parents had. John kept only a few of the traditions, and sadly to Tom, he maintained none of the traditions, except for going to Church well-dressed on Christmas day. Tom's tradition, and probably the one way he had found to connect with his brother, was to make a day out of trimming his Christmas tree with his brother.

Claire and Tom had a lazy Sunday morning. Tom awoke at seven and made coffee. He was nearly finished with his second cup when

Claire came out of the bedroom. "Good morning, sleepy head," he greeted her.

"I didn't sleep well," she said back. "I woke up, almost every hour, thinking about all the awful things that happened yesterday. I finally got back to sleep by trying to think about the nice things we did. One of the times I woke up, it was really bad. When I awoke I had a very vivid picture in my mind of what happened in the parking lot. It was like I was watching it from far away and seeing all the details. My mind and heart started racing and I had a panic attack," Claire explained.

"I am so sorry, and feel doubly guilty because I had a really good night's sleep. In fact, I had a really nice dream about us," said Tom.

Claire poured a cup of coffee and just like the night before, snuggled close to Tom. "Are we going to be all right?" she asked.

"Yes. The Lord will protect me, and the both of us are going to protect you."

"There is no way we are going to make the nine o'clock Mass."

"How about you chill, I make breakfast, and then we go to Mass at eleven?"

"Will that give us enough time to get to your brother's house by one?"

"Yes, we can leave Mass, pick up a few things for the party, and then go directly to John and Diana's."

The pastor's sermon was timely. He spoke of the importance, given all the problems in the world today, of standing up and act when we see or encounter injustice. He spoke about the persecution of Christians, especially in the East. With visceral anger he expressed concern at the level of abortion in the US since Roe vs. Wade, and the impact that violence and pornography were having on young people in our society. He tied it all together and to Advent with a quote from Revelation about Christ' coming, not just symbolically, but to be prepared for his *actual* second coming which could be upon us at any time. After the closing, Tom and Claire exchanged glances as if to say, "Amen!"

"Did you write that homily for Father and pay him to deliver it?" Claire said outside the Church.

"No, but I could have," smiled Tom. "It was kind of reassuring to hear it at this time though. Did you get the feeling that when he spoke of Christ coming that he meant it for real?"

"I certainly did but I have to admit, given recent events I am a bit attuned to his message, considering it's about all we talk about anymore."

Tom looked at her and said, "Exactly!"

When they came to the lane by the entrance to the parking lot they both carefully looked up and down before crossing. They looked in opposite directions at the same time and laughed out loud, realizing they caught each other being extra cautious. Tom said, "It's good that we can laugh at it today."

They drove to the grocery store and went in together. "Has himself figured out what to bring or did John give you some ideas?"

"John said we didn't need to bring anything, but we should get some good holiday snack foods," Tom said as they breezed through the sliding doors. "I was thinking we could put together a basket with a couple of nice cheese blocks, a box or two of good crackers, holiday cookies, assorted nuts, and . . . a bottle of red, and a bottle of white." said Tom melodically. Claire just smiled and they loaded their cart.

John and Diana lived in a three-bedroom, two-and-a-half bath home in a gated, swim/tennis community just north of the city. The place was immaculate inside and out.

"Tom, Claire, it's so good to see you. We're glad you could make it. It just wouldn't be the same without you here."

John looked at the basket that Tom extended towards him and he grabbed the handle and obligatorily said, "You didn't have to do that; we have enough food in for the holidays already."

"Well in that case, John, you now have more than enough," he smiled graciously. John had purchased a beautiful Noble fir tree that was strung with lights and topped with a classic-looking angel.

Tom and Claire stood at the entrance to the living room admiring the tree. "John, as usual, you have outdone yourself. The tree is absolutely perfect. Claire, we really need to put up a nice tree this year. What do you say?"

"I agree completely," Claire said.

"Before we start decorating, let's grab some lunch. I hope you haven't eaten lunch already."

Claire said, laughing, "We actually haven't eaten anything yet."

John and Diana had prepared a nice buffet-style lunch so that they could eat, decorate the tree, and come back for more whenever they wanted. John had a Christmas playlist playing on his sound system, and they spent the better part of the afternoon decorating the tree. The conversation was all about the ornaments and the warm memories they sparked about special moments of Christmases past. They finished decorating the tree around five. Diana said she was going to go to the kitchen to get dinner ready.

Claire said, "I will give you a hand."

"The Eagles game started at four, and if Tom is up for it, we can watch the game while you ladies work on dinner." Claire and Diana went to the kitchen and John and Tom headed to the family room.

John was really into sports. He had a massive TV and unbelievable sound system. Tom had no desire to have the same set-up but he was very impressed nonetheless. Tom was thrilled to get John alone for a while. He hesitated, not wanting to launch into his mission. He sensed John was not only in a great Christmas spirit but he was also into the game, which was close, full of big plays, and a couple of bad calls. The calls went the way of the hated, at least by Philly fans, Dallas Cowboys. For a true Philly fan, this situation heightened the intensity of the game.

Tom finally found an opening at halftime. John went to the kitchen to refresh their drinks and grab some pretzels. When he returned, Tom wasted no time. "We were at Andy Newcomb's house last week and he told me that he was working on the rationing project. He also told me that you were one of the key holders for the secured elements of PCP's payment system."

John's countenance and posture tensed. "Tom, he shouldn't be talking to you about that stuff, and you shouldn't be talking to me about it."

"Perhaps," continued Tom. "But some circumstances require discussions of confidential matters."

John looked very serious. His face grew red, his swift mood swing somewhat scared Tom. "What circumstances are you talking about," John questioned.

"I'm talking about the possibility that the payment system is going to be used by some bad guys to control who gets food and gas."

John's eyes narrowed as he stared at Tom. "Well, it probably will. There has been a lot of talk about food and gas rationing around the world because of shortages and inequality. Some people have more than they need while others starve," John said.

"Some people may want rationing to close that gap but others will want to use it for the wrong reasons."

"What makes you think that," asked John.

"I have a bunch of reasons. Perhaps the most compelling surrounds the freak accident deaths of the three members of the Universe Card board. Since I started looking into this I have been threatened and attempts were made to kill me and Claire," said Tom.

"Who threatened you," John asked, his alarm authentic.

"Wasim Mirza."

"Holy shit!" John said in disbelief.

"Exactly!"

"Tom, why are you telling me this?"

"You need to watch your back. I think you could be in danger."

John looked really scared, visibly shaken. "What makes you think I could be in danger," he asked.

"You are a key holder."

"Do you think there is anything you can do to help me with evidence of the plot or how to stop it," Tom asked.

"Well, at this point I don't have any evidence. The only thing that seems at all odd is that there are a lot of people working on that project, and my understanding is it hasn't even been approved by the board. And there's something else," John's eyes widened, terror visible from within. "I'm not sure how to explain this but I have had a couple of occasions when I got a really strange feeling when I was leaving the office."

"Let me guess, you felt like there was a presence that you couldn't see near you, and that presence made you feel depressed, like you were in an environment that was dark, dingy, cold, and gloomy?"

"Yes, Tom, that is very close to what I have experienced! How did you know?"

"Because both Claire and I have experienced it."

"Any idea what it is," John asked, his voice riddled with fear.

"Yes. According to an old priest friend of mine it is the presence of evil. Evil, as in the presence of the devil or one of his minions."

John looked winded. "Jesus Christ!"

"Don't take his name in vain! He is the only real defense we have."

"Are you serious?"

"Yes, John, deadly serious."

John was on the edge of the sofa just a couple feet away from Tom. He leaned forward in Tom's direction with his hands held together before him as if he was going to pray. He kept his eyes on the floor as he spoke. "Okay, what can I do to help," he asked.

"First, keep your eyes and ears open. Be on the lookout at work for proof. I have an ally who is high up in the card industry who can help us expose the plot if I can get some hard proof. Second, watch your back; I think you may very well be in danger. Third, pray. Lastly, can you tell me the details of how the process works when changes are being made to the secured parts of the system?" John said he could but he wanted to check on the ladies and re-up their drinks.

Tom called after him as he walked to the kitchen. "John, before you go in there try to lighten up a little. You look like you just saw a ghost."

John's expression remained unchanged. "I think I did," he said. He turned and walked away.

John returned from the kitchen, two beers in hand. They had another forty-five minutes before dinner would be ready, and maybe ten minutes left of half time. "The procedure is fairly simple but it has several steps," John began.

"Each of the key holders use their login credentials to enter a program that issues additional credentials that are only good for the next 30 seconds. They use those credentials to login and obtain their procedure document to permit various code changes to the system. We then perform a detailed review of the release package and code. We also enter any network changes that we were given in connection with the project. I have network changes to make, and so does the other key holder. When our review is complete, we each then review a section of the procedure necessary to permit the head of development, in this case Andy, to roll in the new code. Andy has the code ahead of time and he performs an even more detailed review. Andy posts a completion message that is routed to the key holders when he is done. The key holders log off and the system is again secure."

"John, I have a few questions. Do you know who the other key holder is?"

"I have no idea," sighed John.

"Do you know who prepares all of the procedures that you and the other key holder use?"

"No."

"If you had to guess, who do you think sets it up?" John cupped his head in hands. "I really don't know enough to make a good guess."

"Could you or the other key holder make changes to the code?"

"From what I know of the project, only Andy would have enough familiarity with the code and enough time in final review to make any changes."

"Is Corbett or anyone else ever involved with the change process?"

"I've been involved with four changes a year over the past five years, and during that time frame, I don't know that anyone else was involved. However, I don't know who the other key holder is or where he or she is located. Tom, if you are done with your questions, I have two for you."

"That's fair," said Tom.

"Why do you think Mirza is doing this," John asked.

"I think he's either involved with an extremist group or a linchpin of end times, carrying out the will of the devil."

"Wow, that's pretty heavy stuff. What makes you think you can stop it," John asked.

"I just feel like I have to try. I have faith in God that if there is something I can do to help he will guide and protect me." John looked skeptical but hopeful Tom was correct.

The second half kickoff occurred but John had stopped paying attention to the game, a sure sign he was deep in thought and analyzing what Tom had told him. Tom felt terrible and helpless. He thought he should be able to do more for his brother than tell him to watch his back, but he didn't know what he could do for him.

A few minutes later, Diana entered the family room to let them know that dinner was ready. They sat at the dining room table and picked up where they had left off, recalling fond Christmas moments. The dinner was nothing short of spectacular. Diana and Claire had made a light, but tasty salad, and John and Diana had prepared Beef Wellington, oven- browned potatoes and string beans almandine. As they finished Tom raised his glass, and said, "To Diana, an awesome chef." They clanked glasses. After taking a sip, Diana said, "I really need to share credit with John, who did most of the prep work and

Claire, who helped me pull everything together on time and made sure I didn't burn anything like I usually do." Both John and Claire pushed back saying they did very little.

Tom looked at Diana and said, "Diana, where did you learn to make potatoes like that?"

"John taught me. He said it was the way your mother would often prepare them for Sunday dinner. Did you like them," she asked.

"I loved the potatoes. I haven't had them that way in a long time, and it did remind me of Sunday dinner growing up. Very nice."

Diana gave a warm smile and looked around the table and asked, "Did anyone save room for dessert?"

They all declined and John said, "Why don't we go to the family room to catch the end of the game?"

Claire jumped in, saying, "Why don't you gentlemen go watch your game, and Diana and I will take care of the dishes, unless of course you want to swap those roles."

John looked at Tom and said, "I opt for the game, how about you?"

"Exactly!"

There were only a few minutes left in the game, but they were exciting because the game was still close, and the NFL teams were able to pack so much action into the last few minutes.

"You know, every time I watch an NFL game nowadays it seems like the first fifty-eight minutes are just a warm-up and the only part of the game that really counts is what happens in the last two minutes," said Tom.

"Yeah, a lot of times it seems that way, but I enjoy the whole game even if the game comes down to the end like this one," John responded.

The Cowboys went up by two points with forty-nine seconds to play. They tried a squib kick, hoping to keep the ball away from the Eagles deep return man, but the Eagles were ready for it. The Eagles got the ball on the Cowboys forty-five yard line. They kept the ball on the ground, using their three remaining time outs to stop the clock, and then kicked the game-winning field goal. John was so excited he jumped up and cheered. "Life is sweet! My tree is decorated, dinner was a success, and the Eagles beat the Cowboys."

Claire and Diana joined them, and John filled them in on the reason for the excitement and yelling. The post-game show carried on until the screen went dark momentarily, accompanied by a harsh tone. "We interrupt this broadcast for a special news alert." The reporter explained that an emergency UN meeting had just concluded to discuss the latest drought and disease report from Africa. The number of people that had died in the last three weeks was more than three hundred thousand, and that without substantial emergency relief of food, water, medicine, and medical staff an estimated one million would die in the next two weeks. The UN called for the nations of the world to come to the rescue of Africa. In a statement released by the US president moments later he blamed Congress for inaction on rationing for the United States as the main cause for failure to provide more assistance to the plight of Africa and other suffering parts of the world.

There were several moments of silence as they exchanged uneasy glances. Diana spoke first. "I kinda feel guilty. We had a big lunch, snacked most of the afternoon, and then had a grand dinner."

John lent support to her position. "Yes, we really do need to implement global rationing. Some countries have way too much and others, like parts of Africa, haven't nearly enough."

Tom said, "At the risk of sounding insensitive, I think we need better leaders throughout the world. Our country has always had a big difference in wealth distribution, and it has been mainly based on the amount of effort that some people put in and others don't. More than half the people in the United States don't work, and the other half pay for them. We also send billions of dollars around the world providing foreign aid in the form of cash, medical supplies, food, military, and medical support. How much is enough? We don't take care of our hungry, uneducated, and even our wounded warriors, yet we give money to countries who hate us. So much of what we send to other countries is wasted or siphoned off by crooked politicians."

Claire could see that this conversation wasn't the right one to have at the end of the day and tried to cool things off and shut it down. "Not that I agree fully with what Tom just said, however, do any of you know what foreign aid is?" Tom had heard this one before, but just smiled. John and Diana both said no. "It's when the poor people of a rich country give money to the rich people of a poor country." They all laughed. Claire added, "Well, speaking of world problems, I need to be at work early tomorrow morning." Tom and Claire thanked John and Diana for a wonderful day, and John and Diana thanked Claire and Tom for joining them. Tom pulled John aside for a moment and told him that he needed to be cautious and have complete faith in the Lord, especially when he got that depressing feeling.

The ride home was fairly quiet. Claire and Tom had both over-eaten and the day was really nice. "Tom, did you mean what you said about rationing?"

"Yes and no. I feel bad for the people in Africa, and I also feel bad for the people here at home. We have children who go to bed hungry every night, and today I ate and drank enough to comfortably feed a family of four. On the other hand, it's hard not to be cynical when you know that in this country people are milking the welfare system and others are taking advantage of it. Why should one man have to work beyond what most people think is a reasonable age to retire, like seventy-two, yet some government union worker can retire at fifty-five? And at the same time, we have a government that spends and wastes money like a flotilla of drunken sailors. There seems to be so many things that are unfair, I can't see how you can begin to level the playing field. What I do understand is the world today is ripe for evil to grow," Tom's tone invited a rebuttal.

"Believe it or not, I agree with you. Nothing seems fair, and there are so many problems we do need good leaders to straighten things out, and we need good people if we are going to win the battle between good and evil." Claire started to continue but paused, shifting in her seat. Finally, she seemed ready to ask her question. "Do you think the seals are being opened?" she said. "

"Yes, that is exactly what I was thinking when we heard that news alert."

They wasted no time getting to bed. Again Tom wanted to make love with Claire, but he could tell that she was still uneasy and tense. If it was to be tonight, it would be up to her to make the call. Claire was asleep within minutes. Tom thought about the irony; although just a couple of nights, it seemed like they made love more when they lived separately. *That will change when this is over.* He ran the day through his mind, first recalling the priests' sermon and the responsorial Psalm, "Though I walk in the valley of darkness I fear no evil, for you are with me." This put into words the spirit he needed to dwell on as he went forward. He could sense that he was on a collision course with evil, and the only thing that was going to get him through was his faith in God. "Yes, Claire, the seals are being opened." *Stay the course,* he said to himself, *fourteen days till Christmas.*

CHAPTER NINE

*And when he had opened the second seal, I heard the
second beast say, Come and see.
And there went out another horse that was red: and power
was given to him that sat thereon to take peace from
the earth, and that they should kill one another: and
there was given unto him a great sword.*

Revelation 6:3-4

Rainy days, regardless of the day of the week, can not only get you down, but they also cause us to oversleep. Tom held a cup of coffee in his hand as he gently woke Claire.

As gentle as he was, she bolted up and looked at the clock. "Oh dear God, I'm late! Thanks, love. A few sips and I'll get in the shower. Why didn't you wake me sooner?"

"I only got up about ten minutes ago myself," said Tom. "I'll fix us some breakfast to go while you get ready," he added.

"Okay, didn't we set the alarm," asked Claire.

"We did, but we had a power outage due to a thunderstorm." Tom made egg and cheese sandwiches for both of them and prepared a glass of orange juice and coffee to go in a travel mug for Claire. He got everything done as Claire came out. "Tom, you're a saint." She emptied the juice glass with a few big gulps. "Why don't you get on with your day? I don't need you to drive me to work," said Claire.

"Perhaps not, but I need to drive you to work because I love you and I need to take care of you."

Traffic was especially heavy. They were going from the suburbs to downtown at the height of Monday morning rush hour in the rain.

Fortunately, since Tom was driving, they could use the HOV lane to buy some time. Claire was very punctual, and she chaired an early Monday morning staff meeting. She called ahead to the office to let them know she was likely to be a few minutes late. Only as they pulled up to the building did she realize that she didn't have to park and walk to the office. "Tommy, you're a lifesaver. I am actually going to be on time for my meeting."

"Don't be too sure of yourself," Tom said seriously.

"How's that?"

"I expect a lengthy kiss as my reward for coffee in bed, breakfast to go and limo service," Tom grinned.

She gave him a peck on the cheek. "Sorry, but you will have to wait until tonight for your payoff," Claire winked.

"Okay. Give me a forty-five minute warning before you are done with work and I will pick you up. Love you."

"I love you, too," Claire smiled sweetly. Tom watched her until she disappeared through the revolving door.

Tom had some time to kill. His meeting with Sal was set for a café near PCP's office at 2:00 PM. Universe Card was headquartered in San Francisco, but several staff people whose functions were closely linked to technology operations had offices in the Primary Card Processing building for better coordination. He planned on first going to Mass, then for a run at a nearby downtown park, weather permitting, and then heading back to his place to check on things. He needed to pick up some clothes and other items to move to Claire's house, get some work done, order the new saddle for Claire, and plan dinner before picking up Claire in the evening.

The skies didn't clear, but the rain did stop. As he ran, Tom realized that although he wasn't feeling scared, he was constantly vigilant. When he drove he paid particular attention to the behavior of other cars, watching closely if someone matched his movement. When he parked, he looked to see if another car was parking nearby, behind or in front of him. When he ran he looked well ahead, occasionally behind, and turned widely around the edge of buildings, aware that someone might be waiting to ambush him. He hadn't felt the cold darkness, the presence of evil for quite some time now. He wondered if that meant it was gone or if his faith was protecting him from feeling it. He ran really well. The combination of going to church and then running in the brisk fall morning air gave him that fresh, clean, invigorating, uplifting, and positive feeling that he loved. It made everything he did feel easier. He swore it produced better outcomes.

Before he knew it, it was time to head for his meeting with Sal. He had only completed about a third of his to-do list, but that could still work out, depending upon how long his talk lasted with Sal. Tom arrived at one fifty, ordered a cup of coffee, and picked a table in the rear so that he could see the entire café entrance and Sal when he arrived. He had looked Sal up on LinkedIn, and Sal had posted a picture of himself with his family. Sal entered the café at exactly two o'clock and looked all about the café. Tom waved to him. When Sal saw him he smiled and walked toward the table. Sal was a true South Philly guy with a bounce in his step when he changed directions and a confident strut that you recognized when you saw it, but couldn't describe. Tom's father had grown up in South Philly and had the same strut as Sal. Sal was only about five foot four and had dark olive skin. He dressed casually and carried himself more like an automobile mechanic than a network technician.

"Tom?" he guessed.

Tom rose from his chair and extended his hand. "Hi, Sal, it's nice to meet you."

"You too, Tom. I see you have some coffee, if you don't mind I am going to grab a cup as well."

"Sounds good!"

Sal sat down and said, "I looked you up on LinkedIn and saw that you do management consulting and specialize in card payment processing."

"That's funny, I looked you up online as well, mainly to see if you had a picture posted so that I would know you on sight."

"Well, at least some of the stuff that's posted online has a use. What can I do for you, Tom?"

"Well, actually, I think the question is what can I do for you?" replied Tom.

"I don't understand," Sal said, quizzically.

"Sal, I believe that you may be in danger."

"You don't know me. And I don't know you. What makes you think I might be in danger?"

"Sal, are you aware that three board members of Universe Card have died recently?"

"Yes," answered Sal.

"There is an upcoming board meeting to decide whether or not to use the card processing systems to control the rationing of essentials," Tom went on.

"Sure, I am aware of all that," said Sal. "The board members died accidentally. What's that got to do with the vote on rationing?"

"Sal, you seem like a street-wise type of guy; what are the odds of three board members dying accidentally within three months. What are the odds that they were the only Christians on the board?"

"I guess the odds are pretty high, but so are the odds of winning the lottery and I still buy tickets."

"Are you aware that PCP and Universe Card are developing the software to implement rationing, even though the government and the board haven't made a decision yet," said Tom.

"Yeah, but that just means is it's a done deal. Working, middle-class Americans are always paying for everybody else in the world. Why not automate it and make it fair." Sal saw the situation at face value.

"Suppose someone wanted to use the system in a way that wasn't fair, let's say, not based on per capita consumption, but based on your race, your color or creed."

"Who the hell would do something like that?"

"Good question. Maybe a terrorist group, maybe the devil himself," said Tom.

"You know, Tom, you seem like a nice guy, and you probably mean well, but I ain't sure I want to continue this conversation. I don't want to offend you, but you are starting to sound crazy," he added.

"I can understand you're feeling that way, Sal. Suppose I told you that since I started looking into this that I have been warned, threatened, and attempts have been made to kill me and my girlfriend?"

"I would say it might have something to do with it and it might not. There are a lot of crazies running the world nowadays."

"Come on, Sal, I can understand you're being skeptical about something like this coming from someone you never met before, but you got to agree that there are too many coincidences in this story for it to be a coincidence," implored Tom.

"I would. But I would have to believe everything you are saying in order to come to that conclusion, and I am not calling you a liar, but I don't have any proof that what you are saying is true."

"Sal, the threats I've received have come from people you work for."

"Namely?" asked Sal.

"Wasim Mirza."

"That doesn't mean anything. He threatens everyone," Sal sounded relieved.

"Not the way he threatened me, and after he made the threats I started having bad feelings. I was followed, and then an attempt was made on my life."

Tom could see from the look on Sal's face that he had struck a chord with his last statement by the way Sal suddenly sat up. Sal's back straightened, eyes opened wide, as he folded his arms. "What kind of strange feelings? Did you see who was following you?"

Tom described the cold, empty darkness, the sadness, the damp air. He told Sal about the menacing shadow in the trench coat and fedora."

Sal suddenly lowered his defenses. He glanced down at his coffee and said, "I've had that feeling and when I had it, it was after I was followed by a guy who matched your description. I got a good look at his face. He looked evil."

"Sal, are you at all religious?"

"Yes, I am a practicing Catholic, and believe strongly in God."

"So, if you believe in God and that God is good, I assume you believe in the devil and that he is evil?"

"Of course," replied Sal.

"I explained to someone very high up in the Catholic Church about the feelings that you and I have had, and he explained to me that it is the presence of evil, and that it's very real. I also told him that I thought there were people who wanted to get control of rationing for the wrong reasons. He told me that he thought I was on target, and encouraged me to move forward with my investigation."

"Assuming what you say is true, why do you think I might be in danger?"

"Because you are a key holder," said Tom flatly.

"Who the hell told you that?" Sal was aghast.

"I have my sources, and it really doesn't matter."

"Like hell it doesn't matter! That is highly confidential information. No one is supposed to know that."

"Sal, I am sorry to upset you. If someone wants to use rationing for the wrong purpose, especially if they don't actually get approval to use the payment system for rationing, then they would need access to the system to do want they want to do. That puts a target on your back," Tom's concern for Sal was sincere.

"I sure as hell hope you're wrong."

"I do too, but I am certain. If I wasn't one hundred percent sure, I wouldn't put myself and those I love in harm's way. My purpose today was to warn you and ask you to keep your eyes and ears open. I have an ally who is high up in the card industry who will help, but like you he is skeptical, and wants proof. I am hoping that you can help me get proof."

"If I see or hear anything I will get in touch with you."

"I appreciate it. Here is my card, although if you have something it would be best to get it to me in person. I have no doubt that my electronic records are being monitored. One other thing; I haven't felt the presence of evil since I visited with an archbishop who, among other things, told me to put my faith in God and fully believe that he would guide and protect me."

"I'll give that a shot, Tom."

They stood, shook hands, and Sal simply said, "Thanks."

Tom held on to his hand a moment longer, looked Sal intently in the eye and said, "You're welcome. God Bless you!"

Tom had a quick cup of fresh coffee before he left the café to digest the outcome of his talk with Sal, but wasted no time getting back to his to-do list. He figured Claire would probably call him around six fifteen and that should be enough time for him to get everything done.

He felt good when he ordered the replacement saddle for Claire. He paid a good bit extra for it to be delivered to her house by Friday so she would have it for the weekend.

Claire called at exactly six fifteen. "Is this the Atlanta limo service?"

Playing along he answered, "Yes, ma'am, most reliable wheels in town, catering to the rich and famous, or beautiful Irish redheads as long as they are able to pay."

"Well, I am not sure I am fully qualified for those categories, but I can pay the fare, and do need reliable wheels and a safe driver," said Claire.

"You got it. What time shall I pick you up, me lady?"

"Driver, you may collect me at 7:00 PM sharp."

"Okay, love, I will see you then."

The rain had picked up, which meant that rush hour traffic would again be slow, if not gridlocked. Tom didn't want Claire waiting alone in the lobby and allowed the full forty-five minutes he had available to make the twenty-minute drive. He arrived at six fifty-five and was fortunate to get a parking spot in front of the main entrance to Claire's office building. He was watching the people walking along the street. He questioned his eyes when he noticed two men skulking along the sidewalk wearing trench coats and fedoras. The 1940s-ish style had made a comeback among the hip, and especially with guys in college. Each time, he watched them closely. Getting unnerved at the thought that Claire might get bushwhacked walking out to the car, he retrieved his umbrella and walked into the lobby to wait for her. Claire didn't come down until almost seven thirty.

"I am so sorry, Tom, all hell broke loose right after I called you. We had to redo the front page and change our lead stories."

"What's the deal?"

"You didn't *hear*?"

"No, I left right after you called and didn't turn on the radio," said Tom.

"There is a new breakout of a deadly virus in Peru that is spreading like crazy. They think it has a 21-day incubation period which means it could already be all over the world. There was also a major announcement about the New Kingdom extremist group. All of the extremist factions, globally, have united under The New Kingdom. They have seized control of several countries with nuclear weapons and assimilated their armies. They have pledged to follow a newly elected leader that seems to have come out of nowhere. All we know is that he is young, handsome, educated in the US and is very charismatic," said Claire.

"You're not shocked by either story are you?" she asked.

Tom looked straight ahead at the road. "Tom, did you hear what I said?"

"Yes, Claire—I heard you. The seals are open, the trumpets are sounding and the devil is on earth."

CHAPTER TEN

And when he had opened the third seal, I heard the third beast say,
Come and see. And I beheld, and lo a black horse; and he that sat
on him had a pair of balances in his hand.

Revelation 6:5

For the second night in a row, Tom wanted to make love with Claire, but after a light dinner, she got her things ready for work in the morning, put on some cozy pajamas, lay down in bed, and was asleep by nine. Tom was sitting in the living room with his laptop, checking on e-mail, and looking at his schedule for tomorrow. He had a conference call at eleven to go over the agenda for the meeting he was having with the prospective customer he was scheduled to meet with tomorrow and he had a two o'clock meeting scheduled with George Corbett at his office. Not a busy day, but acting as chauffeur and cook would keep him busy enough. He paused, thinking about Claire and how tired she was. He thought all things considered she was actually handling the situation very well. He was called on for this, but she was just an innocent bystander, and her life was in danger because of his mission. What a bunch of cowards to try to use Claire to get him to back off. She didn't have an easy day job, either. World affairs were growing more complicated day by day and every word was scrutinized, not just for accuracy, but also for political correctness. There were political, social, and religious lines that could not be crossed without becoming the target of some blogger whose criticism could go viral and cause the downfall of a business or newspaper or ruining the people who were involved in creating the issue. It made sense that Claire would be beat at the end of her day. He smiled as he thought that now that he was living with Claire, they would probably be more like a married couple and have sex less. He decided to do some backlog reading for business so that he would tire himself out, get to bed at a reasonable hour, and be able to function more closely to Claire's schedule.

It worked. He was able to get to sleep by ten thirty and woke at five fifty-two; eight minutes before the alarm went off. For the second day in a row he gently woke Claire, greeting her with a cup of coffee as she awoke. Today, he was received with, "How sweet! I could get used to this."

Tom said, "I hope so, that is at least part of my plan." Tom fixed breakfast while Claire prepared for work. They were out the door before seven. Tom used the same routine as the day before, getting to Mass and getting in a run in plenty of time before his conference call. The call went well. He was confident that the meeting tomorrow would be fruitful and that he would have another lucrative consulting engagement lined up for January. He had picked up some lunchmeat the day before and had a simple lunch while watching TV.

Tom felt apprehensive about going to the Primary Card Processing's office building to meet with George Corbett. He was concerned that he might bump into someone, like Jim, Andy, or Sal, and especially Mirza, but there wasn't any way that he could get George to meet him on neutral ground. Fortunately, there were less than ten Universe Card staff in the PCP building, and George Corbett's office was in a part of the building where he was somewhat secluded from both the PCP executive offices and technical staff which was where both Andy and Sal were located. He felt more comfortable once he arrived at George's office, although his name was now on the visitor's book for anyone else signing in that day to see.

"Hey, Tom, it's good to see you again. Any trouble parking?"

"No, I told them I was meeting with you and they waved me through."

"Yeah, PCP's security really sucks, but the elevator from the parking garage doesn't go any further than the main floor. You either need to have an up-to-date security badge to get in, or sign in at the guard's station. PCP will be upgrading to use fingerprint recognition within the next year, just like we have at the Universe Card's offices in San Francisco."

They shook hands, and George motioned Tom to sit at the small conference table that was closer to the window. "George, you have a really nice office and a great view of Atlanta from here."

"Yeah, it's not bad considering that I am sort of an outcast in this building. The exec offices in San Fran and here at PCP are all palatial, so why should I be any different."

The truth was that although he had a West Texas twang and carried himself like a good ol' boy, he had been a spoiled only child who went to private prep school. His parents insisted that he attend a local college, so they could help him with anything he might need during his college years. He was no slouch though. He was a good manager and knew the technology side of the business extremely well, both at Universe Card and PCP. On a personal level, he expressed his spoiled nature by doing everything over the top. He had to drive a Ferrari, live in a Buckhead estate home that appeared to have been spared by Sherman, and have a string of trophy wives of which, he was now on his third.

"So, Tom, if you are not going to try to sell me on a consulting engagement, what can I do for you?"

"George, it will probably sound a little odd, but I'm actually working on a consulting engagement for a religious institution and I wanted to discuss it with you to get your insight."

"Okeydokey, Smokey, what do you need to know?"

"The institution is the Roman Catholic Church. They are interested in determining if it is possible that the payment system could be manipulated to determine who gets food and who doesn't. It's kind of like what many interpret is described in the Bible under Revelation," said Tom.

"No shit. Those guys are serious about that?"

"Well, I wouldn't call it serious, but serious enough to hire a consultant to help them determine if it is at all possible."

"Well, not sure if you are aware of it or not pardner but a little thing called rationing is being considered," said George in full twang.

"Yes, I am aware of it, but rationing would, as I understand it, use the payment system to make sure that everyone got more of a fair share. The Church's concern is that such a system could be used to determine who does or doesn't get food and gas because of their race, color, political, or sexual orientation, or particularly because they are not of a certain faith or follow a religious or political leader."

"Well, pard, I guess in this world anything is possible, but I am here to tell you that it ain't gonna happen."

"How can you be so sure?"

"Because I am very close to the process that keeps the system secure and controls the changes to the system, and that ain't gonna happen on my watch."

"I don't doubt your veracity, George, but suppose you are replaced? Or the responsibility is reassigned, or God forbid you get run over by the beer truck?"

"It ain't likely that any of those things are going to happen. My job is quite secure because I know the territory and I manage it well."

"That leaves the beer truck," said Tom.

"I would doubt someone would kill me just to get into the system," George noted.

"They might, depending upon who 'they' are and how important it is to them."

"No, Tom, it just can't happen. We have good security procedures that involve several people, several layers and checks and balances built in . . ." he shook his head left and right several times. "It just couldn't happen."

Tom asked George if he had heard about the Universe Card board members and their untimely deaths.

"I am. Damn shame," said George. "What of it?"

"What are the odds of that happening?"

"I don't know. Pretty high I reckon."

"Did you also know that they were the only Christians on the board and that at the next board meeting a vote would decide whether or not to allow use of the Universe Card system for rationing?"

"Tom, are you saying that you believe the board members were killed so that rationing would be approved and that a non-Christian group is behind it?"

"I'm not saying that but the Catholic Church is wondering if it is possible," Tom replied.

"I don't think it is possible and even if they did, like I already said, we wouldn't let it happen."

Tom wondered how far he should push the conversation. He wasn't sure if George was in denial, or if he was completely unaware. It could also be he was either confident enough in his role that the system wasn't vulnerable, or if he was in it up to his eyeballs and wanted to deny everything. Tom concluded he needed to push it a bit, for intel, but there was too much doubt in his mind about George to try to gain an ally. His instincts told him George was lying. "George, I can understand that since you have responsibility for the security of the card system you might feel it's secure. I can also understand that a lot of people would accept the untimely death of a few board members as coincidence, despite the odds. But I have heard through the grapevine that the rationing system is already being worked on. Are you aware of that?"

"Hell no. We wouldn't waste time and money working on something that might not be used." George sounded pretty convincing. They were only fifteen minutes into the meeting and Tom felt awkward about ending it abruptly but he now knew based on that answer that George was lying. So that most likely means that he was in on it. "George, considering what you have said, and given your position with Universe Card it sounds safe to say this would all be very unlikely. More so, as long as you are on duty it isn't possible," summarized Tom.

"You got it, pard. I don't care if the devil himself or Wasim Mirza tells me to do it, there ain't enough juice or money for me to be doin' anything that ain't right," George vowed.

"In that case I'm going to get out of your hair. I greatly appreciate your time. You have put a completely different perspective on this assignment for me," Tom hoped this was working. George walked Tom to the door, shook his hand, and asked him to keep in touch.

* * *

Tom wondered as he got in the elevator if he took the wrong approach with George, or if the outcome might have been different if he had dug deeper. He shook his head. *He was lying because he is in on it and he even told you why . . . money and power. There is always enough of that on earth for someone who can't get enough and has to do everything over the top.* It also occurred to Tom that using the Church as a client was a good way to start the conversation, but it didn't help him uncover anything he wouldn't have found out if he was representing himself instead of a client. He did hope, though, that George wouldn't say anything to Mirza about their conversation. George just might believe his story about working for the Church and he might think that Tom accepted his lies as truth. Overall, the meeting was unsettling on several levels.

Tom didn't expect the meeting to be so short. He now had some time to kill. He decided to swing by his place and work until it was time to pick up Claire. As he pulled up, his pulse quickened. His front door was open. He entered cautiously, and yelled, "Hello! If you are robbing me you need to give yourself up. I am armed and have already called the police!" He checked each room carefully, repeating his warning as he moved around the house. He found that nothing was missing. It appeared the intruder went through the papers on his desk and a couple of the drawers were open, as though someone had closed them in a hurry. He packed the things he would need for the next few days and decided that he better check on Claire's place. While he hadn't armed his alarm system, he distinctly remembered Claire had set hers before they left this morning. He made a mental note to set them both in the future. He was hoping that Claire's house would not be trashed, but if it was, he wanted to know about it so that he could manage breaking the news to her. If someone did break into her house, though, she would have been notified by the security company. He decided not to leave anything to chance, despite the fact that he would now spend most of the rest of his day driving.

When he arrived at Claire's he was relieved that the alarm was on; nothing appeared to be missing or damaged, nor was anything disturbed. He thought he should tell her about the break-in at his house knowing that she would be disturbed but also that she should know, despite the realization that it would be very disturbing for her. If she wanted him to leave because of the danger he would do so; however, he felt whether he left or not, her association with him was still a cause for concern. All things considered, she needed to know, and he needed to take care of her.

* * *

"This is Wasim."

"Wasim, this is George. I met with MacDonald, and he was indeed snooping around asking questions about someone being able to control the payment system to decide who does and doesn't get food and gas. He said he was working for the Catholic Church."

"Did your detective find anything at his house? Anything that would indicate if he is working for the Church or for himself?"

"No, sir. Our meeting didn't last very long. I tried to drag it out, but he asked some questions, I told him that there wasn't any way that someone could get control of the payment system, and he seemed to buy it and give up. Wasim, I get the impression that he knows more than he is letting on and that he is working for himself. If he was working for a real client like the Church, he would have to have a lot more details to support his conclusions, and he didn't get into any details with me. I think this guy could be trouble."

"I will take care of it, George. You need not be concerned."

"I think I need to be concerned. Wasim, I am willing to help, but this guy gives the impression that the system is going to be used for the purpose of evil. I don't want to do something that will put me in jail." Wasim exhaled impatiently. "George, I just told you I will take care of Mr. MacDonald. All you need to be concerned about is getting your job done so that you earn your bonus."

"Okay, Wasim. I trust your judgment." Mirza simply hung up.

* * *

Tom pulled up to the front of Claire's office building at exactly six thirty, which was the time Claire said she would be done. There wasn't a parking spot available, but as he slowed down he could clearly see her enter the lobby by the bank of elevators. He double parked and blinked his lights, but she apparently didn't see his car. He sent her a text. "I'm here. I'm double parked directly in front of the door." "Be right there," Claire responded. She hopped into the car, leaned over and gave him a nice, but brief kiss. "Good evening, love. How was your day?" asked Claire. She seemed to be in a great mood and he hated to ruin it, but he figured he better get it over with. "It could have been better. My meeting with George Corbett didn't last long, although I did determine something important from him, and when I returned to my house I found the door was open and someone had searched my desk. Nothing was taken, and it appeared that very little was disturbed."

"Did you call the police?"

"No, I am pretty sure I know who did it, and why, and why they left in a hurry."

"How's that?"

"George strongly denied the possibility that anyone could hijack the card payment system. He was so over the top about it—it was

175

weird. I think he is in on it, and I think that either he or Mirza had my place searched while I was meeting with Corbett. Since the meeting ran short they probably had to call the person who was searching the house and tell them to leave. That would explain why the place wasn't turned upside down and the door was left open."

"Tommy, that's a nice theory and seems to make sense, but you aren't sure if it was a robber or those guys, and in either case, you ought to go to the authorities. The whole world hasn't turned bad, and there must be people with the local police or other investigative authorities that could help you."

"You could be right, but as everyone keeps reminding me, I don't have any real proof."

"No you don't, and not to make you feel worse, but it doesn't appear that you are getting any proof. You can report the threats, and attacks on us, and the ransacking of your house. You can even tell them your theory about Mirza hijacking the card payment system. Let them look into it. They have the tools and you will be left alone," Claire sounded drained.

"This thing lives at the top, the top of the payment system, government, and social media. If I report it, I am most likely to have two or three groups of people coming after me. No, I am going to stay the course," Tom said resolutely.

"Thick-headed, stubborn Irishman. Be on with you," she said in her full, now fake, Irish brogue. "I hope they didn't break into my place."

"They didn't, I already checked."

"Wasn't your security system on," asked Claire.

"No, I forgot to turn it on when I left there last."

"Did you hear the latest catastrophic news?"

"No, I've been on the move most of the day and my mind was processing too much to even turn on the radio. What now," he asked.

"Tom, there was a devastating earthquake on the Pacific Coast today. It affected most of Canada, Northern California, and had a huge impact on Central and South America. The death toll is already estimated to be over 100,000, and they've barely begun to scratch the surface of the damaged buildings. It's really odd too—the area most susceptible to quakes around San Francisco experienced only tremors and minor damage. The footage was horrible. I couldn't keep watching it," Claire's eyes misted.

By the time they finished talking about the day's events, they'd arrived at Claire's house. They worked on dinner preparation together. Tom had put on a love song playlist to purposefully avoid the news on TV and radio, and also to set a romantic mood without being too obvious. As they worked on dinner they sang along with some of the songs.

"So, I take it I won't have your chauffeur services tomorrow," Claire asked.

"Only if you want to leave at 5:30 AM and if I get back in time, which is possible."

"That wouldn't make any sense. You would be driving for two hours in the direction that you would then retrace. I am sure I will be all right."

Tom looked at her, concerned and serious. "I want you to promise me that you will sit in your car in the morning until someone else is near you and walking to the elevator, and that in the evening you have a guard walk you to your car."

"I promise, I will take those precautions."

When "My Endless Love" came on, Tom took Claire's hand and led her to the open area of the living room floor and they started to dance. As the song progressed they kissed, and without a word went to the bedroom and made love.

Afterward, Tom said, "Claire, I love you."

"I love you too, Tommy," smiled Claire.

Tom thought again about the deepening affection he had for Claire. He thought that it might be because of the danger, it might be because of the family life he realized he was missing when he stayed with Mo or it might be that he simply was coming to the conclusion that you could have more than one trip to the stars. It didn't matter. *When this is over, I will ask her to marry me. Hopefully this ends, and she says yes.* He smiled. *Thirteen days till Christmas.*

CHAPTER ELEVEN

*And when he had opened the fourth seal, I heard the voice
of the fourth beast say, Come and see.
And I looked, and behold a pale horse: and his name that sat on him
was Death, and Hell followed with him. And power was given unto
them over the fourth part of the earth, to kill with sword, and with
hunger, and with death, and with the beasts of the earth.*

Revelation 6:7-8

Tom and Claire were both leaving at 6:45 AM. They stopped at the front door before going to each of their cars and kissed passionately. Tom held Claire tightly and close. "I think we should go back to bed and pick up where we left off last night and let the world fend for itself today," he said.

"As nice as that proposition sounds, I need to let the good people of Atlanta know how the world is turning, and you need to line up some work for next year so that you can support me in a manner in which I wish to become accustomed," joked Claire.

"Well, if you're sure. I will call you and let you know my ETA. Be careful, and remember your promise about being cautious."

"I will, and you take good care of yourself, boyo."

Tom liked trains much more than planes, but except for the lack of productivity, he loved road trips. He especially liked the trip up I-85. This was the route he took when he first moved to Atlanta and would visit family and friends a couple times a year. He would get that warm, fuzzy, going-home feeling, which was always nice. The scenery was for the most part gorgeous. Much of the road was bordered by tall pines and mild, rolling fields. Passing between Georgia and South Carolina, the I-85 bridge passed over Lake Hartwell. This morning the sun was shining brightly, and the air crisp and moderately blowing caused a shimmer to shine all over the lake. He felt exhilarated. He brought an iPod loaded with a three-hour Christmas song playlist for the trip. He had all the classics as well as some recent releases by both country and pop artists. If this didn't get him into the Christmas spirit, nothing would.

Tom thought about his family, the meeting that he was going to, and Claire. The thought that Satan and his minions were hard at work, tried to push to the surface of his mind a few times, but for this trip he was managing to put them in the background. There wasn't anything he could do about that situation today anyway. The time passed quickly, and before he knew it he was pulling into the parking lot of America's Bank.

The meeting was long and trying, but unbelievably fruitful. The more they talked, the bigger the project grew in both scope and depth. After five hours, which included a working lunch, they had defined a project. Tom had given them a preliminary time frame and ball-park price quote. They were amenable to both. Tom was to follow up in a few days with a full proposal outlining the project in detail as they discussed, including the task list, phases, time estimates, and cost. The project was roughly scoped out to take five to six months for a fee of $250k, plus all expenses. The project would probably consume about eighty percent of his time. This deal would make his year, regardless of what else he might land for the second half. A good result would open the door to a lot more business with the bank.

The meeting ended at three o'clock, and he got on the road right away. He was thinking that he would drive into town and follow Claire home. The only block in that road would be traffic in Atlanta. The sooner he got there, the better.

The morning had been exhilarating, but now he had that post-deal high. He decided he would push the envelope a bit when he set the cruise control, cool it with the coffee to limit bio stops, and to blast the Christmas playlist again. He made great time going through the Carolinas. There were often backups due to road construction, rain, or traffic congestion passing through some of the major towns like Gainesville or Spartanburg, but today was clear sailing.

The beauty of Lake Hartwell distracted him as he entered Georgia. Between the overwhelming beauty of the scenery and sounds of the season blaring in the car he didn't see the two black cars coming up on him until it was almost too late. At the point where it crosses the lake, the interstate is only two lanes heading south, and the two black cars each occupied a lane. Tom was going 85 miles an hour, but the cars were closing on him quickly. He knew they were coming for him. His car wasn't fancy, but it had a lot of "guts" as his father would say. He floored it, and though he didn't gain any ground, he stopped them from gaining on him. There were cars up ahead. It looked like they were trying to box him in with one car directly behind him and the other on his left side to try to run him off the road. He would have to outrun them. It started off smoothly as he sped past two trucks in the right lane. He continued to push his speed, approaching a truck in the right lane and a car in the left lane. They were moving at the same speed, blocking his path. His heart raced knowing they would catch him. Then he saw an opening. If he was going to make it he would need the car in the left lane to pick it up. He started flashing his lights and honking. The driver gave him the finger in the rearview mirror, floored it and pulled away. It was enough to leave Tom a gap. The two black cars were just about on top of him and had lined up directly behind him and beside the truck. He quickly swerved to the right in front of the truck and exited to a rest stop. He positioned his car at the end of the parking lot so that if they doubled back he could jump on the road ahead of them at high speed. When they didn't come he realized this was only beginning. *They were going to be waiting for him. He needed a plan.*

He saw a Georgia state patrol car pull into the rest stop. Tom figured the statey wouldn't be long, and he would either follow the patrol car out of the rest area or squeal his tires so much if the black cars entered the rest stop area, that the patrol car would then follow them. The patrolman was there for only about ten minutes. Tom followed him out of the parking lot. He was hoping and praying that the patrol car was headed all the way to Atlanta. He knew that wasn't very likely, but if he at least got close and he hit traffic he would be in the clear.

They had gone down the road no more than a mile when Tom saw the two black cars parked on the shoulder. Their reaction was too slow. The patrol car put on his party lights and pulled over to check on the cars. Tom hadn't counted on this, but it was the perfect scenario. The patrol car would tie them up for at least ten minutes checking out their license and registration information. With any luck something would show up. The thing that Tom could never figure out, in fact, most honest people can't, is the way the criminal mind works.

As soon as the patrolman excited his car, two men jumped out of one of the black cars with guns drawn and ordered the patrolman to put up his hands. They placed his own handcuffs on him and shoved him into the ditch on the side of the road. Tom had gotten too far ahead to see anymore, but he knew that these guys were playing for keeps and that he'd better step on it. He slammed on the gas pedal. The whole situation was becoming surreal. He had bad guys in black cars chasing him while a forties crooner was singing Silent Night. *Dear Jesus, please help me. I am not sure what to do. I am seriously out numbered.*

Although he was still well outside of the Atlanta area, he was getting closer, and it was coming up on five o'clock. Traffic was getting heavier. The men in the black cars would have to weave through traffic to catch up with him. He figured he probably had four miles of breathing space between himself and the bad guys. He did what he figured they would be doing. He was averaging about 80 miles per hour, weaving in and out of cars to push forward. He had seen people drive like this on the road before and always felt that they were—and referred to them as—total assholes. It fit. A half-hour passed. He was sweating, and his eyes were glued to the road in front of him. He would only look back when the road was open before him. His hands grasped the wheel so tight that they would probably be sore for the next couple of days. He was grateful he had filled the tank before the meeting. A pit stop could be a real problem.

Suddenly, the two cars appeared in his rearview mirror about a mile back. They were at a point that Tom knew well. In another ten miles he would be in heavy traffic. Unfortunately, several cars entered the highway in front of him at the next exit impeding him. He had to slow down. He finally managed to get past one just in time. The two black cars were only about 100 yards behind. There were cars ahead of him, but he went back to high speed bobbing and weaving. He looked ahead and in the gully between the north and southbound lanes there were two police cars. When he was about 100 yards away from them they turned on their lights and started to pull out onto the expressway. By the time they pulled out they were behind the two black cars. The police pulled them over and Tom moved on. He figured they would radio ahead with the description of his car so he exited to change the settings on his GPS so it wouldn't use major highways. The route he took was a familiar one. It was unlikely the tails would find him. As he started moving forward he smiled again, realizing that the Christmas playlist was still going. He left it on.

The hour approached when Claire would be getting off work. He called her to say he would meet her at her house as originally planned. When asked about how the trip went, he said that the meeting went well and the ride was interesting. He didn't want to alarm her for her ride home. "What time do you expect to get home," asked Tom.

"Probably around seven thirty. How about you?"

"The GPS is saying seven forty-five, but I think eight is more realistic."

"Okay, I will get dinner started as soon as I get home. Are you hungry?"

"I am famished for both food and affection," Tom said with more meaning than he could convey.

"Well then, you are in luck, I have plenty of both for you."

Claire had dinner ready when Tom arrived, and greeted him at the door with a hug and a big kiss. She was really excited. The saddle that Tom had ordered had been delivered that day. "I made your favorite, steak, potato, and salad. Why don't you pour us each a glass of wine while I plate dinner?" Claire was in high spirits. Tom told her all about his ride up to Charlotte, the Christmas playlist, and the memories that the combination conjured up. All she said was, "Lovely." She raised her glass to toast him when he told her about his new consulting engagement. Her light mood shifted when he told her about the cars that tried to run him off the road.

"Tommy, please just contact the authorities. Tell them everything and let this go before it costs you your life!"

"I wish I could but I wouldn't be surprised if telling the cops would cost me my life at this point. Besides, I decided a while ago that there really isn't any turning back. I am just sorry that I have gotten you involved," Tom said sincerely.

As they cleaned up the kitchen Claire said that she learned at the office there would be some significant news breaking that evening but they weren't given the details. It was nine-thirty when their program was interrupted for breaking news. The deadly virus that the CDC and other government agencies, including the White House had said was totally contained, had spread to Spain. Based on this news, those same authorities were suddenly labeling the virus a worldwide pandemic capable of taking out 25 percent of the world's population if not contained within Peru and Spain.

"I will have to get into work early tomorrow morning and try to get our story straight. They label it pandemic with horrific projections, while at the same time talking about containment. I am going to get to bed." Claire rose, shaking her head. "It's going to be a long day tomorrow. You," Claire asked.

"I will be along shortly. What time do you want to leave?"

"I would like to be out the door by six o'clock."

"I will set the alarm for five fifteen and fix us some breakfast to go."

"Sounds good. I appreciate it, and I love you."

"Love you, too, sleep well."

He used his anonymous e-mail to let Nelson Glassman know that he was continuing to seek proof. At the moment all he had were the physical threats on his life and he was more confident than ever that what he was doing was the right thing. He told Nelson that he wanted to discuss the situation with him on the phone tomorrow. He sent a similar message to the archbishop. Tom admitted to himself that he was feeling pressured. His attackers seemed to be very careful. Tom realized that they were playing for keeps, but they were still trying to make his death appear to be an accident. That could change. He received a response to his e-mail from Gene Thompson at Giggly. Gene said he was not only receptive to meeting with him and aware of the rationing project, but he wanted to meet with Tom as soon as possible to discuss it with him. They arranged to meet in Chapel Hill on Friday evening over dinner.

As Tom closed his eyes he thought about the day, and thanked God for helping him escape. He asked Him to give him the strength to continue with his effort. *Please keep Claire safe.* He didn't realize the increasing significance of the date as he thought, *only 12 more days until Christmas.*

* * *

"Hello.

"Nelson?"

"Yes, this is Nelson Glassman."

"Nelson, this is Wasim."

"What can I do for you, Wasim?"

"I want to be assured that if my board decides to go forward with rationing that your board will do the same."

"Wasim, I haven't discussed it with each of the board members, but if your board votes for it, I am confident we will follow suit."

"I would like something more solid than your confidence," hissed Wasim.

"Why don't you talk to each of them and find out if there are any members who might oppose the measure?" he suggested.

"I guess I could, but like I said, it is very unlikely that if Universe Card passes the measure that we would create a road block," Nelson replied.

"I thought the same, but when I spoke with my board members I found several who were opposed. I had to make sure that they would not continue with their opposition. You may have the same problem. If you do, I would like the opportunity to address the situation," said Wasim.

"Very well, I will get a reading in advance of your board meeting," agreed Nelson.

"Please do so soon, as I am moving up the board meeting."

"What date are you moving to?"

"To Christmas Day," Wasim said flatly.

"Christmas Day?" exclaimed Nelson. "I don't understand. Why would you do that?"

"The president and several other world leaders think it is important to make a significant symbolic gesture for the program," Wasim showed no emotion.

"Well that is certainly symbolic," Nelson said.

"Nelson, have you met with a gentleman named Tom MacDonald recently," Wasim asked.

"Yes, I had a luncheon meeting with him. Why do you ask?"

"What was the purpose of the meeting?" Wasim probed.

"Uh, he is a consultant with whom I have worked with several times over the years. He approached me to ask if I had any upcoming projects that he might help with."

"That's interesting," mused Wasim. "I approached him recently about working with my company and he told me that he was currently on an assignment and unavailable."

"Why do you ask, Wasim?"

"He seems to have trouble minding his own business. Did he ask you about the upcoming board meeting and rationing?" Wasim asked.

"No it seemed like he was just looking for work."

"You let me know if he approaches you about the vote or rationing," Wasim demanded.

"If you wish."

"I do, and I would appreciate it if you would make sure your board is in favor of rationing." Mirza hung up.

Nelson thought about the implications of the phone call. How did Mirza know about his meeting with Tom MacDonald? He didn't say that he convinced the board members opposing rationing to change their minds. His wording sounded like he somehow guaranteed they would not oppose the program. Moving a board meeting to Christmas Day would certainly be symbolic. Perhaps it could be spun as a Christmas gift to those starving in the world, but having a board meeting on Christmas was a precedent that could also be viewed as anti-Christian. Our job is not to be for or against social and economic issues, but should be focused on whether or not it is appropriate for the cards and the processing system to be used for the purpose of rationing. Perhaps MacDonald was right, that Mirza has more motivation than he should. He wasn't sure if he was in favor of letting the payment system be used for rationing, let alone how Mirza and others like him might want to use the system. He certainly wasn't going to try convincing his board members that they should vote for or against the program. Let Mirza do his own dirty work.

CHAPTER TWELVE

And when he had opened the fifth seal, I saw under the
altar the souls of them that were slain for the word of God,
and for the testimony which they held:
And they cried with a loud voice, saying, How long, O Lord,
holy and true, dost thou not judge and avenge our
blood on them that dwell on the earth?

Revelation 6:9-10

Morning came quickly, but Tom and Claire both jumped at the sound of the alarm. They left the house within a minute of Claire's targeted departure time. The ride was short, and much of the time was spent eating their now standard getaway breakfast of egg, cheese, and bacon sandwiches. The early hour also resulted in plenty of available drop-off space in front of Claire's office building.

"Once again, your personal services were par excellence."

"Then I shall again expect a reward this evening."

"Count on it, just so long as the world isn't falling apart and I'm not dead-tired." said Claire as she shut the car door.

Tom had extra time so he went for a really long run and then to morning Mass. His nerves were steady but he was now beyond vigilant. He frequently looked in the rearview mirror when driving, and was constantly looking well ahead and frequently behind as he ran. He was able to occupy his mind as he ran though by mentally laying out the details needed to document the engagement proposal letter. He was at his house by 10:00 AM and had a draft of the document put together by 1:00 PM. He would sleep on it and send it out tomorrow morning with any final changes.

After a light lunch and shower, he decided it was time to use his burner phone to talk to Nelson and the archbishop.

"Hello."

"Nelson, this is Tom MacDonald, how are you doing?"

"I could be better," Nelson said honestly.

"In general or in relation to me?" asked Tom.

"Both. But before we go on, are you calling me on a safe phone like I asked you to do?"

"Yes, of course. It sounds like there is a problem." said Tom.

"I received a call from Wasim Mirza last night. He had some things on his mind."

"Okay," Tom said with a questioning tone.

"He wanted positive assurance that my board would vote in favor of rationing. I told him that I was certain that if Universe Card's board approved the program that my board would do the same. He said that wasn't good enough. He wants me to speak to each of them and let him know if they are in agreement. He added that a few of his board members had been opposed to rationing and he had to 'overcome their opposition.' "

"What did you tell him," asked Tom.

"Mirza doesn't expect you to disagree with him and it is pointless to try. If you don't say anything, he assumes that you will do what he wants you to do. I let him assume that because I have no intention of discussing this matter with board members on an individual basis. I meant what I said to him; if Universe Card's board approves the measure, I have little doubt that my board will approve it except for one member." said Nelson.

"Can you tell me who that might be," asked Tom. "Yes. That might be me," Nelson said.

"And why is that," asked Tom. "Because I believe that you might be right. I don't trust Mirza. I think that he is pursuing this too hotly. He seems self-motivated, and anything that self- motivates him isn't a good thing," said Nelson.

189

"He also wanted to know if I met with you recently," added Nelson.

"What did you say," asked Tom.

"I told him that you were seeking my help to stop him from hijacking the payment system to control access to food and gas."

"Did you really?"

"Of course not." They both laughed, Tom nervously.

"I told him that I had you work with us on several projects and that you wanted to see if I had anything that could use your help. He said that he had contacted you recently and you told him you were too busy. When I asked him about the nature of his inquiry he said that you needed to mind your own business. Obviously, he knew that we met, and he no doubt suspects that we discussed rationing and your conspiracy theory," said Nelson.

"Do you still think it is a theory," asked Tom.

"No. There is a conspiracy and Mirza is a part of it, if not leading it," said Nelson.

"So now that you believe me, will help me," asked Tom.

"I mean, I would love to help you, Tom, but we don't have anything other than our suspicions."

"We have much more than suspicion. They've tried to kill me and my girlfriend. The key holders are shaken up. They think they're being followed. I also have an archbishop who could someday be pope encouraging me to move forward and do whatever I can."

"Tom, I don't doubt you. To the contrary, I agree with you. The problem is that you don't have enough hard evidence for anyone in a position of responsibility to act upon. And you are not sure of the motive. Without those two things I don't know that we can do anything more than go to the cops and tell them what we know. You certainly should, so that maybe you, your girlfriend, and the key holders can get some protection."

"Nelson, are you invited to the Universe Card board meeting in January? Can you get me into the meeting?"

"Well, first of all, and I planned on telling you this, the board meeting has been moved up to Christmas Day."

"Christmas Day! Who the hell holds a board meeting on Christmas Day?!" replied Tom.

"Considering your Revelation theory, I could say that's a rhetorical question."

"That's funny, Nelson, real funny."

Nelson laughed at his own joke. "Seriously, why is he doing that," asked Tom.

"Symbolism. Many would conclude it is a Christmas gift to the world to balance the distribution of food, but cynically you could view it as a slap in the face of Christianity."

"Going back to my question, are you invited, and can you get me in?" Tom pushed.

"I am invited, no doubt to provide assurance that my board will follow Universe Card's lead, but I intend to send my regrets," said Nelson.

"Why would you do that? If you are willing to vote against rationing at your board meeting, why not go to Universe Card's meeting and speak up in opposition?"

"Because that would be suicide—for me and my career."

"Do you think that you can get me in to the meeting," asked Tom.

"It's by invitation only."

"Suppose I crash the meeting," said Tom.

"You'd either have to present your name and have your fingerprint pass the biometric reader for a specific member or be listed as a guest, show ID, and have the guard contact someone to confirm and approve your admittance."

"Since when do they check fingerprints for board meetings," asked Tom.

"It's not just for board meetings—it's used at the security gates in the lobby of the building. No one gets into that building without passing security. We will be installing the same system and procedures early next year. We need to beef up security in every area to protect against all the different types of threats we encounter. Tom, I would like to help, but I don't see how. Like I said before, if you come up with some real proof, I will get further involved. For now, I see nothing but risk. I encourage you to do the same. You are going to get yourself or someone close to you killed. If you feel you have to do something, then you should go to the authorities. They know how to handle these things, and despite what we both think about the government, there has to be enough good people high up in the organization to make a difference."

"I appreciate your concern and your help but I feel I have to keep going."

Nelson sighed and shook his head. "Well, all I can say is good luck then," he resigned.

"Thanks," replied Tom.

"Goodbye."

"Goodbye Nelson."

Tom was rattled. He thought that Nelson would be an ally, but he proved to be like all too many other good people who, in the face of real, ruthless evil, simply cower and look for the easiest way out. They expect someone else to carry the flag and make the sacrifice. Some dimwit who cares too much and thinks too little, and is willing to take the risk. *Dumb shit like me, exactly!*

* * *

"His Eminence, Archbishop Gleason's office, may I help you?" He couldn't remember the lady's name. "Yes, this is Tom MacDonald. Is the archbishop available?"

"Please give me a moment and I will check."

A moment passed and the bishop spoke. "Tommy, how are you doing?"

"I'm doing well, Frank. How are you?"

"I could be better."

Déjà vu. "Because of what we recently discussed or just in general," Tom asked.

"Both, actually."

Déjà vu indeed. "You know, Frank, this is the second phone conversation that I've had today that started the exact same way."

"It seems that you are the common denominator to things not going to well then, Tom," the archbishop said.

"Perhaps. The reason for my call was simply to check in with you. The good news I have is that the crucifix you gave to me and the prayers have helped immensely. I haven't had the bad feelings, and I have escaped a couple of serious threats that I don't believe I would have eluded if it were not for the Lord."

"True faith in God can be a very powerful thing. I believe the most powerful on earth," replied the bishop.

"I haven't gotten any proof to substantiate my suspicions of a conspiracy, and the ally I thought I had has pretty much abandoned me. I'll continue to look for proof, but as it stands right now, all I have is my convictions and my desire to do the right thing."

"That and your faith may be all you need. Are you tarrying or at all afraid?"

"I feel a bit weary. I am looking over my shoulder a lot," added Tom.

"I took another shot at my boss."

"Really, how did that go," asked Tom.

"It could have gone better. He called me to tell me that I was again under consideration for promotion to becoming a cardinal and asked me how I felt about it, knowing that I have not been receptive to it before. I told him that I had personal reasons that caused me to shrink from the position, but if it was the Lord's will and if he felt that I could best serve the Church in that capacity that I would accept the honor and position. He thanked me. I asked him what he thought we, as Church leaders, should be doing considering the continuing rise of Christian and Jewish persecution, and the spread of radical and now organized New Kingdom extremist rebels who seem bent to attack us. He said that the Church, in modern times, had to stay out of the affairs of governments and concentrate on being religious leaders. I won't go into detail, but I pushed him pretty hard. He said that his life has been threatened for remarks that he has made in the past, and that if he tried to form an alliance or apply influence to form an alliance that the Vatican would be destroyed."

"Did you tell him about our conversation," asked Tom.

"I did. In fact, I shared with him the details of the conversation."

"How did he react?"

"You have to understand that people hang on every word the pope says, and that he can't really trust anyone. That said, his reaction was very much like mine, although he never explicitly said so. He asked me what I thought, and I told him that given my faith, I accept that I will not know when we are in the end times, but it sure seems like we are. I told him that your analogy between what is going on in the world and the seals and trumpets discussed in the Book of Revelation seems to hang together pretty well. I told him that I felt as church leaders we should at a minimum be very vocal. I also told him that I felt that we should be influencing world and financial leaders. He disagreed vehemently and told me very nicely that I needed to stay in line."

"Well, Frank, it looks like I am in this alone."

"Maybe not," said Frank. "I may go rogue. You know, it just occurred to me that you have broken radio silence."

"I am using a phone that is untraceable," replied Tom.

"Yes, but we are talking over my phone line, which probably is traceable."

"We haven't mentioned too many names or specifics. Plus, I'm not sure how much good trying to fly under the radar has done for me. The bad guys seem to know every move I make," said Tom.

"So, who else knows every move you make?" asked the archbishop.

"Claire, but I trust her completely."

"I won't tell you not to trust her but do be careful how much trust you place and in whom you place your trust. I am saying special prayers for you every day."

"I appreciate that. Is it likely you will be promoted to cardinal soon?"

"Yes. It is a done deal and will be announced on Monday."

"Do you still have concerns," asked Tom.

"Plenty, but I think at this time I need to conclude that this is a call from the Lord and the Church, and that I should take the advice I am giving you and have great faith."

"Good luck in your new job, Frank," said Tom.

"Thanks."

"I better let you go," said Tom.

"God bless you, Tom."

"And you, Cardinal Francis Xavier Gleason."

The moment the call ended his cell phone rang. "Tom, do you have some time this afternoon? There is something I would like to talk to you about." It was John and it sounded urgent.

"I take it you are at your office, what is a good place and time for you," Tom asked.

"Can you make it by three thirty to the café across the street from the office?"

"Yes, if it is that important to you," Tom questioned. "It is and I can't talk about it on the phone."

"Okay, John. I will see you then."

His brother, John, was already seated at a table near the back of the café with a cup of coffee when Tom arrived. He waved, and Tom motioned back to him that he was going to get a cup of coffee as well. As they shook hands Tom said, "John, you seem really upset, what's happening?" John looked around the café as if to make sure there was no one there he might know or that anyone would be able to hear.

"Tom, I am getting that feeling that someone is following me as well."

"Do you feel like they mean to ambush you or are they just following you," Tom asked.

"I guess they are just following me. It doesn't appear like they are trying to get close. They aren't being real careful about not being seen though either." John looked exhausted, dark circles formed under his eyes.

"I see. You need to be very careful. Have you given any thought to carrying a gun," Tom asked.

"No. You know me. That's not my style. I'm not sure what to do, but I felt like I needed to talk to someone, and I knew you would understand."

"I've been going to church every day that I can and have put my faith and my fate in God's hands. That, and carrying a gun seems to be helping. That's the only real advice I can give you," said Tom.

They talked a while about family members and Christmas plans, and John seemed to calm down a bit. "Well, I better get back to work. Since you seem to be in tight with the Lord, please say some prayers for me."

"I will. Take care of yourself, John."

* * *

"Good Afternoon, Mr. Corbett's office."

"This is Wasim. Is he in?"

"I believe he is in the office, but let me see if he has anyone with him. Just a moment please."

George was staring out the window, deep in thought, when the phone buzzed. Startled, he swung around his chair and slid toward his desk. He picked up the phone. "Yes, Susan?"

"Mr. Mirza on line one for you, George, shall I put him through?"

"No, tell him I will call him back when I damn well feel like talking to him," he paused, she waited, and then he continued, "and that would be right now. Yes, Susan, put him through." George rolled his eyes to the ceiling and swung his chair back around so he could look out the window. "George, this is Wasim. Give me an update on the project." "OOOOO . . . K," said George dramatically. "Andy's team is on schedule and the code looks good. Giggly says they have completed their incoming and outgoing interface code and they have submitted their test scripts for review, and we are in the process of reviewing them. I am reviewing Andy's completed code and it looks good. Bottom line, we are on schedule."

Wasim raised his voice. "On schedule isn't good enough! The coders and technicians are always on schedule until it is time to be done and then they suddenly have a week left, which turns into two and then there are problems, which takes another week or two. I want these people working night and day to get this done ahead of time."

"Wasim, the only people that I can directly control on this project are Sal and myself. I can't tell Andy to work and have his people work around the clock! Hell, they aren't even in our company let alone under my control," George had officially lost it.

"If you act like they're under your control they will be under your control. Use your phone and keep on top of them. You haven't done any coding in years; who's checking your work?"

"Wasim, I may not have coded in several years, but I am damn good at it and it's just like riding a bike. Skills that are ingrained bounce right back. Plus, if I let someone check my code they are going to know exactly what we are implementing and could blow the whistle."

"Use Sal to check your code!"

"And how am I supposed to keep him quiet," asked George.

"I will make sure he keeps his mouth shut," barked Wasim. "Since he is one of the key holders he is already dispensable," he added.

"Wasim, I signed up to do the job you asked me to do and to keep it secret, but I didn't sign up to hurt people, especially good people who are just doing their job."

George sucked in air and braced for the imminent tirade. After a seemingly interminable pause, Wasim exploded. "You agreed to do all that was necessary to earn a ten million dollar bonus. You will do what I tell you is necessary to earn it. Are . . . we . . . clear?"

"Yes, sir." George knew it as coming but he still flinched when Mirza slammed the phone down.

* * *

Claire called Tom at five forty-five and told him she would be late because of a breaking story. She said she expected to be done at seven thirty, but she would call him to confirm about forty-five minutes ahead of time. She wasn't done until eight fifteen, and he planned on picking up a Greek salad and pizza on the way home. She hopped into the car at exactly eight twenty and although she looked beat she was smiling, and leaned over to give him a kiss that was part passion and part relief.

"I guess you had a rough day?"

"No rougher than usual, but significant late-breaking news always causes chaos at a newspaper."

"I haven't been keeping up, what is the evening's big story?"

"More of the same stuff, only it is spreading and getting bigger. Several major South American governments are declaring emergency food shortages and prices are skyrocketing. The leaders of Venezuela, Brazil, and Peru have all called for emergency relief from the United Nations. Concurrently, the Eastern nations are slowing down oil production and gas prices are soaring internationally. The president is taking advantage of the situation to make political points by continuing to blame Congress for inaction on rationing," explained Claire.

"Speaking of food, I got tied up this afternoon and wasn't sure when you would be done, so I haven't planned on preparing anything. Is salad and pizza okay with you?"

"Absolutely, in fact, it is exactly what I was thinking."

"Great—I'll call and place a to-go order." Tom could tell they were being followed and mentally made a joke about it but kept it to himself. *Perhaps we should order extra and ask the guys in the black Mercedes what toppings they would like.*

"This is good pizza, but it doesn't come close to the pie the cops shared with me in Jersey." Claire was too busy eating to respond. She didn't have lunch and was absolutely famished.

Tom continued, "Since I will be in Chapel Hill tomorrow and can't chauffeur you, is it possible you could work from home?"

"Afraid not. There is too much going on for me to work from here, in fact, there has been some talk about me and my crew having to stay in town at a hotel for a while to stay on top of things," said Claire.

"Please, please be careful when you are going into and leaving the office. And Claire, I know you are anxious to get to the stable, but please don't go there without me."

"I promise."

By the time they finished dinner and cleaned up it was time to go to bed. Claire was mentally spent and fell asleep within minutes. Tom was tired, but couldn't shut down. He had purposefully held back from telling Claire about his conversations with Nelson, Frank, and John. He knew it would only upset her and add to the burden she now carried because of him. He retraced the conversations. His assessment was that he needed a breakthrough as much as he needed a break. He hoped that Gene Thompson at Giggly could help, and he prayed that Claire would be safe. It was near midnight when he finally fell asleep thinking *eleven days until Christmas and the board meeting.*

CHAPTER THIRTEEN

And white robes were given unto every one of them; and it was said unto them, that they should rest yet for a little season, until their fellow servants also and their brethren, that should be killed as they were, should be fulfilled.

Revelation 6:11

Two road trips in one week might have been fun if the first one hadn't ended so dangerously. Still, as he started north toward Chapel Hill, North Carolina, for his meeting with Gene Thompson, he did again feel the same exhilarating feeling that stemmed from road trips and vacations in the Northeast. He would vary his playlist this time. The ride was an hour and a half longer each way. In addition to the Christmas playlist he brought country music, which seemed to work well driving through the Carolinas. The weather was cold for the Deep South this time of year but the sun was shining. He was hoping for a good meeting. He was hoping for some sort of lead or sign. He was hoping for an ally.

Gene originally wanted the meeting to be over dinner. Tom explained that if they met at dinner he would have to stay overnight or not get back home until after midnight. He didn't want to leave Claire alone, and Thompson finally agreed to a two o'clock meeting. Driving ten hours for a 1-hour meeting seemed insane, but it wasn't unfamiliar territory for Tom. He had taken many long road trips to sign up a consulting engagement. He considered flying to Raleigh, but the security measures have tightened so much that it's faster to drive.

Ironically, Tom had met Gene when he was working on an assignment with Jim Martin early in his career. Gene was well liked by Wasim and especially Jim. He was in his mid-forties and was now a bit overweight from too much desk work and not enough exercise. His hair was receding and thinning, but in his late twenties he was in great shape. He was good-looking, and like Jim, he had a roving eye. The big difference between him and Jim when it came to drinking and women was that Gene knew when to stop drinking, and despite his many affairs, he always made it home by midnight. Jim was clearly the bad influence, and Tom's understanding was that since his departure from Primary Card Processing seven years ago, Gene had ceased drinking and philandering. Maybe it was Jim's influence, maybe it was reduced stress from not being around Mirza, or maybe he just got older, fatter, and balder but he was now a real family man. He had two children and a dog. He had a boat on a nearby lake, which is where he and the family would usually spend Sunday afternoon. He belonged to a country club where he would play a full round on Saturday and nine holes in the evening a couple times a week. He was in charge of all new development at Giggly and Easy Pay, which was the new digital payment system they had developed. Chapel Hill was an ideal spot for Giggly and Easy Pay development because of its proximity to the technology triangle and two major university campuses. There was no shortage of young, bright, open-minded programmers within a hundred-mile radius.

The ride north to Chapel Hill was uneventful and peaceful. He picked up a burger, fries, and a diet coke and ate lunch while driving to make sure he would be on time. He pulled into the parking lot and looked for a spot up front in the visitor section, but the lot was full. As he glanced around the lot he noticed that almost everyone he saw was in blue jeans, a hoodie, or colored t-shirt and carried a backpack, with one exception. Walking two parking lanes over to his right, in the same direction and almost even with him, presumably having just parked, was the man in the trench coat and fedora. Tom continued at an even pace. His follower must have caught Tom's glance. He hung back. Tom entered the building, signed in, and after the security guard called Gene he was directed to Gene's office on the tenth and top floor. Tom looked around the lobby and outside while the guard was confirming that Tom had a meeting with Gene Thompson. There was no sign of the man in the trench coat.

Tom was accustomed to meeting with financial institutions where the office décor was very conservative, adorned with large, wooden desks, dark leather chairs, expertly chosen wall art and sculptures, and exotic plants. Giggly's offices were closer to what Tom would describe as adult-sized pre-school design. Lots of metal, glass, and break rooms with ping pong tables, free coffee, tea, water, and juice, with slouchy, colorful chairs, chairs on wheels and portable desks. Everyone in sight held a lap top, tablet, or smart phone as if they were as essential to their being as breathing. Both males and females seemed to be in two tight ranges comprised of those who looked hip and those who looked like nerds. Tom felt like a Neanderthal man.

"Tom, it is good to see you! Thanks for making such a long trip. Was the ride okay?"

"Yes, it was actually quite nice."

"Great! What do you think of our offices here? A bit different from the old days, aren't they?"

"That's for sure. I am used to the stodgy old bank buildings."

"Yeah, the difference is really the outlook of the people who design buildings now. They feel that the casual, colorful, comfortable environment results in more productivity. Our people are productive and happy. Tom, I am glad you called me about the rationing project. I have had some concerns about it and haven't been sure what to do about them," Gene closed the door to his office and took a seat.

"What are your concerns," asked Tom.

"Well, our role is pretty minor. We are to supply information in response to inquiries we receive from PCP to allow them to authorize or deny transactions. It is a relatively simple interface, both in and out. What is really strange is the data that they are requesting from us. You may not be aware—at least no one is supposed to be aware—that in

202

addition to all the data that we collect, we have an interface with the government where we provide complete profiles on people. When I say complete, I mean complete. Not only is it an invasion of privacy, it is a complete inversion of treating race, creed, or country of natural origin, equally. We have full access to all of the government databases, in the United States and most of those with whom we carry on trade and view as friendly. It's also only known, by very few, very senior people that we have just as much information on those who aren't friendly. We just don't have a lot of use for that information, yet. As a result, we have the most complete personal and business profile in the world. Neither the United States government nor the major card associations have approved rationing, yet we are not only implementing systems to do it, but I was pressured to have it done by the end of the year. And we've done it. We are ready to go, but PCP isn't. There's something else that's really troubling as well. Our response is not only household or company or fleet count information, as would be expected for rationing. It includes financial information, political persuasion, sexual orientation, race, religion, memberships, and subscriptions . . . Tom, it appears that they want to be able to decide who gets food and who doesn't, who gets water, who gets gas based upon other factors. It seems like someone is behind this—driving it forward, manipulating the system. I hope you don't think that I'm a whacko for saying this, but when it looks like shit and smells like shit, it probably is shit. I only have a few people working on this interface and it is the same people who have worked on the current government interface that has been in place for years. These people didn't like the idea of working closely with Big Brother before. They've all come to me individually and recently as a group, wanting to know why we were compiling this information. They want to know why we're turning it over to the government and a card processing network. They think it smells funny, as do I. Tom, what do you think?"

"I agree with you and your people, which is why I called and asked to meet with you in person. Before we go further, is your office bugged," Tom asked.

"I don't think so, but who knows these days. I may be filmed all day for an upcoming reality TV show. Let's go down the hall to an open area conference room. We won't have total privacy, but no one will hear what we are saying and I am pretty sure nobody would place a bug there."

Tom filled Gene in about the board members, his conversations with Jim Martin, Mirza, the archbishop, and Andy Newcomb, and the attempts to kill him and hurt Claire. Gene listened carefully, but didn't seem surprised or upset by the story. He didn't even blink when Tom told him that he thought that their intentions might be aligned with the prophecy in the book of Revelation.

"So where do we go from here," asked Gene.

"I don't know. I thought I had an ally at World Passport Card, but he doesn't want to rock the boat. I was hoping to have an ally within the Catholic Church, but as high up as he is he can't speak out freely. Several people have told me to go to the authorities, but I don't know that that will do me any good. I don't have any real proof—just theories."

"If it makes sense to us, then why wouldn't it make sense to the authorities," asked Gene.

"Because it would appear that people in very high places with significant resources are the ones who are leading this situation."

"Well, that definitely adds up. I've received phone calls from Mirza, and I even had a call from the vice president, who called on behalf of the president, indicating that the rationing project was very important to him; the president and the American people."

"Can you shut it down, Gene," Tom asked.

"I have nothing to do with the operational side of things. Once I complete a project, which we have done, we turn everything over to

Ops for final quality assurance, review, and testing. At this point it is out of my hands," said Gene.

Suppose we go to your boss."

"I did go to my boss. He told me that he didn't want to have to appear in front of Congress again, and that every time we balk at working with the government about giving them information we are threatened with an anti-trust suit and our stock drops. No, he won't do anything."

"Gene, I appreciate your time and your openness. If anything should change, please get in touch with me. As I have said to some other people, please keep your eyes and ears open. Oh! I almost forgot. Have you had any strange feelings or noticed anyone following you?"

"No, not at all. Should I?"

"No, I guess not."

From the time he got off the elevator until he got into his car Tom looked around frantically for the man in the trench coat and fedora and didn't see him. As he pulled out of the parking lot he was there. Tom saw him in the rearview mirror walking into the building. *What the hell? The shadow had come to pay Gene a visit, bringing with him the presence of pure evil.*

Gene had seemed convinced that the rationing project was not what it seemed and with questionable motivations. Gene was already thinking something was wrong. The meeting also resulted in achieving one of his objectives, which was gaining an ally. Nevertheless, he felt extremely tense. He knew that he was spinning his wheels. He was running out of time and options. He could give up which seemed to be the approach du jour; he could take his chances with the authorities; or he could shake a few trees and see what fell out. He decided to shake a few trees. He didn't want to waste any time, either. It was only three thirty in the afternoon and he had another four-and-a-half-hour ride home. He decided to circle back to Jim Martin.

"Jim Martin's office."

"Hi, this is Tom MacDonald. Is Jim available?"

"Just a moment, sir, and I will check for you."

"Hey, Tom, how are you doing?"

"I've been better."

"Well, that doesn't sound good."

"No, it isn't. After our dinner meeting, things have not gone real well for me," said Tom.

"How so?"

"I got a call from your boss that was threatening in nature, and since then I have been followed. Multiple attempts have been made on my life and one on Claire's. Jim, I know I'm right about this thing. I also know you must have told Mirza about our discussion."

"Tom, you're barking up the wrong tree. Yes, I admit I told Mirza about our conversation, but my reason for telling him was simply that it is the business I am in. If there is something bad going on then I need to know about it and I need to do something about it. So I went to the source and let him know what kind of questions are being asked."

"And what did Mirza say," asked Tom.

"He said it was nonsense. He said that the rationing project was inevitable. I asked him about all the data that was being collected and he said that they were just making sure they had plenty of flexibility built in, just in case the governments want to change their approach to rationing. He said it was nothing for me to worry about."

"I have a hard time buying that, Jim. Some really scary people are following me. All of this started within hours after our dinner meeting. Regardless of what Mirza said to you I'm convinced that he is up to his eyeballs in this. I also find it hard to believe that you are not involved considering it's your people who are implementing what he wants. You have to be either uninformed or lying."

"Are you suggesting that I'm either incompetent or a liar," asked Jim rhetorically. "I guess you don't care about working in the card industry anymore," he added.

"In a couple of weeks there won't be a card industry!"

"Tom, I think this conversation is going nowhere. You won't accept the truth from me and you're resorting to personal attacks. I hope you can get your head turned around before you get yourself into real trouble. Good day."

Tom sat for a moment, wondering if he accomplished anything with the call. His conclusion was that Jim might not be incompetent, but he could be misled. Tom stood by his observation from the dinner meeting. Jim's parting words that night were a threat. Jim was lying. The only thing he accomplished with that call was heightening the danger for him and Claire. He was rattled so he said a few prayers, called Claire's office to make sure she was safely there and let her know when he would be home. Still uneasy, he turned on the Christmas playlist.

An hour passed before he began to get tired of the Christmas and country playlist and he turned on the radio. Tom said to himself, "So much for calming down."

"We are interrupting our program for a special WKBY Gainesville Radio News Alert. The deadly virus, CHIM, that is spreading without check through Peru and Spain, is now breaking out in Ireland. The CDC has identified a clear link to travelers who were in Peru where the virus was first detected. The CDC is working closely with Peruvian officials to contact all those who departed from Peru in the last thirty days. The CDC has strongly urged the governments of Peru, Spain, and Ireland to cancel all outbound flights to other countries and to identify and isolate anyone who travelled from an affected country within the last thirty days. They further indicate that the number of people who have possibly already been infected and travelled to countries all over the world is significant. The CDC is urging all governments to voluntarily curtail all international flights until the virus is contained or a vaccine developed. So far, there is no vaccine that has shown the ability to alleviate or protect against the virus. The CDC indicates that this is the worst pandemic in history. Worldwide, airline and airline-related companies' stock prices are down over 60% in just the last thirty minutes.

Several major stock markets in Asia, Europe, and the Americas have halted trading on several major airlines serving the three countries where the virus is spreading. Stay tuned for additional information."

Tom thought about how this news would affect Claire. She would be distraught. There was no question that she was American, but there was still a part of her heart that belonged to Ireland. She still had and kept in touch with family there, and although it made him feel a little jealous, she would likely think about the boy she left behind.

* * *

"Mr. Mirza's office."

"Gene Thompson calling for Wasim."

"Just a moment, Gene, and I will check to see if he is available."

"Yes?"

"Wasim, I met with MacDonald and played along with him to see what he knew. He knows more than I thought he would. He suspects that the card associations and the governments are behind it."

"Will he go to the authorities?"

"No, he doesn't trust them. He also knows that beyond the attacks on him and his girlfriend he doesn't have any real proof. He said he thought he had allies at World Passport Card and someone high up in the Church, but neither are willing to do anything."

"Good work, Gene."

"Wasim, there was a guy in a trench coat and hat asking questions about MacDonald. Do you know what that was about?"

"Yes, he is one of our people. We just wanted to make sure that you were the only person he met with and that there was no evidence of MacDonald's visit."

"How would there be no evidence of his visit," asked Gene.

"He removed the sign-in sheet. If he claims that he met with you and that you agreed that the rationing project was bigger in scope there would be no proof that he had met with you."

"Yes, but there would be a big gap in the log," said Gene.

"No. The log was removed just before he arrived and immediately after he left. The only thing missing is his sign-in."

"We have security cameras that would show that both MacDonald and our guy, who doesn't blend in this building, were both in the lobby."

"Our guy took care of that as well. You will be rewarded well for your work, Gene." Mirza hung up. Gene gazed out the window and thought about how nice it will be when he replaces Jim Martin.

* * *

"Mr. Mirza's office."

"Is he available?"

"Just a moment, Jim, and I will check."

"Yes?"

"Wasim, I just got a call from Tom MacDonald. He was really angry with me. He said that since meeting with me that he received a threatening phone call from you. He said that he was being followed, and that attempts had been made to kill him and his lady."

"A coincidence, I'm sure," replied Wasim.

"He doesn't seem to think so. He thinks that we we're behind it."

"If he had any proof he would do something. He is just one of those crazy end of times conspiracy theorists with an overactive imagination. I doubt he will call you again. There is no need for you to worry about him. Just do your job, Jim." Mirza hung up.

* * *

Tom arrived at Claire's house a few minutes after 9:00 PM.. The return trip was uneventful despite his growing paranoia. Claire had prepared a simple but nice dinner and tried as best she could to hide the fact that she had been crying.

"I listened to the radio on the way home and heard that CHIM had spread to Ireland," he said.

She immediately wrapped her arms around him and put her head on his shoulder. She started sobbing. "This is so horrible. That little country will be devastated like it was during the potato famine. I have so many friends and relatives there. I sent e-mails to everyone I keep in touch with and urged them to isolate themselves as much as possible. What will we do, Tom?" Claire sounded drained of hope. She was clinging to him as if she would never let go. It was worse than he thought. "I was barely able to hold it together while I was at the office. I tried to hold on until I got home."

"Claire, we need to have faith in each other. We need to have faith in God like never before, and pray to him for our safety and the safety of those we love. I'm afraid the devil and his minions are among us now," said Tom.

The rest of the night was quiet. They lay in bed. "Will you take me to the stable in the morning? I want to try out my new saddle," said Claire.

"Absolutely. We'll stay as long as you want."

Claire reached over to hold him and kissed his neck. He wasn't sure what it meant, but one thing led to another. They made love slowly and tenderly as if they were consoling each other for feeling the problems of the world. Despite the world coming down around him he was content, as he closed his eyes to rest. *Only ten days till Christmas. Hang in. Exactly!*

* * *

Tom woke early the next day for church and his daily run. As he had hoped, when he returned to the house Claire was still asleep. He fixed a light breakfast and served it to her in bed. "Well, boyo, you are really trying to score points today. Did you do something wrong," Claire asked.

"No, I'm just trying hard to do everything right."

"You sleep OK," Claire asked.

"I slept very well. Last night was really nice and I was completely relaxed."

"What time do you want to leave," she asked.

"Take your time. I have some work to do. Just let me know when you are ready to go," Tom replied.

Claire was so excited about her new saddle and seeing Celtic King. This had been the longest time in a couple of years that she had gone without at least visiting him. Claire saddled up and was on her way in a few minutes. She had a routine where she would start by riding around the large outdoor or indoor corral, depending on the weather, and then circle the field outside all of the corrals. If she had time she would either do some riding around barriers or go off into the woods. The weather was good, and Tom watched as she circled the outdoor corral a few times and moved around some barriers to get the feel of the new saddle. She wore a smile the entire time. After a few turns she had Angel open the gate and she started her ride around the field. On the second time around, by the far corner of the field, Celtic King reared up. Claire was able to stay on the first time, but when he reared the second time he made a sharp turn to run, and threw Claire. Tom and Angel ran out to check on her. Before they got there Claire had risen to her feet and waved.

"Claire! Are you all right?"

"Yes. I am fine."

"Was it the new saddle?"

"No. Angel would you get after Celtic King and bring him back to the corral, please?"

Angel ran after the horse as Tom and Claire walked back to the stable. "What happened?"

"The saddle seemed fine, a little stiff but that would affect me not King. I think it may have been something else," said Claire.

"Any ideas?"

"I got that feeling in the corner of the field. That feeling that the archbishop told you was evil. Do you think it could affect Celtic King," asked Claire. "It could," Tom shivered.

When they reached the corral, Tom asked Angel if he could use his horse.

"Yes, Mr. Tom, you can use him. I didn't know you liked to ride."

"I usually don't because I am not skilled at riding, but I want to ride over to that area and see if there is a snake in the grass that could have caused King to throw Claire." Angel accompanied Tom on Celtic King to see if both horses got the jitters in that part of the field. As they approached the spot, neither horse got spooked. They found no sign of real snakes or anyone who was acting like a snake. In fact, they rode about the area and uncovered nothing.

When they returned to the corral, Claire wanted to ride more. At first Tom objected, but Claire said that it was important for riders who get thrown to get up and get back on right away. Angel backed up her story. Tom relented and agreed, as long as Angel would let him use his horse to accompany her. They circled the field a couple of times and then went for a long ride through the woods. Claire seemed to erase being thrown and thoroughly enjoyed the ride. Tom had no such luck. He couldn't put it out of his mind and surveyed the forest vigilantly as they rode. He was not very good at riding, and Claire wasn't giving him a slow, easy ride. She pushed through, up and down hills, with or without trails, and broke into a gallop whenever they were in an open field.

By the time they returned to the corral, to which Claire seemed to navigate with ease, Tom was surprised to have found their way back, and was convinced he wouldn't be able to sit on his butt for several days. Claire laughed uproariously as he dismounted and tried to take a few steps. "Does himself have a wee bit of a sore bum this morning?"

"Exactly, and I don't think it's funny!"

They drove back to a restaurant near Claire's house and had lunch at the mall. They did what Claire said would be her final

Christmas shopping, went grocery shopping and prepared Christmas cards while drinking wine by the fire. They had dinner, and not once did Claire mention being thrown. Tom was certain that she would ask him to back off again or go to the police. Nothing. Maybe she knew it was pointless. Despite the fall it had been a wonderful day until Claire received an urgent e-mail from the weekend crew. China announced that their food shortage was reaching critical levels and that they would soon take whatever actions they deemed necessary and appropriate to resolve the plight of their people.

Tom and Claire spent Sunday morning quietly. Tom went for a run while Claire prepared breakfast and then they went to Church together. They picked up where they left off on Saturday with final Christmas preparations and spending quiet time together. Unfortunately, the day ended much like Saturday, with Claire getting an urgent text from her weekend staff followed by a call from the editor in chief. When she got off the phone Tom thought that someone must have died. She looked both troubled and sad.

"What is it, Claire?"

"I am not sure where to start. The world is coming undone. My boss is putting up my entire staff in the hotel down the street from the office. He's putting us all on shifts leaving just enough time to eat and sleep. He said that this approach is necessary to keep up, and will continue indefinitely, including Christmas if necessary. CHIM has spread to China. People in China live on top of each other and it is expected that the virus will spread quickly. China is calling all their loans to foreign powers to be paid in cash, medical support, and food. Their stock market will not open tomorrow, and they have asked that other markets not trade their stocks or currency until they can stabilize their food and medical supplies and restructure their economy."

"Oh my God, that's incredible! If other governments don't pay off their loans they could be attacked, and if they do, many of their governments will go bust as well."

"Tom, it is worse than that. The New Kingdom extremist have announced that they have formed an air force, tripled the size of their army and they have threatened nuclear strikes on Israel, Rome, London and Paris."

"Their motivation or terms?"

"None, just the threat, but those are the capital cities of the countries most active in the Crusades. The editor also wants us to do an editorial discussing the possibility that these catastrophes are tied to end times prophecies," Claire added.

They sat staring at each other. Neither knew what to say, but they both knew what they were thinking, and they were thinking the same thing. Claire spoke first. "I need to pack and go. Will you keep an eye on Celtic King for me?"

"Sure. I have a very serious question for you though."

"What's that?"

"Are you allowed to have visitors?"

"Yes, but I will only have time to eat and sleep."

"We can make that work."

Tom dropped Claire off at the hotel. "Are you sure you don't want to invite me up for a drink," he asked.

Claire responded, turning on her brogue, "I am sure I do, but that is not what I need to be about doing tonight. I will let you know when you can come and visit. I am certain we will be off for Christmas Day, and that's only eight days away." She gave him a long and intense kiss, as if to make sure that he would miss her. Tom realized that for the first time in his life he would not be home for Christmas, even if he managed to stay alive. He kept this to himself.

CHAPTER FOURTEEN

*And I beheld when he had opened the sixth seal, and, lo, there was
a great earthquake; and the sun became black as sackcloth of hair,
and the moon became as blood.*

Revelation 6:12

Tom woke early feeing alone. Although he often travelled alone
on business, this was different. On business trips he was in complete
work mode and would be occupied with the client from morning till
late in the evening. Now, he was completely alone. There were no clients, and Claire was the one who was working from morning to night
and staying in a hotel. He felt lonelier still as despite well wishes, he
had no allies or supporters. He was alone on an island with the animals
closing in for the kill.

Christmas and the board meeting were now a week away. He
had to get into the boardroom. It was his only chance. He had to convince the board members that Wasim's intentions for rationing were
dangerous. He needed proof, and he needed a way to get into the
meeting. He also needed to stay alive between now and then. He felt
more comfortable with Claire being cloistered. She would be around
people. Staying in a hotel within a short distance of her office should
keep her out of danger, he hoped and prayed.

It was now clear to Tom that Wasim and his minions were trying to stay below the radar of the authorities. They had to make all
their dirty deeds look like accidents. Tom decided that he needed
to change up his routine. He had three places where he could work
during the day and sleep at night. He also had two cars that he could
use. He decided that he would do his running only in daylight, and in

a different location each day. He would also continue to go to Mass daily, but would attend at a different location, and not always the location closest to where he spent the night. It's hard to plan an accident unless you know in advance where someone will be and when they will be there.

Claire called Tom mid-morning to let him know that the president was going to make a special announcement on national TV around noon, and the rumor was that the news was going to be really big. Tom was at his house when Claire called around eleven. He turned on the TV to a network channel and went back to checking on his e-mail. The president came on the air at a few minutes after noon. He announced that he had just signed an executive order approving rationing within the United States, and to extend the United States' participation in international rationing as soon as the UN and the payment systems companies had worked out the rules for those programs. He also addressed the Chinese ultimatum. He indicated that America would repay China with food and medical support, but we don't have the money to repay loans. Then he dropped the bomb." If China should press military action for cash, then the United States would have only two alternatives; war, or the utilization of corporate and citizens' individual retirement accounts." He noted that the world markets had been informed of the speech he was making a few minutes before noon and advised they close their stock markets to allow the markets to digest these actions with forethought and avoid a financial crisis. Tom couldn't control himself and yelled at the TV as if the president could hear him. "Bullshit! You didn't have to say war or confiscation. Having said it, the markets will crumble and currencies will fail as soon as they reopen. You are posturing you demonic scum. You son of a bitch." What was conspicuously absent in his speech was any mention of the formation of the New Kingdom army and their nuke announcement. *I guess he couldn't use the New Kingdom extremist crisis, or more likely, he was supporting them. Asshole!*

Tom received a call and then a follow up e-mail from the contact person at the prospective client with whom he hoped to seal a deal. His proposal was accepted as is and they signed the agreement. The consulting engagement would start on January 2 of the new year. None of his other prospects were close to closing. This wasn't too troubling, considering he needed all available time between now and Christmas to undo Wasim's plans.

* * *

"Mr. Glassman's office."

"I would like to speak with him."

"Who shall I say is calling?"

"This is Mr. Mirza. Let him know my call is important."

"Very well, Mr. Mirza."

"Hello, Wasim, what can I do for you?" said Nelson.

Mirza was angry. "You can stay the hell away from Tom MacDonald and do what I tell you to do." Wasim shouted.

"Wasim, what's the problem?"

"MacDonald is telling people that you are his ally. I know you met with him. You lied! You said he was looking for work," bellowed Wasim.

"And what I told you was the truth. Who did he supposedly tell that fairy tale to?"

"It doesn't matter; what matters is that he told him that, and I don't think he would unless there is some truth in it."

"And on what matter or matters am I allegedly his ally?"

"That doesn't matter either. What matters is whether or not you are his ally or mine," shouted Wasim.

"On any current matter, I am nobody's ally or pawn. I will do what I think is right."

"Like hell! You will do what I tell you to or else, is that clear!" Wasim erupted.

"Is there anything else you want to talk to me about," Nelson asked.

"Yes, there is. I called several of your board members and they all said that you had not talked to them about the rationing program. You were supposed to speak with all of them and make sure they are lined up. They haven't heard word one from you."

"Is there anything else on your mind," asked Nelson. Wasim knew that Nelson was annoyed and blowing him off.

"Yes, I will repeat what I said a minute ago. Do what I tell you if you value your position and your life." As was his custom, Mirza slammed down the phone.

Nelson was not at all rattled. He had conversations like this before with Mirza. The big difference this time was that he not only threatened the loss of his job, but also the loss of his life. He now had the same type of proof that Tom MacDonald had and it was suddenly enough.

"This is Tom."

"Tom, this is Nelson Glassman, how are you?"

"Good, but this is not my secure line."

"Can you call me back quickly," asked Nelson.

"Yes, give me a few minutes," replied Tom.

"Tom?

"Hey Nelson, what's up?"

"I just got off the phone with our friend Mirza. He was breathing fire angry about a couple of things. He said that you told someone that I was your ally." said Nelson with a questioning tone.

"I told a few people that I had had an ally, and that the ally was high up in the card payment business, but I never mentioned your name to anyone who would repeat it to Mirza," promised Tom.

"Did you mention my name to someone you felt wouldn't repeat it?"

"Yes, two people. I mentioned it to Archbishop Gleason and to Claire."

"How can you be sure that neither of them told," asked Nelson.

"Because I am absolutely certain they didn't. My guess is that he put two and two together. He knows that I met with you, and someone I told about having a senior-level ally in the card business told Mirza. He's guessing it is you," Tom sounded positive.

"That could be, or it could be that one of your trusted sources can't be trusted," Nelson responded less positive.

"Nelson, I am sorry if I implicated you."

"It's fine," sighed Nelson. "But I do think it highlights the need to be as covert as possible and be careful what we say. He checked to see if I had talked to all my board members about rationing and found that I had not. He was just as mad about that. He demanded that I get them all lined up if I wanted to keep my job, and my life."

"Holy shit, Nelson, I am so sorry. This guy is over the cliff!"

"Yes, he is, and I may literally be over the cliff soon. I want to be your ally. And honestly because of the way Mirza is acting, I don't really see any alternative. If you are still interested, I will get you into the board room."

"Nelson, that's great. I think that is the best and possibly the only thing that we can do to stop him," replied Tom.

"Do you have a plan?" Tom asked.

"I think so. Let's fly into San Francisco on Christmas Eve. I'll tell the guard who you are and that you are working for me. If we're lucky it's the guard that is usually on duty, named Peter, and he will most likely let you in on my say so," explained Nelson.

"And if Peter isn't on duty that day," asked Tom.

"Then I either talk the guard on duty into it, or I carry the ball myself. I'll set my itinerary today and send it to you, so we arrive at roughly the same time and stay in the same hotel. That should allow us to meet up before the board meeting and we can ride over there together. Any questions," asked Nelson.

"No, I'm good," replied Tom. His expression narrowed. "I think it was Gene Thompson at Giggly who told Mirza I said I had an ally. I say that because I very recently met with him, and Mirza reacts quickly to news."

"Well, now we know we can't trust him," said Nelson. "See you in San Francisco," he finished.

"Sounds good. Thanks for doing this. Beyond just having help, I was starting feel pretty lonely in this," confessed Tom.

"No worries, Tom. We will bag this son of a bitch and nail his hide to the board room wall." Nelson was fired up.

Late in the afternoon, Claire called Tom to let him know that she would be working even later than what was becoming the usual. "Oh, Tom, I almost forgot to tell you. Did you know that your archbishop friend was elevated to the position of cardinal today by the pope?"

"Yes, he actually told me that the other day," replied Tom.

"He is going to have a televised ceremony and press conference tomorrow. I heard he is going to be making some interesting announcements. I saw his picture today. What you told me about some women throwing themselves at him made sense. He is very handsome. Unfortunately, the reports about him are sprinkled with innuendo about possible affairs over the years. The release is considered world news since it came out of Rome. I wanted you to know that I had my staff remove the innuendo."

"Thanks. It's good to have friends, and a lover, in high places," said Tom.

"I better get back to work. I miss you and love you."

The rest of the day flew by with some pre-engagement planning the client wanted done and changing his base for the next 24 hours from Claire's house to his. He picked up some to-go food from a nice nearby Italian restaurant and sipped wine while he made travel plans based on Nelson's itinerary. Having Nelson on board brought some relief. He felt more confident. Having one more than his usual two glasses of wine didn't hurt either. He tried to fight the urge to turn on the news knowing it wouldn't be good. He wanted to hang on to the mellow feeling. His sense of duty eventually won. He pulled up a news website, and was not surprised at the dire headline. The Pacific was rocked with a major quake. A massive tsunami was predicted to hit the coastlines of Japan and China in a few hours. Evacuations were in process, but there was no way that all the people on the coast could be evacuated in time. There was also a strong possibility that the quake would cause a less severe tsunami on the western coast of the United States.

He grabbed the phone and dialed Claire, knowing she would be up and working. "This is Claire O'Reilly."

"It's me. I just called to say good night and tell you I love you," said Tom.

"How sweet and thoughtful. I love you, too."

"I saw the latest catastrophe on the news and figured you would still be at work covering the story," said Tom.

"Yes, it is going to be so terrible on the coastlines of Asia. The saddest part is that many of the areas have no real means of communication and limited transportation. In the areas where there are good roads and cars, the emergency exit routes will be jammed. The quake was unfathomable. The tsunami will be worse. There is very little reaction time. The death toll will be massive," Claire sounded numb with sorrow.

"That's so horrible. I'll pray for their souls. God help them," said Tom somberly.

"One other thing before I let you get back to work. Do you think you can join for me for dinner tomorrow night and have me as a guest in your hotel room?"

"Sounds great, I will make the time and look forward to your conjugal visit."

"That tells me you know at least one of the things on my mind. I'd better let you get back to work. By the way, in case you have lost track of time, there are only seven more days till Christmas," Tom said, sounding hopeful this might make her smile.

"Thanks for reminding me. I hope to be able to get out of here by then."

"Good night, Claire."

"Good night, my love."

* * *

Tom was halfway through his morning run when he felt his personal cell phone vibrating. The caller ID flashed on the screen "Office of Cardinal FX Gleason."

"Good morning, Your Eminence."

"Cut the crap, Tom. I am still Frank to you."

"Are you still concerned about any dirty laundry? Claire told me that the rumor mill was buzzing about your alleged affairs. She told me, though, that she made sure her organization cut out all the innuendo," said Tom.

"I am only concerned about the effect it has on the Church. With all the sex scandals the Church has endured it doesn't need the sins of its newest cardinal on the front page. I'm at peace with what I have done and if it comes out, I am prepared to own up to it and ask for forgiveness."

"Do you think it will come out," asked Tom.

"I hope not, but it might."

Tom wanted to change the direction of the conversation. "Well, now that it is official, congratulations!"

"Thanks, Tom. I wanted to give you a heads-up. At one Eastern time today I am holding a press conference. I'll try to be diplomatic, but I'm going to speak out against several matters that the pope would rather be left alone. This may very well be the shortest time in office of any cardinal in history."

"Frank, as we discussed recently, we all must do what our conscience and our God tell us to do."

"That is exactly how I feel. I believe it is the Lord, not the pope, who has given me this office, and given me the grace I need to accept my role in spite of the attacks I am sure to receive from both inside and outside of the Church."

"All that is necessary for evil to succeed is for good men to do nothing. You're a good man, Frank, and in spite of your trouble with celibacy, you're also a good priest. You'll be a great Cardinal. This fight doesn't just need a leader right now. It needs a hero."

"No pressure," laughed Frank nervously. "I will do my best. How are you faring, Tom?"

"I am well. I am not getting those feelings you helped me deal with lately. And I think I might have found a way to fight this in my own way," said Tom.

"I'm glad to hear it. "Call me if there is anything I can do," offered Frank.

"There is one thing," started Tom. "What will you be doing on Christmas Day at 9:00 AM Pacific time?"

"Most likely starting Mass."

That's what I figured. If you remember, and if you can, please say a very special prayer for me at that time," asked Tom.

"You can count on it. Tom, I need to go. May God bless you, in Nomeni, Patri, et Spiritu Sancti."

* * *

Tom tuned in at twelve fifty-five to view the cardinal's address. It was billed as a press conference, but the announcer explained the cardinal was going to deliver a short speech.

Momentarily we will bring you an address by the newly appointed Cardinal Francis Xavier Gleason. The charismatic Cardinal Gleason was, until yesterday, the archbishop of the Archdiocese of Philadelphia. The product of a large, middle class Irish Catholic family, Cardinal Gleason was born and raised in Philadelphia and attended Cardinal Dougherty High School and LaSalle College. He entered the seminary immediately after graduating college. He was ordained a priest at the age of 27. Many attribute his swift rise through the ranks of the Church to his charm and dashing good looks. He is also well known for his ability to use those characteristics to get things done. He practices great piety, living strictly off of donations from family and friends. He is a brilliant mind. Many have suggested he would have been named cardinal years ago were it not for reports of slips in his vow of celibacy. The pope, in his statement appointing Gleason to the office of cardinal, added to his duties the role of special emissary to the United States. The site the cardinal chose for his address this afternoon is on the steps of Independence Hall. We don't know if he chose that site expecting a large crowd, but if he did, he chose the correct spot. The entire Independence Mall area is packed with a crowd estimated to be over 500,000. The larger than anticipated crowd may be related to growing speculation that the next pope is here today in America. Cardinal Gleason is making his way to the podium in front of Independence Hall. We take you there live at this time.

Cardinal Francis Xavier Gleason took to the podium like the captain of a football team about to speak to the student body at a pep rally. He was dressed like a regular priest apart from the Cardinal's cape draped over his broad shoulders. He stepped forward. A gust of wind blew his hair to the non-parted side. When he reached the podium the gust subsided and he flipped his head, moving his hair back into place. He looked across the Mall and struck a commanding pose, his powerful stare oscillating over the crowd. He had them mesmerized.

> *Good afternoon. I want to thank you for taking the time to come here today to hear what I have to say. My remarks will be embarrassingly brief. Embarrassing, because so many of you have gone to so much trouble to come here on short notice, and I'm only going to speak for a few minutes. He motioned to the area where the politicians were seated. There are so many here who have demonstrated their ability to speak at length, regardless of how little they actually say.*

The crowd erupted, and roared with both laughter and applause.

First, I want to thank the pope and my Lord God for entrusting me with the office of cardinal. The pope has seen fit to make me his special Emissary to the United States. The United States, like so many other parts of the world, is in dire need of God's grace and guidance. I, very humbly, will do my best to, hopefully, help Christians to hear his word, receive his grace, and follow his guidance. I also want to talk about some problems in the world and here in America that need attention.

For centuries, people of Christian and Jewish faith have been persecuted. These persecutions were cyclical in the sense that through some means they were overcome, for a time, and subsided. The Persecution of Christians was rampant during the times leading up to the Crusades. The genocide of Jewish souls during the Holocaust was an unbelievable horror. Yet it was not the primary reason that countries fought against Nazi Germany, but it should have been one of the primary reasons.

For several years now, people of Christian and Jewish faith have been more than persecuted around the world, and especially in the East. The Church has spoken out against the persecutions, but I do not think it has spoken with the frequency or the intensity that has been warranted. World leaders have said little and done less. The Church, especially here in the United States, has become paralyzed by the need for separation of Church and State. All religions should have freedom of expression. We are not only paralyzed, but have grown confused. There is a huge difference between turning the other cheek, freedom of expression, and cutting someone's head off. As Emissary to the United States, today, I am calling upon the leaders and the people of this great country and other countries around the world to recognize that Christians and Jewish people are being persecuted around the world at a level that is genocidal. It is time for our leaders to take action to stop it.

The crowd instantly roared and rose to its feet as one in thunderous applause. Despite the fact it was an obvious slam on the politicians, at seeing the crowd's reaction, they too quickly rose to their feet and applauded.

There is so much trouble in the world today. We are being ravaged by drought, famine, geological disasters, disease, sinking currencies and economies. The planet is in chaos and the bad news seems to grow daily. Many believe we are in the end times because they find, or think they can find, similarities between the visions in the Book of Revelation and today's world events. They think that these tragic events are the result of evil winning in the world and God's wrath upon us. Maybe they're right, perhaps they're not. The Lord said that he would come again and that we would not know the day or time, but we should be ready. Ladies and gentlemen, we all need to examine our lives and our actions and ask, what are we doing to prepare for the coming of Christ? Are we ready? He may be retuning in six years, six months, or six days.

There are some who say that the answer to our problems today is rationing our finite resources. Certainly, we need a fair way to better distribute the necessities of everyday life, but I question whether or not rationing is the answer. Rationing should not be needed if we would open our eyes, our ears, and our hearts to Jesus' message of love. He said to love one another as we love ourselves and to give to the poor. There is enough food in the world for us all. There is enough gas in the world for us all. Wouldn't it be better if those of us, who had more than enough, in each country, gave to those who didn't have enough? We can do that ourselves. Wouldn't it also make sense for the leaders of countries who have more than enough, to work with the leaders of countries that don't have enough to make sure that everyone at least has what they need to survive? Real leaders could work out an approach that would solve the problem. I am willing to bet that if they knew that Jesus was coming in six days and that he would judge them on how well they were doing their jobs, they would undoubtedly figure it out real fast.

We need to be careful about the power we place in systems like rationing and social media. Jesus is coming, but we won't know when. The devil is already here. He's present in the persecution of good people of all faiths. He lives in the corruption of governments and businesses. I have no doubt he lives in the bowels of society, weaving in the dark edges of the web, influencing the horrific content children and young adults are exposed to on the Internet. We need to be aware and wary of the things we let Satan control.

People, world leaders, heads of major corporations, operators of web services and social media—are you ready for the second coming of Christ?

He paused. He looked out toward the crowd, pointing out as he moved his arm from the left to the right over the crowd. Then loudly he asked, "*Are you ready for his return? Are you prepared to face his judgment? Thank you and may God bless you.*

The Cardinal stepped to the side of the podium and blessed the crowd. The crowd was standing and applauding; many were crying. The Cardinal's miter was placed upon his head and his shepherd's staff in his hand. The crowd was still cheering. He returned to the podium to give a final blessing.

Tom was floored, as was the news announcer.

Wow! In case you weren't sure what you just heard, Cardinal Gleason just called out the world leaders to act against the religious persecution of people of Christian and Jewish faith. He also slammed government and business leaders for not doing enough to combat evil and promote the common good. He spoke about the problems of the world, and although he said he didn't know when Jesus was coming, he challenged everyone to get ready and be prepared. He minced no words. While he called on leaders to act for good and against evil, he also cautioned people to be wary of their leaders and the power they give to them. He mentioned, almost as if an example, rationing in the United States. It appears that the pope's new cardinal is prepared to make a stand.

Tom started flipping channels. All the news channels were buzzing as a result of Frank's remarks. It appeared that the vast majority favored what he had to say, but doubted that the political and business leaders would heed his words without public uproar. Many likened his message to that of Christ. Tom waited a few hours and then called Frank. As he expected, the line was busy. Cardinal FX Gleason was now in high demand. The Church now had a real leader in America.

Tom chose a restaurant within two blocks of Claire's office for dinner. He wanted a quiet atmosphere, valet parking, and good food.

Despite everything he wanted the evening to be special. He could pick her up at the front of her office building, valet park at the restaurant, and then park in the lot below her hotel. He arranged for door-to-door service. He wasn't taking any chances. Claire was able to get off work at eight fifteen despite the frenzy in the news room.

As soon as she got in the car, she leaned over and they kissed like they usually did when he had been out of town for a couple of weeks. "Wow, I guess absence does the make the heart grow fonder," Tom said.

"Absolutely. I think it is because this absence is enforced and being caused by circumstances that you and a growing number of people think portends the end of times."

"Yeah, I am getting to the point where I don't want to hear the news. It seems like every day there is another calamity."

"Well, I guess you haven't yet heard today's calamities?"

"No, I haven't, and it sounds like there is more than one."

"There is, and the second one is close to home."

Tom was not deterred. He asked Claire to share the news with him on the ride to the restaurant so that they could then enjoy the rest of their evening together. She dove right in, "The first case of CHIM was diagnosed in New York today. The victim had been to Peru and returned to the United States before the flight restrictions were put in place. She's a teacher. She's had a lot of contact since her return with family, friends, co-workers, and students."

"Well, that certainly does hit close to home," said Tom

"That is not the news item that I was referring to when I said that."

"Okay, what then were you referring too?" said Tom. His expression was dark as he realized the shadow sweeping the world was inching toward him.

"Well it gets very close," said Claire with obvious apprehension. "I was talking to my mom tonight and she told me that there's a story that was released by—of all sources —Giggly—containing information about Cardinal Gleason's affairs with women during his priesthood.

She said they were trying to fact check it to make sure that the information is legitimate and was legally obtained."

"Isn't that common practice," asked Tom.

"Yeah but Giggly isn't being forthcoming about how they obtained the information, which makes it suspect. The API doesn't like to sit on these stories. They'll probably release it in the morning on a 'use at your own risk' basis," said Claire. "Tom, I don't think I will be able to squash this story. I'll do what I can. Maybe I can try to push through a piece suggesting this is an attempt to tarnish the cardinal. I'll blame it on the politicians suggesting he appears to have struck a nerve with some big wigs or something," said Claire.

"I appreciate whatever you can do to counter the attack. It seems the devil is always at work and knows no bounds. I see his work in this," Tom sounded distant. The weight of this burden was taking its toll.

As they crossed the threshold of the restaurant, Tom intended to turn the conversation and kept it centered on Claire, Celtic King, and Christmas. He waited until the entrées arrived to get to the real point of the evening. He told Claire he wouldn't be home for Christmas. He told her about his plan to attend the Universe Card board meeting that morning.

Clare took it worse than expected. "How are you even going to get in let alone survive it," Claire asked. Tom explained his plot with Nelson and how Mirza's threat had won him an ally.

Tom felt time racing forward. He knew the moment was all he had. "Claire, I love you very much, and recently I have come to realize that you were always the right girl for me. We both went into our relationship with the notion that you get only one trip to the stars, and our trip had been cancelled years ago. I have also realized that there is a part of our life that I put on hold without ever realizing I did. That part is a family life. When I recently went to Philly and stayed with Mo's family, I came to that realization. Claire, I'm asking you to marry me. Will you?" Tom hung on expectantly.

Claire sat back in her chair looking at him intently. She gracefully picked up her glass of wine and took a sip. "When," was all she asked.

"This Saturday," Tom replied.

"You don't think you are coming back and you want to marry before you go," Claire calculated.

"I have every intention of coming back and spending the rest of my life with you," Tom didn't expect this twist in the conversation.

"So, what's the rush?"

"We have waited too long already. I want to marry you before Christmas and yes, should I leave this world, I want to leave it knowing that I finally did the right thing."

Claire tortured him for a moment with a blank stare but finally a smile snuck up, lighting her eyes. "I will marry you on Saturday, but it must be in a Church, with a priest, two good friends as witnesses, and we have to have a more formal ceremony and wedding reception later."

"You got a deal," said Tom, relieved.

"And you have a fiancée, if I can get off from work." They kissed. The restaurant wasn't very busy, but the half-dozen couples who saw what was happening clapped. Claire blushed. Tom presented the engagement ring over dessert and she turned crimson red.

Claire had to check her e-mail when they arrived at her hotel room. She had one alert, which she kept from Tom rather than spoil the rest of their night together. The API had crafted the story about Cardinal Gleason. The story would be released in the morning.

CHAPTER FIFTEEN

And I will give power unto my two witnesses, and they shall prophesy
a thousand two hundred and threescore days,
clothed in sackcloth.

Revelation 11:3

Claire awoke well before Tom. She ordered breakfast for two, and prepared for work. She needed to get to the office early, but didn't want their time together to end. She knew that Tom was putting on a brave face for her and she loved him. She waited until the last minute to wake him for breakfast. "Last night was wonderful, Tom. I am looking forward to being Mrs. Thomas MacDonald."

Tom looked at her and smiled. "If being married includes making love like we did last night and room service, it would seem I have made a great choice." They both laughed.

"Tom, the story I told you about was released last night. It will be all over the media today."

"It's not a surprise. Mirza and those involved with him will do whatever they have to do to proceed with their plans. I'm afraid they'll do a lot more before we can stop them. Frank was prepared for this. I think he'll deal with it pretty well. I just hope the combination of speaking out yesterday and having this news come out today doesn't cause the pope to fire him," said Tom.

Tom changed into his workout clothes and walked with Claire to the lobby of her office building. "Tom, I am hopeful that we will have the weekend together, but I can't promise you that. I will take off at least Saturday for our wedding and honeymoon."

"Sounds good. Take care of yourself for me."

"And you do the same for me." They kissed and said good-bye.

Tom went to his house, gathered a few items, and drove out to Claire's place. He made Mass, checked on Celtic King, and got in a good run before lunch. The winter air was crisp. He felt exhilarated, high from the prospect of marrying Claire despite the storm surrounding him. There were now only five days till Christmas.

He was surprised when he received a call from Frank. "Frank, thanks for getting back to me. I am sure your time is now more precious than ever."

"You got that right. It seems I have caused quite a stir."

"Did you anger the pope?"

"No, he said he wasn't surprised that I spoke out. He said I spoke well, and that I should stay the course. I actually got the impression that he wanted me to do exactly what I did, and that it provided him the cover he feels he needs."

"And how did he feel about the news of your affairs?"

"I had already confessed those to him and he approved of the way I planned to deal with the news if it was released."

"How's that?"

"Tune in later today and you will see."

"What time should I tune in?"

"Around 6:00 PM. It will be a small press conference, but I am hoping for world coverage."

"I am sure you will do well. By the way, Frank, your address was really awesome yesterday. I was so proud to know you and for what you did. It is about time that people spoke the truth and for leaders to lead."

"Thanks, Tom. We are now in the fight together. I won't ask you what you are doing, but I will pray for you, especially on Christmas morning as you requested."

"Take care, Frank."

"God bless you, Tom."

When their conversation ended Tom was feeling pretty damn good. The euphoria didn't last long. Mid-afternoon, Claire called him and told him to check on the financial news. He did. The principal, global financial organizations were calling for a move to a single currency and card payment system. The president of the United States and the chairman of Universe Card, Wasim Mirza, were putting the measure forward. The action was being framed as absolutely necessary to stabilize failing currencies and to provide the necessary infrastructure for the equitable distribution of food, gas, and other necessities of life. An emergency meeting would be held no later than Friday, and the measures were expected to pass. Tom was shaking as he listened. He knew the real reason behind this play. He felt like he was sinking. They even had the audacity to frame the story as though it was in response to Cardinal Gleason's call to action of world leaders. Damn the hypocrites. It pained him even more when he thought about how skilled these people were at making something so wrong sound so right. He was so incensed he almost missed the next news item.

It was much worse. *We are saddened to report that the head of World Passport Card, Nelson Glassman, died in a tragic accident this afternoon. He was travelling by car to a meeting in Purchase, New York, from his home in Connecticut. Investigations are ongoing but he appears to have lost control of his car while crossing a bridge. He crashed through a guardrail and into the river. The car was quickly recovered, but Glassman did not survive.*

Greif and anger flooded him. *Accident my ass, they ran him off the road, just like they tried to do with me. Bastards.*

Tom sat quietly for a while, discouraged and sad. He tried to stifle his emotions and approach the situation logically. He needed a new plan to get into the board meeting. It was the one thing he thought he could do to stop Mirza. For almost an hour he drifted between prayer, moments of irrational thoughts and visions driven by fear. After thinking and praying, it suddenly came to him. He looked at his watch and said to himself, *you've got one shot, and it is a real long shot. Take it.* He drove to his house, found what he was looking for, composed a brief note, and drove to the UPS store. He used his burner phone to call Mo's husband, Bill.

"This is Bill."

"Bill, this is Tom, how are you doing?"

"I am doing well. This is a first. Is there something you need help with?"

"Yes, Bill, and it is very important. I am overnighting something to you. There is a handwritten note with an object, requesting that you get something done for me with the object very fast and then send the result to me at a hotel in San Francisco."

"Okay, do you want to just tell me what it is you want me to do while we are on the phone?"

"No, and you will have to trust me, it is for a good reason. Please don't call me unless you can't fulfill my request or do it within the time frame I am requesting."

"Okay, will do. Take care, Tom."

"I will, and you do the same. And tell Mo and the kids that I said hello and that I send my love."

* * *

John MacDonald had gotten tied up at work and was leaving the office late. It was dark, raining lightly, and cold. He had walked about twenty yards down the street before he realized it wasn't the weather causing him to feel weak and depressed. He picked up the pace. He heard footsteps behind him, growing louder as his follower matched his pace. He went faster still as he turned the corner toward the parking lot and quickly crossed the street. His follower did the same. John fought his welling fear and turned to face the shadow in the trench coat. "What the hell do you want?" John shouted. A powerful blow struck his head. A black limo raced toward them. A man dressed in black emerged from the car. He opened the trunk and helped the assailant shove John inside.

                                    * * *

Tom got back to Claire's place just before six. He turned on the
TV. A reporter appeared on the screen. She said that they were waiting for Cardinal Gleason to make a statement. It was expected he
would respond to the allegations against his celibacy. Frank was playing it smart. He was fully attired as a cardinal sans the hat. He was
sitting calmly at his desk, flanked by pictures of the pope and Jesus on
the wall behind him. His stare never looked down, up, or to the side.
He looked straight into the camera—confidently. His penetrating gaze
was focused directly as though he could see the audience through the
camera. He began speaking. Tom knew that Frank was prepared to
beg forgiveness for his sins. Not only was his apology well executed—
he decided to hit back.

> Ladies and gentlemen, I do not deny that in my younger
> days I succumbed to temptation, and had affairs with sev-
> eral women despite my vow of celibacy. I want to say first,
> though, that it is no coincidence that this information has
> been released to the press at this time. There are those in
> powerful places who feel it is necessary to diminish me,
> thinking that by attacking my reputation my message to
> you, which is Jesus' message, will be likewise diminished.
> Please, do not be confused. I am a man like you, nothing
> more, nothing less. Like you, I have sinned. That fact does
> not change my message. It does not change Jesus' mes-
> sage, and it should not hinder you from hearing the mes-
> sage. If anything, it underscores my point concerning the
> caution you need to have with your leaders. This informa-
> tion was not obtained by normal and ethical methods. We
> believe illegal use of surveillance tactics on my personal
> e-mail and phone call recordings occurred. Do not be
> fooled. Do not be distracted. They gathered and released
> this information to discredit me in your eyes.

I am here to confess my sin and ask for forgiveness. I seek forgiveness from my family and friends, all people, and the pope. I beg for forgiveness, especially, from the women with whom I had affairs, and from my Lord and Savior. Judge me if you wish. Judge me harshly if you wish. Dismiss my words if you feel I am unworthy. But, please, remember what Jesus said, "Let he who is without sin cast the first stone." Thank you. Good night, and God bless you!

Frank smiled like the little boy who had just been forgiven by his mother for breaking the window. You had to love him. Tom wondered how many offers to break his celibacy this would yield.

Tom had dinner alone and thought through his new plan. He had to laugh at the outlandish request he asked of Bill. He wondered what the chances were that he could get it done in time—but if Bill couldn't who could. Bill was the only person he knew with the connections, technology and ability to lift fingerprints from a glass and make a copy of the print that he could place on his finger. Tom planned to use this ability to get by security and into that board meeting. And he wouldn't know if it was going to work until it was done. The buzz from his third glass of wine helped reassure him.

When the phone rang around ten thirty he was certain it would be Claire calling to say goodnight. "Hello?"

"Tom, this is Diana. I am sorry to call so late, but I was wondering if you've heard from John. He is never this late coming home from work. I called the office and his cell phone, but he didn't answer. I left a bunch messages for him, but I still haven't heard back."

"No, Diana, Tom was shaken, "I haven't heard from him. Try calling the front desk at the office building and ask if they can tell you if he left the building and when."

"That's a good idea, Tom. I will try that."

"Let me know either way if you find out something, and don't worry about the time."

"All right, good night."

"Good night, Diana."

Diana seemed grateful for any kind of guidance as she was immobilized with worry. As soon as he ended the call his phone rang again. He hoped it would be John, but this time it was Claire. "Good evening, my love. Are you still at work, or safely in your hotel room?"

"Good evening to you, sir. I am done work for the night, I think, and I am not only safely in my hotel room, but snugly in my bed."

"Now that's a good vision for me to have this time of night. What did you think about the archbishop's news conference?"

"Your friend handled himself extremely well. I watched it closely, and I was thinking as I watched it that many women were wishing he wasn't celibate."

"Exactly!"

"Tom, I am sorry, but an alert text just hit my phone. I will have to check on this."

"Okay, call back if you can before midnight, otherwise we can touch base in the morning. I love you."

"Love you, too."

Tom waited for his midnight cutoff to try to doze off. Neither Claire nor Diana called back. This left the explanation to his imagination which fed on his paranoia. Maybe there was another disaster, maybe John's been hurt or even killed. At one thirty he turned on the news. On his way to early Mass the leader of the Orthodox Catholic Church, Patriarch Bartholomew II of Constantinople had been killed by an assassin on his way to early Mass. He was spiritual leader to 300 million Christians. The Orthodox Church is the third-largest body of Christians behind the Roman Catholic Church, followed by all Protestant denominations. Despite the late hour every channel was covering the story, and they had already brought back in their anchors and several commentators. It was big news by itself, but the fact that Bartholomew was supportive of Cardinal Gleason's remarks, while the pope remained silent, amplified the relevance of the news. A large portion of the Orthodox Church was in the East where the New Kingdom extremist were gaining support and spreading. He poured a large glass of sherry and stayed glued to the TV until two thirty. Speculation pointed to the New Kingdom extremist as the culprit. The pope, the president, and other world leaders all issued their typical statements of sadness for such a great loss, and condemning the cowardice and senseless nature of the shooting.

Tom had planned on going to bed at ten with nothing, but thoughts of his upcoming wedding to Claire and Christmas. It was now close to 3:00 AM and he was wide awake, worried about Claire, John, Andy, Sal, and himself. He lamented the loss of Nelson and the patriarch of a Christian Church. Circumstances had worsened rapidly. There were only five days left before the board meeting. *Do what you can. Do what you must.* Finally, he fell asleep.

CHAPTER SIXTEEN

And when he had opened the seventh seal, there was silence in heaven about the space of half an hour.

Revelation 8:1

Tom woke just a few hours later feeling down. As he sipped his first cup of coffee he thought about the reasons why. He felt his world bottoming out. It wasn't just the loss of sleep. He knew the dark finale was fast approaching. He was getting the uneasy feeling he recognized so well when something big was coming up. The desire to do a good job and be successful always caused him to become increasingly tense as time decreased and the deadline approached. The constant weight of the tragedy brought each passing day was piling up, and suffocating him. He couldn't contain his worry for his brother, John. John was a between-the-lines kind of guy, very organized and thoughtful. Rarely would John fall behind on a project and need to work late. He would always stay in touch with Diana. Something was wrong. He could feel it, but he didn't know what to do, what he *could* do. He felt the void caused by Nelson's death, that in this moment he was alone.

His sense of depression was exacerbated by the solitude in his home. When he was travelling on business he would miss Claire, but that was different. It was little consolation to think that she was travelling on business. She wasn't; she was simply away, incarcerated by the constant press of the horrific news from around the world. Tom was constantly worrying about her—her safety was questionable. They could come for her at any time. They likely were planning to as soon as an opportunity to make it appear accidental presented itself.

He didn't feel like going about his daily routine. He wanted to retreat to his room and hide like the rest of the world seemed to be doing. Let the so called "leaders" figure it out. *God, I wish today I was a slacker. Have one more cup of coffee and get your ass in gear.* He called both Diana and John, but neither of them answered.

* * *

John was dazed, and in a lot of pain, but felt somewhat relieved by the knowledge that outside the sun was rising. After enduring a hellish, torturous night, he had not given up his key codes. He didn't know he had it in himself to sustain such a severe beating without talking. He kept reminding himself it was his duty to keep the codes secure. If they wanted them that badly they were going to have to hurt him a lot more. Lives hung in the balance. He found strength in the knowledge that if they wanted the codes they couldn't kill him. They weren't wearing masks and used their first names. Since he could iden-tify them he had no doubt that they would kill him as soon as he gave them the codes. The scenario wasn't anything like what you would come to expect from all the torture scenes in the movies. You would expect a torture chamber—a dark room with a single, low-wattage light bulb in the center— walls dark with sewage water dripping down them. His torture chamber was a pretty nice hotel room. The guys who were beating him were well dressed. They would seem polished were it not for their mean looks, nasty nature, and harsh language.

"Listen, shit for brains. We've been at this now all night. We aren't getting food and rest so you won't either. We are going to keep pounding the living shit out of you until you tell us what we want. So, what are the fucking codes?" John was tied to the desk chair with rope around his chest, arms and feet. They beat him senseless, moving from closed fist to striking him with a hose. They upgraded from a hose to a chain, whacking him across part of his chest. Pain shocked across his body. His silence garnered more threats and increased violence. John lost track of time. The pain was overpowering his consciousness. They were hitting him on both sides of the torso and legs with the chain. Every inch of him sang in agony.

His captors grew tired. Ali, the mountainous figure wielding the chain spoke. "This isn't getting us anywhere. We need to take the next step."

"I am agreeing with you. I will be back as soon as I can." Saeed was smaller with darker expressions. He gathered his coat, hat, and car keys and left the room.

Ali turned to John. "If beating you won't make you talk we'll have to raise the stakes. Save us all a lot of trouble and give us the codes you stupid bastard."

* * *

Sal was scheduled to complete his review of the rationing code that Corbett had given him by noon on Friday. With one day to go, Sal finally allowed himself to come to a conclusion that scared the hell out of him. He didn't understand all the field names, but it was very clear the code would not be used solely for rationing. The field abbreviations were centered on race, religion and a host of personal information that shouldn't be relevant to the rationing project. Tom was undeniably right. Sal needed to get in touch with him.

"This is Tom."

"Hi, Tom, this is Sal. Any chance you can meet with me this afternoon?"

"Sure, where and at what time?"

"How about three o'clock at the same place we met before."

* * *

A slap lit up John's face, shaking him awake. He had no idea how long he had been sleeping. He eyes struggled to focus. Someone was flailing on the bed. He turned and dread overcame him. They had grabbed Diana and brought her to the room. She had a gag around her mouth. Her hands and her feet were tied. The terror in her eyes was more than John could bear. "You don't seem to care about your body, dick head, so we thought you might care about your wife's. In case it isn't clear how this will go, I will explain it to you. First we will both rape her, repeatedly, while you watch. Then, and only then, will we allow you to give us the information we want. If you do not, we will then begin torturing her, but not as humanely as we have treated you. We will pull out her fingernails, toenails, and teeth, one by one. We will take her apart piece by piece. She will beg you to tell us. Either you will or we will continue. At some point she will die. What do you say?"

John was broken. "Okay, I will give you the codes."

"We're not letting you or her go free until we are able to verify the codes. If you try to give us bad information we'll simply return later and pick up where we left off. Have I made myself clear?"

John nodded. They untied him and he gave them the codes. They then tied him up again and gagged him. They raped Diana and then pulled out a gun, screwed on a silencer, and shot both Diana and John in the head.

* * *

Tom arrived at the café a few minutes before he agreed to meet Sal to check the place out. He figured they were both being followed. The café was near empty. The other diners looked innocent enough. Sal arrived a few minutes after three o'clock. He spotted Tom at the back of the café with his back against the wall, but his eyes darted around the cafe anyway. Tom could tell that Sal was freaking out.

"Thanks for coming on such short notice. I was assigned to check the rationing code for my boss, George Corbett. I'm supposed to be done by tomorrow at noon, but I completed the review this morning. I tried to deny it but there is no question the code is not designed for rationing. You were right. I am sorry I doubted you." Sal, how could you know?"

"What can I do to help?"

"Did you have to make any changes?"

"No, are you kidding? Most of it was written by Andy Newcomb and George Corbett. Those guys are both really good at what they do. I can't believe they asked me to review it."

"Does Corbett know you're done?"

"No."

"Do you think you could alter it?"

"I could, but Corbett would be able to see the changes."

"If I asked you to go public with the information, would you?"

"No. Considering what you told me before, I would be afraid of retribution."

"If I promised to use it discreetly would you sign an affidavit?"

"What do you mean by discreetly?"

"I mean, it would only be shared with senior people at Universe Card, PCP, World Passport Card, or the police."

"Yeah, I would sign it on that basis."

Tom pulled the document from his portfolio. He gave one of two copies to Sal to review and sign. As Sal took the document from Tom his hands were shaking. "I'm a little nervous about all this."

"Understandable, I am nervous as well."

Sal read the document, looked around the café, picked up the pen Tom had placed on the table and then signed both copies.

Tom asked Sal to accompany him to have the document notarized. He agreed. Afterward, Tom asked Sal to go back to the café with him. "Sal, I am not certain what good this document will do, but I appreciate the fact that you took the step to do the right thing." Sal nodded as if to say both thanks and you're welcome. "I want to give you some advice that I hope you will take."

"Okay."

"Go directly home, pack up what you can, and you and your family get out of town as quietly as possible at around three in the morning. Drive far away to a relative's home and stay there until after

Christmas. Call in sick on Christmas morning and send Corbett an e-mail telling him the review was finished with no suggested changes."

Sal looked at Tom and laughingly said, "What are you, nuts? Pack up and leave town four days before Christmas?"

"No, Sal, I am not nuts. I am trying to save your life.

"They know that you know," warned Tom.

"I'll think about it," was all Sal said. They both stood and shook hands.

"Thanks, and good luck, Sal. May God bless you for what you have done."

"No problem, Tom, you take care of yourself as well." Sal turned and headed back to his office. When he arrived he turned in his code to Corbett, thinking that having done his job he wouldn't be a target. As he left the office that night he was met by Ali and Saeed.

CHAPTER SEVENTEEN

And when they shall have finished their testimony, the beast that ascendeth out of the bottomless pit shall make war against them, and shall overcome them, and kill them.

Revelation 11:7

Ali and Saeed were quickly getting accustomed to what made people break. They spent only a short time with Sal before moving in on his family. Ali stayed with Sal and Saeed, the nastier, more frightening of the two, went to Sal's house.

"This Ali."

"Ali, this is Saeed. Put your phone on speaker." As soon as he turned the phone on speaker, Sal and Ali could hear the sobbing in the background.

"Saaallllll," the maniacal voice rose. "You should have talked. I have already killed one of your children so you know that I am serious. Give us what we want or I will have my way with your wife and kill her in front of the children. Then, if you don't tell us what we want, I will take my time killing each of your children."

"How do I know you are telling the truth?"

"You want proof? I will let your wife tell you," Saeed threatened.

Sal's wife spoke next. She was sobbing and told him that Saeed had cut Sal Junior's throat. She sobbed and then loudly yelled, "Sal, tell them want they want to know! I don't want all of us to die!"

Sal was afraid, but he didn't believe them. He said, "You will probably kill us all anyway."

Saeed's evil voice responded in a low cadence. "Sal, you . . . don't . . . know . . .that. What you do know is that I will do what I said

246

I would do if you don't give us your codes." There was a consuming silence for what seemed like an eternity.

Sal then heard Saeed angrily say as he grabbed his wife by the hair, "Come here, bitch, while I show your kids what a whore you are!"

Sal heard his wife scream and couldn't take it anymore. He yelled, "Stop! I will give you the codes."

Saeed came back on the phone and said, "Sal, don't try to give us bad codes. We will not let you and your family go until we have tested them. Since you are smart enough to know that we would keep hurting your family, you should be smart enough to know that your only chance is to give us the real codes. Do you understand?"

Sal's head was hanging down. He was not only in a lot of physical pain, but it was also sinking in that his son was dead and had been brutally murdered in front of his wife and other children. He realized he and his family would probably be killed even if he did give them the codes. He decided it was worth the risk. He told them everything he knew.

Tom was still asleep when Claire called early that morning. "Hello."

"I'm sorry, Tom, I thought you would be up already and I didn't want you to hear this from anyone else."

"You are right; the only one I want to hear say I love you, want you, and miss you after being up most of the night is you."

Claire didn't laugh. "Tom, that's not why I called. The worst possible thing has happened. John and Diana were found dead this morning at their house. The preliminary police report said it was a murder-suicide. I am so sorry, Tom."

His voice shook as he spoke, tears clouding his vision. "John wouldn't swat a fly, and he wouldn't cut Diana's hair for fear he might hurt her. And, he would never kill himself. This whole situation is my fault. I should have gone to the authorities."

"Tom, it's not your fault. You are doing much more than anyone else would, and you are doing what you know to be the right thing."

Tom had no response. "I am afraid there is more," said Claire. "There's a report about another family, a murder-suicide. The man worked for Universe Card. His name is Sal Asante. He, his wife, and children, were all found dead. I was thinking there might be a connection."

"There is. They were all killed by Mirza's people to obtain information he needed for his plan."

"Oh my God, that's what I was afraid of. These people are monsters," whispered Claire.

"No, Claire, they are worse than monsters, they are the spawn of the devil. Mirza had all these good people killed because he wanted a back-up plan. I better go," Tom said.

"Tom, I will come home now if you want."

"No, we both have things to do; I will pick you up this evening as planned."

"I love you."

"Love you too."

Tom was inconsolable. For more than two hours he drank coffee and cried. He and his brother John weren't close, but he loved him, and he loved Diana. He blamed himself for not doing more, and not going to the authorities. He felt terrible about Sal as well. *Sal, why didn't you listen to me?* Finally, he started to pray and put things in order. He came to a simple and pragmatic conclusion that he didn't have time to grieve now. If he survived the next few days, if the world survived the next few days, then he would grieve. Whether he was right or wrong, he knew he had come too far and needed to stay the course. He knew he needed help. He not only had preparations to make for the wedding, but now he had to handle the funeral arrangements for John and Diana. He had to break the silence with Andy Newcomb. Andy would probably be able to do the math but after the deaths of John and Sal, he wasn't going to leave any lives to chance. He called Mo to break the news about John before she heard it on TV. He asked her to make the funeral arrangements and gave her the contact information he found online for the church, funeral parlor and cemetery. Mo was heartbroken. She said that she would fly to Atlanta in the afternoon and handle everything. As sad as she was about the horrible death of their brother and sister-in-law, she seemed genuinely happy to hear that he and Claire planned to be married the next day. Tom hoped she would come to understand why he was going to move forward with the wedding despite John and Diana's death. He asked her to be a witness. "I will be thrilled to stand up for you and Claire, and you don't have to explain anything to me. Your wedding is long overdue, and anytime is a good time for you and Claire to be married."

"Shoot me an e-mail when you have your flight information and I will pick you up at the airport."

"Will do, bye."

"Take care, Mo, and tell the family I said hi."

* * *

"Andy Newcomb speaking."

"Andy, this is Tom, how are you holding up?"

"Working hard. It looks like I'll be working on this project right into Christmas Eve," replied Andy. "I guess you have heard about John and Sal," he asked.

"Yes, Claire called me early this morning to be sure I didn't learn about it through the news. Are you and the family going out of town for Christmas," asked Tom.

Andy was a quick read and realized that Tom was speaking in code and he should follow suit. "I sent the family to their grandparents for Christmas, and God willing they will have a happy and healthy holiday. I will join them when my work is completed.

"Andy, do you think you will be able to get me a gift?"

"I hope so, but time is running out. If I do, I will have to ship it to you. Are you staying home for the holiday?"

"No, I will be out of town so if you do get me something it will have to be delivered electronically. Tom told Andy that he and Claire were getting married tomorrow morning and that he was hoping Andy would be the best man.

"I would be honored, Tom but I won't have time to party afterward," replied Andy.

"There isn't any party. It will just be Claire, my sister Mo, you, me and the priest." He gave Andy the address and told him he didn't need to bring anything but himself.

"I can handle that. Are you going to have a proper celebration someday soon?"

"Yes, and it is important to me that you and your family be there, so make sure you take care of them and yourself." They hung up, promising to see each other in the morning.

* * *

The day was flying by and he was completely off his daily routine. Since Claire was locked up at work, Tom had to make all the final preparations for the wedding, Christmas, the holiday meals, and get everything ready for his trip to San Francisco. He was just leaving the jewelry store after buying a basic pair of gold bands when he felt his phone vibrate. He was startled, and put up his defense screen up as soon as he looked at the caller ID. "Hello, Jim. What can I do for you?" he said somewhat coolly.

"Tom, I am really sorry about your brother."

"Yes, it was totally avoidable, and you and I both know it wasn't a murder-suicide," snapped Tom.

"That's why I'm calling. You were right, Tom. There is obviously a lot more to this than rationing," said Jim. He offered to help. Tom wanted to open up and tell him about the signed affidavit from Sal, and his plan to crash the board meeting. He even considered inviting Jim to the wedding but he didn't. There was too much at stake. He quickly sized up the situation and decided he had more to lose than to gain by trusting Jim. He told Jim he wasn't sure what anyone could do. "Jim, it seems like the whole world is upside down. What's right is wrong, what's wrong is made to seem like it's right, and those that are good, unconfused people seem to get killed

Jim seemed to sense his distrust and tried to convince Tom he was on his side. Tom said he believed him, and would be in touch if he thought of anything they could do to stop this.

Tom felt bad, almost guilty as he hung up the phone. He had always liked and admired Jim despite all of his failings. He felt a little disloyal turning down his offer but he was too close to Mirza and had too much to lose.

The news of Sal and his brother's families' deaths, the preparations for Christmas, the wedding, the San Francisco trip, and the surprise call from Jim were all too much distraction; his reality crumbled into a seemingly hopeless void. He didn't notice Ali and Saeed until it was too late. They shoved him into an alley and swung on him, knocking him to the ground in an instant, without Tom being able to lift a finger. Fortunately, the blow to the head missed its mark. He was more shocked and off balance than hurt as they hoped. As he rolled over he pulled his gun out and shot Ali as he was about to jump on him. Tom was in reaction mode. He fired four shots into Ali's chest, driving him back into Saeed. Saeed was off guard and quickly turned to run. There were pedestrians on the other side of street. Tom didn't want to endanger an innocent bystander and the man in the trench coat and fedora was running away quickly. Nevertheless, he steadied the gun on his knee and took the shot. He saw his target falter but not stop. His action was reckless but he didn't care. He was pretty sure he wounded him. Tom got to his feet. He started shaking uncontrollably. He had never killed anyone before and the feeling was frightening. He was surprised that no one seemed to have noticed what just happened. He put his gun away, took a deep breath, and walked out of the alley. As he heard the Salvation Army trumpet playing down the street he thought to himself, *Peace on earth. Good will towards men.* He would not mention this to Claire or Mo, and he would make tomorrow a wonderful day if it was the last thing he did on this earth. *Exactly!*

* * *

"Mr. Mirza's office."

"Is he in?"

"Yes, who shall I say is calling?"

"The president."

"What firm are you with, sir?"

"The United States of America."

"I see, just a moment, Mr. President."

"Mr. President, how are you?"

"I am well. Have you seen the news?"

"Yes, congratulations. We now have exactly what we need; one currency and one payment system."

"How are things on your end," asked the President.

"I don't expect any problems with the board, but just in case, our back up plan is in place. The rationing system will be rolled out on Christmas Day," said Wasim.

"That's great. Good luck, and keep me posted."

"Yes, Mr. President." They both hung up simultaneously. Mirza looked out the window of his office toward the bay, with fire in his eyes thinking he was triumphant. *There would be no Christ in this Christmas.*

CHAPTER EIGHTEEN

And the third angel followed them, saying with a loud voice,
If any man worship the beast and his image, and receive
his mark in his forehead, or in his hand,
The same shall drink of the wine of the wrath of God, which is
poured out without mixture into the cup of his indignation; and he
shall be tormented with fire and brimstone in the presence of the
holy angels, and in the presence of the Lamb:
Here is the patience of the saints: here are they that keep the com-
mandments of God, and the faith of Jesus.

Revelation 14:9-10, 12

Tom awoke at six thirty to the smell of breakfast. He thought about it for a moment, and realized that there was a distinct odor comprised of coffee, bacon, eggs, home fries, and toast. *That,* he thought, *is the smell of breakfast.* Claire was still asleep in bed beside him, which meant that Mo had decided to treat them all to a wedding and Christmas celebration breakfast. He decided to let Claire sleep a little more since it was the first night she had slept in her own bed in more than a week.

"Good morning, Mo. Breakfast smells heavenly," Tom gave Mo a sleepy smile. "I thought it would be nice for you and Claire to relax before your wedding. Help yourself to coffee."

Tom poured his coffee and sat at the kitchen island counter. "Hey Mo, before Claire gets up, and in fact, for the rest of the weekend, I want to avoid talking about John and Diana. Since we probably have a few minutes now, I just wanted to ask how it went yesterday. Were you able to get all the arrangements finalized?"

"Yes, the viewing will be held on Wednesday evening, and the Mass and burial on Thursday morning. All of the details have been finalized. The only thing I wasn't sure about and didn't address was whether or not we want to have a reception afterwards and if so, where," Mo asked.

"Yes, I think a reception would be appropriate. I will give you the number of a restaurant that has an upstairs space they don't use during the day. Ask them to have an open bar and to set up a cold buffet for lunch." Tom said.

Claire entered the room and said the same thing as Tom. "Breakfast smells heavenly. Thanks so much, Maureen."

"You're welcome, Claire. Have some coffee. Everything will be ready in about five minutes." Claire refused to call Mo, Mo. She said that it wasn't right to shorten a beautiful name like Maureen. Over breakfast they discussed the plan for the day. After the Mass they would go to lunch at a nearby restaurant. Tom and Claire begged Mo to join them for their early Christmas, but Mo said that they deserved time alone, considering it was their wedding day, and that Tom would be out of town for their first Christmas Eve and Christmas as a married couple. Mo insisted that Tom drive to the church by himself, and that she bring Claire to the church. She would not allow Tom to see Claire once she started to get ready. Mo wanted the wedding to be as special as possible. She knew that Tom had compartmentalized the death of John and Diana, and he was doing that for Claire. She could also tell that something else was seriously bothering him. So serious that he wouldn't discuss it with her. She knew this, because she was doing the same for Tom and Claire. She decided that whatever it was that caused them to get married at this time of year, that demanded Tom go to San Francisco, in spite of John and Diana's death, meant they needed her help. She decided she would do whatever it took to give it to them.

Maureen helped Claire dress. Tom left for the church and met up with both the priest and Andy at about ten forty. At ten fifty-five

Tom received a text from Mo telling him to take their positions in the church. They would be there in less than five minutes. Tom stood at the front of the church by the altar with Father Doyle to his right and Andy Newcomb to his left. To Tom's surprise, the organ began to play Canon in D Major. Moments later, Claire entered the church. She was wearing a long white embroidered dress, heels, and a simple white veil draped around her head. Her blue eyes and strawberry-blond hair popped against the all-white clothing and when she was halfway up the aisle, the sunlight coming from the stained glass windows above the altar framed her. She was bathed in a kaleidoscope of colors. The vision of Claire coming up the aisle was nothing short of stunning. The ceremony exceeded every expectation Tom had. Mo had made more than just funeral adjustments. She ordered flowers for the church, an organist and vocalist.

Tom and Claire held hands and never blinked. They looked deeply and tenderly into each other's eyes as they said their vows. Father Doyle remarked afterwards during lunch that he had never before witnessed such an intense kiss at the altar, let alone by a married couple who were already living together. "Father, that's because you never saw anyone marry someone as fair and lovely as Claire," remarked Tom.

Claire blushed. "Thomas, you are probably—no, wait a minute—you are absolutely correct," he beamed.

After lunch, Mo's car was brought around first by the valet. She was going to stay at a hotel for the night and then with Claire while Tom was out of town.

"Mo, thanks so much for everything. I loved all the extras you added to the wedding and I am so happy that you were here with us," he said, his voice full of love and gratitude.

Mo hugged Tom. "It's the least I could do. Also, Bill said your package will be waiting for you when you arrive at your hotel. "Congratulations and Merry Christmas," she waved.

Tom turned to Andy and thanked him for being best man. "Well, I will do a better job next time around. This time I was a little pressed for time but I plan on sending you a useful gift as early as tomorrow," his expression sharpened. "Sounds good, Andy. "Congratulations again, Tom and Claire. I wish you health, happiness, wealth, and at least five kids." They all laughed.

As soon as Tom and Claire returned to their house, they began their preparations to spend the rest of the day combining their honeymoon, Christmas Eve, and Christmas. They worked in the kitchen together for several hours preparing a full Christmas Day feast. Tom had his Christmas playlist on and they sang along with several of the classics. The table was set with Claire's best china and silver, and they enjoyed a perfect turkey dinner by candlelight.

Tom lit a fire in the family room and they spent most of the evening exchanging gifts. When the gifts had all been opened they started to kiss forgetting about dessert and coffee. They made love as though it was for the first time, and vowed that they would try to make every time feel like it was the first time. Claire was content and fell asleep by ten. Tom wished that he could do the same, but having focused on the wedding and Christmas, he now had a lot of coiled-up emotion. He poured another glass of wine, turned on the late-night news and started to check his messages.

Tom's brief stay in fantasyland was short-lived as he was quickly jolted back into the real world that seemed to be tumbling out of control. Every news channel was carrying the same story. Tom thanked God that Claire stuck with the rules and didn't look at her messages all day. Their day would have been ruined, and she probably would have been back at the office instead of sound asleep in bed. The head of The New Kingdom gave a speech declaring that Jews and Christians needed to convert to the New Kingdom beliefs. The ultimatum was aimed directly at the pope and the Prime Minister of Israel. "If the leaders of every world religion do not swear their allegiance to the New Kingdom and their prophet they will be wiped from the face of the earth by midnight on December 25. We will annex Israel and make it part of the New Kingdom. We will use nuclear bombs on Haifa, Varanasi, Lhasa, Pushkar, Rome, Salt Lake City, and New York." The announcer interjected that these cities, except for New York, were considered religious centers for all non-New Kingdom countries. There were others, such as Jerusalem and Bethlehem, but nuclear attacks on those cities, housed many loyal followers to the New Kingdom. The speech had been delivered earlier in the evening and the media was now focused on the breaking news rippling out after the speech. The president of the United States delivered what the announcer said was 'a stunning statement' just a half-hour after Rouhani's speech calling for complete capitulation in order to avoid worldwide nuclear war and extermination. He cautioned world and faith leaders to recognize that the extremist were difficult to identify, spanning every country, ethnicity and social rank. The president of France and the Prime Minister of Israel called for immediate "show of force." The United Nations immediately entered debate on multiple resolutions that had been put forth, including total annihilation of the New Kingdom. A huge crowd had formed outside St. Peter's Square in Vatican City and it continued to grow in size. It appeared that no one was leaving, and soon all of the streets in Vatican City leading to the square would be filled. The pope had appeared once on the balcony of his residence and gave a blessing. He had not made any announcements, and Vatican officials were not responding to press inquiries. Tom suddenly realized that he was sitting on the edge of the sofa, totally mesmerized by what he was hearing. The announcer and his "expert panel" continued to read reports, cut to live interviews, and then return to the panel for discussion and analysis. Leaders in both Houses of Congress were condemning the president's position.

Tom had ignored his phone and e-mail all day. He wondered if he had messages that were related to this madness. When he opened his phone his screen was full, and as he scrolled down through several texts and missed calls there were two that grabbed his attention. A call had come in from Wasim Mirza at about the time he was waiting on the altar for Claire to enter the church. Tom opened the voice mail. "Mr. MacDonald, sorry I missed you on such an important day. I called to extend my best wishes to you and your beautiful bride." Mirza had a tone that was equal parts jovial and cynical. "I wish I were in your shoes tonight with such a gorgeous woman to bed. I also wanted to express my condolences to you on the loss of your brother and sister-in-law. I suppose you are struggling on this joyous day to deal with the tragic deaths of others in the industry with whom you have recently met. It seems your bad karma is spreading to others. Hopefully, you will be able to keep your bride, her prized horse, and yourself safe from such karma. Enjoy your wedding and Christmas holiday."

Tom was shaking, not with fear, but with anger. He wanted to press "call back" on the phone and verbally tear into Mirza with every-thing he could think of, regardless of whether or not it was the smart or right thing to do. He filled his wine glass and went to check on Claire. She was sleeping like a baby. He called Angel and asked him to check on Celtic King. He was surprised to learn that Angel was at the stables. Angel explained there was a strange character lurking around all day so he stayed. He said the man made the horse jumpy. He told Tom he would spend the night there and would call the police if the man came back. He vowed he wouldn't let any harm come to Celtic King.

Tom hated to do it, but he had to take all precautions. Mo sounded groggy—he could tell he woke her up.

"What is it Tom?" she said with more concern than annoyance in her voice.

"Mo, what time are you coming over here in the morning?"

"I have a cab scheduled for nine. Why?"

"At seven call the cab company and tell them you had a change of plans. That will get you here before eight, which is when I am leaving for my flight. I don't want to leave Claire alone. Please don't ask questions." Mo agreed. Tom wanted to tell her to watch her back, but he didn't want to add to her stress level.

Tom took a big sip of wine and went back to his phone messages to listen to the second voicemail that he was sure would be interesting. The Church was under attack and he was getting a call from its newest prince. "Tom, this is Frank. I am so sorry for your loss. Be assured your family is in my prayers. Hold fast and strong to your mission, and most importantly, remember, I have asked Jesus and the Blessed Virgin to guide and protect you and your family. The pope has summoned me to the Vatican without delay. No matter what is happening, I promise to pray for you at the time you requested. Please pray for me as well. Despite my transgressions, I sense I am about to be called upon. Have no doubt, nor harbor any fear; hell is on earth, and the Lord God Jesus Christ is coming. Stay strong with unquestionable faith in Jesus. God Bless you, Tom."

There would be time to sleep on the plane. He stood guard until Mo arrived. Claire was still asleep. He gently woke her with a kiss and a cup of coffee. "I have to leave now, my love. Mo is here. Under no circumstances are you or Mo to leave here until you hear from me. I am your husband now and yesterday you promised to obey me," Tom smiled knowing this would get her to laugh.

"That's a bunch a crap, boyo, but yes, I promise. Take care of yourself."

"I will, I have much to live for," said Tom.

CHAPTER NINETEEN

*And he had power to give life unto the image of the beast,
that the image of the beast should both speak, and cause that as
many as would not worship the image of the
beast should be killed.
And he causeth all, both small and great, rich and poor, free and
bond, to receive a mark in their right hand, or in their foreheads:
And that no man might buy or sell, save he that had the mark, or the
name of the beast, or the number of his name.*

Revelation 13:15-17

Tom was surprised there were as many people as there were flying from coast to coast on Christmas Eve. The few he spoke to while waiting to board and those whose conversations he overheard all had one thing in common, and that was to make it home for Christmas. No one asked him if he was going home. He guessed they all assumed he was. He was glad no one asked so that he didn't have to lie. Who would believe you were leaving home on Christmas Eve, especially the day after you were married, and only a couple of days after your brother and sister-in-law were murdered. He tried to ignore the painful reality of what he was dealing with and keep his mind on what he had to do. Although the plane was nearly empty, there was another person in the same row. Tom moved to a different row and was asleep in less than five minutes after the plane took off. He didn't wake until he was startled by the jolt caused by the wheels touching down in San Francisco. He thought for sure the flight attendant would have woke him and made him sit up for the descent and landing. A few minutes later she told him that he looked too peaceful and in need of sleep to wake.

Claire answered the phone on the first ring. "Hey—how are you? Are you okay," she questioned.

"I'm good. I slept the entire flight and just now landed. I just called to let you know I arrived safely, and I miss you and love you."

"I love you, too. Please be careful." She was clearly on edge. Tom was both careful and watchful as he made his way from the plane to ground transportation. If someone was following him, they were being very inconspicuous.

* * *

When Andy returned to the office the day before from Tom and Claire's wedding, he was told by George Corbett that he had to roll out the code. Andy promised George that he would as originally scheduled. He told George he needed until noon on Christmas Eve to prepare everything for rollout. Corbett gave him a hard time. He even had Mirza call Andy, but there wasn't much they could do. Andy was trying to buy time. He had to leave them with no time to check his final release while giving himself the time he needed to insert a Christmas gift for Tom.

Andy had anticipated that he would be murdered. He was on the inside without being an insider, and in the end they could not risk him letting the cat out of the bag too soon. The code was specified to have an external switch to turn it on for true rationing, and a switch to modified rationing. It could be switched back and forth between the two. It could be turned off, used to target people specifically, and Andy added a simple switch that allowed the modified rationing to be flipped. The flip would give resources to those that were to be denied authorization and those that the bad guys wanted to be authorized would be denied. He also used a technique that he learned when he was a programmer trainee. He was assigned to fix a program that had been developed by the company's lead programmer, who was considered to be a wizard. Andy later learned that this was a test that was given to all trainees, and all of them, up until Andy, had failed. All those before him, and those after him, gave up after about two days, exclaiming that it wasn't possible for the program to do what it was doing. Therefore, the change that they were supposed to make could not be applied. What Andy found, and the others didn't, was that in another part of the program, when a particular condition was met, it would then alter the program where the fix was to be applied. As such, the code that was on the screen in that section of the program was being modified, on the fly, in another part of the program. Unless you were able to find the other section of the program where the modification was taking place, you would never figure this out. Andy used this routine to activate the flip. He sent an encrypted e-mail to Tom, using an anonymous e-mail address, giving him the credentials to get into the system and the code to activate the flip. It wasn't fool-proof, but it would buy some time.

At exactly noon, Andy's phone rang. It was George and Wasim. They wanted an update on the rollout. "It's time to roll out the code. Are you done?"

"Yeah, it's done, but I'm not rolling it out. This code isn't for rationing. You guys are gonna use it to decide who gets food and who doesn't."

Wasim blew up. "What the fuck are you pulling? You roll out the damn code or your entire family will be killed," his voice was like rolling thunder before intense lightning.

"My wife and kids are in a safe place, so don't try to pull that con job on me," said Andy. Andy heard Wasim tell someone to get Kumar on the other line right away. Suddenly his confidence left him. He felt his stomach sink and the hair went up on the back of his neck.

They waited and Wasim spoke. "We know you moved your family to your uncle's house in the middle of the night. We are holding them captive. What have you told MacDonald about what we are doing?" Wasim was calm, always a step ahead.

"All he knows is that I am working on the rationing project. He doesn't have any details at all, nor does he know what this project is really about," Andy tried to hide his panic. Wasim put them on hold for a moment while he bridged the call. He proceeded one by one to put Andy's family on the phone so that he would know that they were all in danger if he didn't rollout the code. "How much longer will it take to roll the code out?" Wasim asked, knowing his blackmail would prove successful.

"I will have it done in twenty minutes," Andy folded.

"You either have the code out in twenty minutes or your entire family is dead. Is that clear?" Wasim's voice trailed off with a hiss.

"Yes, I understand. Let me go so I can get it done," said Andy. In just under fifteen minutes he called George and told him that everything was complete.

George tied Wasim into the call. "Wasim, this is George and Andy. It is finished."

Mirza sounded calm and reassuring. "Andy, you need to keep your mouth shut if you want your family to live. I want to assure you that they are fine and will be fine. They will think it was extremist who were trying to force you into something so they would have money for their activities. Tell them that you had to do what they said so that they could live. They will love you for it," said Wasim. Andy began to believe he and his family might make it through.

* * *

Tom went to pay for his cab fare and the cabbie told him his card was declined. He retrieved another card from his wallet and it, too, was declined. Finally he tried his American Express card, confident that card would work. Declined. "It has begun," he whispered, eyes wide. The cabbie looked at him and asked what had begun. Tom didn't think it would have any meaning to the cab driver but had lost all filter. "The devil controlling payments," he blurted out.

The cab driver looked at him knowingly. "I wouldn't be surprised. Half the fares I've tried to collect the past hour have been denied. It's either the devil or people running out of credit from overspending on Christmas gifts." Tom had enough cash to pay the cab fare. At the front desk he had the same problem with his card. Fortunately he had enough points available from all his business travel to cover his stay. He was thrilled when the desk clerk said there was a package for him. He glanced at the package and smiled when he saw that it was from Bill. He got into his hotel room at 6:00 PM Pacific Time. As soon as the door closed behind him, he called Claire to check on her. Claire answered. He could tell by her voice that something was wrong. She had been crying. "Tom have you heard any of the news."

"No, I just got into my room. What is it?"

She couldn't talk without sobbing. "The pope . . . the pope had just started the midnight Mass when he was gunned down by three extremist wielding machine guns."

"Oh my God. It's all coming down on Christmas Day."

"It seems the pope had expected this and he had summoned Cardinal Francis from Philly to Rome. The pope left a document indicating that your friend was to be the interim pope until the conclave could be assembled and elect a new pope. Pope Francis III immediately had locked up the archbishop who would normally succeed the pope. He's been implicated in the assassination," explained Claire. She was managing to tell the story but she was still sobbing heavily.

Tom said, "Claire it will be okay."

"No it won't! Like you said, it is all coming down. Andy, Barb, and the kids were found dead this afternoon. It was reported as a murder-suicide. Supposedly Andy shot Barb, the kids, his aunt and uncle, and then killed himself." The dam broke and Claire was now sobbing uncontrollably. Tom wasn't sure what to do. He didn't want to leave Claire in such a state, but these developments were breaking him down, and he knew he had to stay strong no matter what happened.

"Claire, I know this is terrible but I think we can still survive this. We have to believe that God will help us make it through," implored Tom.

"I am trying," said Claire. They swore their love to each other, and Tom tried to refocus.

He called room service and ordered a bottle of wine, salad, baked potato, and a New York strip steak. He was going to have to pay cash since his points would only cover the cost of the room.

Tom opened the package from Bill as if it were a Christmas present. There were four little envelopes and a piece of paper with typed instructions on how to use the fingerprint covers. There were four clear-to-flesh colored extremely thin finger covers made of a latex material. There was one for his right thumb and the first three fingers next to it. That made sense, since neither he nor Bill had any idea which finger they would use. Nelson probably didn't use his pinky finger when he held the glass. Fortunately, Nelson had only touched the glass once or twice, so it was unlikely the prints were smudged. Tom looked over the instructions and the finger covers carefully. *This is going to work.* He would put them on just before he left in the morning.

Tom had the TV on so he could listen for any news updates from the Vatican. The anchor said they were expecting Pope Francis III to make a statement very soon. He turned on his computer to check his e-mail while he waited for dinner to come. As expected, there wasn't much e-mail. The business world really slows down on Christmas Eve. His eyes were instantly drawn to the e-mail from Andy. It felt so strange reading an e-mail from a man who was now dead. Andy had modified the rationing system so that it could be flipped. There was a knock on the door. "Room Service," a man announced. Tom was very cautious and looked through the peephole before opening the door a crack. The man in the doorway seemed to be a bona fide waiter delivering his meal. It looked good—as it should, for $75.00 without tip. When he was done eating, he poured a fresh glass of wine and decided to try Andy's program flip. He proceeded cautiously and followed the link Andy provided. He triple checked the ID and password as he entered them. The change was easy to implement. He waited a few minutes before calling the front desk. "Yes, good evening. This is Tom MacDonald in room 724. I had some trouble checking in with my credit card, but I have since contacted my bank and I think we have the problem resolved. Could you please run my card number and see if it's working now," Tom asked. After a moment's pause the answer came. "Mr. MacDonald you are back in business. Your card was approved."

* * *

Wasim Mirza was at dinner with two board members and was closing out his check. The server came to the table and with great discretion, whispered to him that his card was declined. He looked like he would burst. His eyes flashed left and right, and finally he reached into his suit coat pocket and pulled out his billfold to present another card. One of the board members realized what was happening. "Wasim, I didn't think your card would be declined regardless of the balance," he said facetiously. The board member wore a wry smile and exchanged a baleful glance with a few of the other members. Mirza looked at them with putrid disdain. "This isn't funny," he snapped. The server returned in less than a minute with more bad news. This time Mirza went ballistic. "It must be your system! I am the chairman of Universe Card and there is no possibility my card is not good. Get the manager out here!" The board members were amused, but they knew Mirza well enough to know they better not chide him anymore about the situation or he might launch on them.

The manager came to the table having been undoubtedly briefed by the server. He apologized for the inconvenience and said he would comp the entire check. Mirza felt vindicated and flashed a smug grin. He stormed out of the restaurant, leaving the board members alone at the table.

Mirza's chauffeur saw him come out of the restaurant and darted promptly toward the entrance, cutting off the valet. The valet had to slam on the brakes to avoid hitting the limo. Another valet opened the rear door for Mirza before his chauffeur could get out of the car. Mirza sat down and called George Corbett.

"George, I just had two of my cards declined. What the hell is going on?" shouted Mirza. Corbett was dying to ask if the accounts had good funds, but knew Mirza wouldn't respond well to a joke.

"I am not sure. We turned on the rationing program as you instructed for an hour to run a live test and we got a lot of declines. As far as I can determine, the first cards we declined were those of high-earning Catholics, but then it turned around and started declining high-dollar non-Christians. Since volume was down because of the hour and the day, we let it go a little longer to try to debug it on the fly. We finally decided a few minutes ago to turn it off." Mirza was fuming. "I don't care WHAT the hour or the day is—figure out what is wrong and fix it. I want this system turned on by 10:00 AM Pacific Time tomorrow morning!" He ended the call and told his driver to take him to his mistress' apartment.

* * *

Tom was tired, but he was anxious to hear what Frank had to say. The news anchor said that the pope's address was expected to be at 1:00 AM EST. In the interim they ran a story about a string of inexplicable card declines that occurred on Christmas Eve. The restaurant must have leaked the details about Mirza's card being declined and it was included in the story, mocking his bad experience. Tom reared back on the couch, laughing with joy. He wished he could have seen it happen. At 10:00 PM PT, Pope Francis III appeared on the balcony of the pope's apartment overlooking St. Peter's Square. There was a bulletproof shield covering all sides of the balcony. Frank looked different. He was not Frank anymore. He was transformed physically as well as the way he carried himself. He was now clearly Pope Francis III.

"We are saddened by the great loss we have experienced today. Nevertheless, it is important that we recognize our Lord is with us. Hold fast to your faith in Jesus and he will protect you. Speak out, and when necessary, defend yourselves from the forces of evil that surround us." He asked the crowd to join him in prayer. He led them through the entire rosary, citing the joyful mysteries. When the rosary was done, he looked to the sky, and raised his hands toward the heavens. "Jesus, on the blessed day of your birth, come to us and give us your loving peace and protection." He looked back to the crowd. He smiled like a father would smile at children he loved so dearly. He blessed them and wished all the people of the world, Christians and non-Christians, a joyous and blessed Christmas Day.

Tom took Pope Francis' words to heart. He finished the bottle of wine, and went to bed. His last thought was that *Christmas and the day of reckoning have come.*

CHAPTER TWENTY

*And the kings of the earth, and the great men, and the
rich men, and the chief captains, and the mighty men, and every
bondman, and every free man, hid themselves in the dens and in the
rocks of the mountains;
And said to the mountains and rocks, Fall on us, and hide us from the
face of him that sitteth on the throne, and from the wrath of the Lamb:
For the great day of his wrath is come; and who
shall be able to stand?*

Revelation 6:15-17

*And out of his mouth goeth a sharp sword, that with
it he should smite the nations: and he shall rule them with a rod of
iron: and he treadeth the winepress of the fierceness
and wrath of Almighty God.
And I saw the beast, and the kings of the earth, and their armies,
gathered together to make war against him that sat
on the horse, and against his army.
And the beast was taken, and with him the false prophet that
wrought miracles before him, with which he deceived them that had
received the mark of the beast, and them that worshipped his image.
These both were cast alive into a lake of
fire burning with brimstone.
And the remnant were slain with the sword of him that sat upon the
horse, which sword proceeded out of his mouth: and all the fowls
were filled with their flesh.*

Revelation 19:15, 19-21

Sometimes you wake up in a hotel room after the first night and you are not sure where you are. Sometimes, the first night in a hotel room, Tom would have trouble sleeping. This time he had slept through the night like a baby, and he awoke as the first light came between the slit where the two drapes didn't quite meet in the middle. He knew where he was. His heart rate and blood pressure soared. He was wide awake. *Yes, this is a big day and butterflies in the stomach are natural, but you can handle this; the Lord will be with you.* He took several deep breaths, said a quick prayer, and within a few minutes he had gained his composure. Tom had ordered breakfast the night before and requested it be delivered at seven thirty. That left him plenty of time for a leisurely cup of coffee, shower, shave, and time to get dressed.

Tom had packed his best clothes. He planned his attire as a boardroom presentation outfit. White shirt, three piece tailored Brooks Brothers blue pinstripe suit, dark cordovan wingtips and matching belt, and a blue and silver tie. He spent extra time this morning, as he would for all big meetings, making sure that his shirt was neatly tucked in military fashion, and that his tie fit the "v" in the collar as though it were sewn in. Not a strand of hair was out of place and his part was perfectly straight. He was ready for business.

He avoided his cell phone and e-mail so that he would not be distracted. He knew that he would need absolute concentration. He even prepared a checklist to make sure he didn't miss anything. He brought his thin, lightweight briefcase, into which he placed copies of Sal Asante's affidavit, his written summary of what he knew of the conspiracy, his hand gun, which he would ditch when he arrived at the Universe Card office building, cell phone and lap top. He carefully put on the false prints that Bill procured for him. He felt fully prepared. He told himself he had done his homework and was ready for the test. He looked at his watch and, seeing that it was time to go, he made one final check in the mirror and walked out of the hotel room.

He didn't want to be a sitting duck waiting in line for a cab nor sitting in one. He planned to walk the four blocks from the hotel to the office building. He wanted to stay moving so he took his chances on foot. The street was still crowded with people rushing to work. He walked briskly, keeping an eye out at all times. Whenever he had to stop he would look over his shoulder. At the second light, he turned his head and saw Saeed staring at him from across the street. As their eyes met, they both reached for their guns. Saeed carried his pistol in a shoulder holster and drew it faster than Tom could open his brief-case and pull out his gun. As Saeed leveled his gun at Tom a lady screamed and the man standing next to Saeed pushed his arm up into the air. A shot slammed into the side of the building next to Tom. Tom went into a policeman's firing stance and took down Saeed with three rapidly fired shots that all slammed into Saeed's chest, knocking him backward. The people all around the intersection ducked or dove to the ground when the lady screamed and the gunshots roared. Tom walked across the street. He casually continued walking past Saeed's lifeless body. The bystanders were so stunned that no one said a word or attempted to stop Tom.

When he crossed the last street and was no more than twenty yards from the Universe Card office building he dropped his gun onto the street and without missing a step, kicked it into the culvert. He didn't want to draw any attention to himself as he entered the office building.

Tom arrived fifteen minutes early because he wanted to get the lay of the land at the security desk that led to the executive elevators. Between eight forty-five and eight fifty-five, a steady stream of chauf-feured limos pulled up to the door and dropped off a member of the board. One by one they entered the building, approached the guard station, placed their index finger in the bio reader, and were allowed to pass through the metal detector and enter the elevator. The last to arrive was Wasim Mirza. He waited for his driver to open the limo door and then walked into the office building with a posture and bearing telling the world that he was the lord and master of Universe Card and this building. The expression on his face was the only tell that he was in a foul mood.

Mirza strode past the guard station toward the metal detector. The guard informed Wasim that he had to be positively identified by fingerprint to enter the building. "Peter, you know who I am, and I am sure you also know that there is a disease spreading around the world. I do not want to expose myself just to satisfy a requirement that should not apply to me," said Wasim impatiently.

"Mr. Mirza, I have my orders and procedures to follow. No one, under any circumstances, can be allowed to enter the executive offices of Universe Card without a positive fingerprint identification. There are absolutely no exceptions."

"If you value your job you will let me pass." Mirza pushed Peter aside and walked around the metal detector and directly into the elevators.

Tom was concerned. Peter was the guard that knew Nelson Glassman. Peter said something to the guard at the metal detector station and the guard moved over to take Peter's place at the primary guard station. Peter walked about five steps to the side of the station and, looking at his cell phone, was calling someone. Tom guessed he was obliged to report any disregard for security procedures to his boss. Tom saw his opening. Tom stood only two steps away from the guard stand, when Peter stowed his phone away and headed back toward him. "The boss isn't available," Peter said to the other guard. "You can go back to your station."

Peter turned to Tom. "Good morning, sir. Here for the board meeting?"

"Yes, I am."

Tom placed his finger into the reader. He was close enough to see the display screen. Whoever Bill hired was an expert. The name that appeared on the screen was Nelson Glassman. Peter looked perplexed. "Sir, I know Mr. Glassman, and you are not him. Who are you?"

Tom didn't hesitate. "My name is Tom MacDonald. I am a management consultant and I was invited to the board meeting by Mr. Glassman prior to his untimely death."

"Well, Mr. MacDonald . . . ."

Peter was cut off by a voice to Tom's right that he instantly recognized. It was Jim Martin. "Peter, I'll vouch for Mr. MacDonald."

"Mr. Martin, I know you, and know you are on the list, but I can't let this gentleman in. Especially, since he seems to have lifted Mr. Nelson's fingerprints. My job is already in jeopardy. If I let this man in without proper credentials I'll lose my job," explained Peter plainly.

Jim looked at Peter with great sincerity. "Well, Peter. I know this is a difficult decision, but Mr. MacDonald and I need to let the board know about something that is vital. Who would you place your trust in, me and Nelson Glassman's substitute, or Wasim Mirza?" Jim responded with equally plain terms.

"Mr. Martin and Mr. MacDonald, you may proceed. I have no doubt I am going to get fired today one way or the other."

Both Tom and Jim simultaneously said, "Thank you," and laughed at themselves. Jim thought it was funny. Tom's laugh was nervous relief.

Inside the elevator and headed to the thirty-seventh floor, Jim looked at Tom, shaking his head. "This would have been easier if you had trusted me from the start."

"Sorry, Jim, but I didn't think there was anyone I could trust. Thanks for getting me in here. My plan wasn't working," replied Tom.

"So, now what are you going to do?"

"Try to convince the board that they aren't voting on rationing but something very wrong and dangerous."

As the elevator slowed and just before the door opened, Jim got in a few last words. "Good luck. It's your show now, and where I can, I will support you."

The hallway leading to the board room was stately, with plush blue carpet, dark, heavy wainscoting on the walls and pictures of the previous chairmen of Universe Card. Jim opened the board room door for Tom and he entered, with Jim right behind him. The room was both impressive and intimidating. The walls were solid wood, with glass panels from floor to ceiling, spaced evenly every ten feet on the wall facing the outside of the building. There was a skylight that gave a slight glow from natural light on the table and the edges of the room had a similar but subdued lighting that came from concealed points in the ceiling. Mirza was seated at the table in between two of the glass panels, as if to highlight his importance and position among the board members. There were two empty chairs almost directly across the board room table from Mirza. Tom and Jim started to move toward the chairs as if they belonged in the meeting. As Tom approached the first empty chair, he noticed that the man seated to the right of the chair he was going to take looked at him with a faint, knowing smile on his face. It was the "minister" he had met on the flight to Philadelphia. Tom was focused on his mission. He did not acknowledge the phony minister.

Mirza was about to burst a blood vessel, his head seemingly swelling with rage. Each hand grasped the edge of the table like he was going to try to shove it so that it would press Tom against the opposite wall.

He finally exploded. "What do you think you are doing barging into this board meeting, MacDonald?"

"Well, since you asked, I am here to tell your board members that they're not here to vote on rationing. This whole agenda is a ploy for power so you can determine not how much food someone gets but rather whether or not they get any food at all," Tom's words hung in the room as Mirza scanned the room for reaction.

"Get the hell out of this room, MacDonald, or I will have you physically removed by security!" Mirza rose from his chair and started toward the door.

One of the board members looked at Tom. "Sir, who are you, what do you do, and why should we listen to you?" Mirza stopped walking and looked at Tom.

"My name is Tom MacDonald. I am a management consultant specializing in the payments processing industry. I've worked with Jim Martin—he will vouch for me. I'm filling in for Nelson Glassman. Nelson planned on saying to you today what I would like to say. Unfortunately, Nelson was murdered because of his knowledge of Mirza's plan and his intentions," Tom's glare poured into Mirza as the board processed what he was saying.

Mirza stepped up to the table and slammed down his fist. "That's a damn lie!"

The same board member who asked the question calmly spoke. Wasim, I'd like to hear what he has to say. I think this board can judge whether or not his story has any proof or merit." Mirza started pacing as the gray-haired gentleman looked at Tom, saying, "You have fifteen minutes, Mr. MacDonald. Please proceed."

Tom opened his briefcase as he began his story, starting with the three dead Christian board members.

* * *

Pope Francis III did not forget his promise. He moved the Christmas Day Mass from its usual time to exactly 9:00 AM PT. As he stood on the altar waiting for the procession of the co-celebrants to ascend to the altar with him, he prayed that the world would be at peace today and that his friend, Tom MacDonald, would do his part. The pope's homily would be centered on the idea of each person on earth treating one another, each day of the year, the way that they would treat their most cherished loved one on Christmas Day. He would call for peace and charity throughout the world to replace war and poverty. Although that is what he would say, as he stood waiting, he could not help but think about the briefing he received the day before. There was a significant bounty offered to all New

Kingdom extremist for his assassination. In addition to the bounty, there were no less than five cells of extremist who were prepared to act on well-planned assassination attempts. They wanted the pope of the Catholic Church dead no matter what the cost. There were nuclear bomb threats on the Vatican that were deemed legitimate by global intelligence agencies. Pope Francis III had been told at the briefing that he needed to be shielded at all times and that it would be best if he made no public appearances until "the current imminent crisis had passed." He thanked his advisors for their thoughtful wishes, but for the very reasons they stated, and because of his duty to the flock, he needed to demonstrate his faith in God. He needed to be visible and unshielded. As he reflected on this information, he reassured himself that the Lord was with him and would protect him, and that he needed to give all around the world, not just Christians, the firm belief that no matter how bad things seemed that they must maintain their faith.

* * *

Asad Rouhani was at his desk and on his phone at 9:00 AM PT when he called his generals, giving the order to proceed with the ground invasion of Israel and to launch the nuclear attack on the ten largest religious cities in the world.

* * *

At noon ET, the president of the United States and his family were seated in Pew 54 of St. John's Church, known as the Church of Presidents, which is located across the Lafayette Square from the White House. All eyes, including the minister's, were on the president as the service began. He looked calm and confident.

* * *

Tom told the story from beginning to end and had allowed a few minutes for each of the board members to read his and Sal's affidavits. He included each attack and threat on his life. He recounted the painful, gruesome deaths of Sal, his brother, John, and Andy Newcomb, and their families. As Tom spoke, Mirza paced back and forth within ten feet of his chair. He would occasionally look at Tom with a look on his face of total hate and rage.

When Tom finished mounting the charges against Wasim, the gray-haired board member spoke. "That is a very interesting story, and I certainly subscribe to the theory that where there is smoke, there is fire, however, as Mr. Glassman said to you we need hard proof. Can you provide it," he asked.

"Yes, but not until the rationing protocol is implemented. When it is, I can assure you that my credit and debit cards will not work. It was turned on briefly last night. My card was declined as I attempted to pay for my cab fare and register at the hotel. I used the codes and the procedure that Andy Newcomb sent to me to me to flip it back. Either that procedure worked or the protocol was turned off," said Tom.

The gray-haired board member's eyes scanned between Tom and Mirza, scrutinizing both men, sizing them up. "I find that interesting," he replied. "What time did you make the switch Mr. MacDonald?" he asked.

"It was a little after 7:00 PM Pacific Time, sir."

He mused, "Very interesting. We were at dinner last night and as I recall, Wasim, you had trouble closing out your check at about that time, didn't you?"

"Yes, I did, but it was a card reporting problem. That had nothing to do with this preposterous accusation," said Wasim.

"Mr. MacDonald, is there anything else that you can offer in the way of proof," asked the gray haired man.

"Sir, you and the other gentlemen sitting around this table are the board of directors of Universe Card. You have a serious responsibility to card holders and in this case, world security. I think you should have the rationing code reviewed—" Tom stopped. Mirza's arms flew up in exasperation and rage as he ran at Tom. The time was exactly

9:17 AM. Most earthquakes, Tom thought, started with a rumble. This quake was instant and fierce. The building swayed, windows shattered and glass showered the boardroom. As the earth shook and the building trembled, Wasim and many other board members were unable to keep from falling out of the now open windows. Mirza's face, framed by the hollowed out window panes for his final moments on earth were disbelief and fear incarnate.

* * *

At 9:17 AM Pacific Time, Pope Francis III was about to rise from his chair and deliver his homily when he saw two men step out of their pews. They were both in the second pew; one at the end of the left aisle and the other at the end on the right. They both started walking toward the altar slowly removing large-caliber handguns. As they reached the first altar steps they lifted their guns toward the pope. Everyone on the altar rushed forward, prepared to give their lives to protect the pope. The congregation was stunned, wide-eyed, and many with their mouths agape, but not a sound came forth. The assassins suddenly vanished. The pope stood, raised his hands and signaled for them to be calm and to rise. He walked to the pulpit and made one small change to his homily. "Surely, the Lord is with us this day."

* * *

At exactly 9:17 Pacific Time, with all eyes in the church still upon him, the president of the United States disappeared in plain sight of all in attendance at St. John's. Asad Rouhani disappeared, as do numerous other global business and government leaders.

***

The New Kingdom Army was in and had already travelled across most of the desert, headed toward Israel, when Rouhani gave the order to advance. The Israeli Army was prepared and was headed toward the New Kingdom Army with every man and weapon available to them. The air forces of both armies were now engaged in a fierce air battle in the air space above the New Kingdom Army. Witnesses, mostly members of the Israeli Army, report that they saw a great white cloud, shrouding a blinding light beaming down from the sky. The light swept across the dessert. The New Kingdom Army was massive and in clear sight when the cloud enveloped them. In but a few minutes the entire army was gone. Some of the witnesses swear they saw what they would have imagined to be Jesus flanked by angels in battle attire, like in the paintings in churches. The cloud went back high in the sky and then vanished at nine twenty. The Israeli Air Force reported being "swallowed by a cloud, blinded by a light, and then suddenly the cloud and the New Kingdom Army and its planes were gone."

* * *

At 9:10 AM Pacific Time, the New Kingdom Army launched ten missiles, as threatened, at the ten most religious cities in the world. All other nations with nuclear weapons were already on high alert, prepared for immediate retaliation. At most of the command centers, the same scenario playing out at NORAD was occurring. Major James Wilkinson was not surprised when one of his operators reported missile firings in the East. He was not surprised when his other operators reported moments later that launches were taking place in other countries, and signals indicated that they were both retaliatory and aimed at targets of opportunity. Although not surprised, Major Jim, as his men affectionately referred to him, was scared to death. He was a seasoned veteran of the Middle Eastern wars. He looked down at his hands, clenching and releasing to steady them from trembling. He knew his biggest fear, the possibility, which they had always talked about, was about to play out in front of him; an all-out nuclear war. The reality was worse than anyone's fears. The muffled voice of one of his operators shook him from his waking terror. "Major, my read is that all, I repeat all, nuclear missiles have been launched. Sir, there's been an override. It looks to have effected more than our base. Sir, every nuke on the planet is in the air."

* * *

The quake quickly reduced to moderate shaking and within twenty seconds subsided. A guard entered the board room. "Gentlemen we need to evacuate the building. I will lead you to the stairway, and ask that you calmly and quietly leave the building." As they started to proceed from the room, the gray-haired board member looked at Tom. "Please send us an invoice for your services." The gray haired man turned to face the surviving board members. "It appears we need to find a new chairman. I will reschedule our meeting."

* * *

The relief of feeling the sun on his skin as he exited the building quickly changed as Tom saw the scene outside. He and Jim ran to the side of the building where Wasim and the other board members fell. There were several bodies on the ground. They were all attended to by ambulances that had rushed to the scene and good Samaritans who were trying to help those who were knocked over by the quake or struck by debris that had fallen from the buildings. It looked like a war zone. "I don't see them anywhere," said Jim.

"Neither do I. They must be here, though. Let's split up. I'll cover the other side and you cover this side. Yell if you find something." After a few minutes they met back in the middle of the street. Tom walked slowly toward Jim, their expressions deflating as they realized the other had found nothing. "Tom, they're not here. It's like they vanished into thin air." Then it began. The greatest fireworks show in the history of man. Smoke filled the air. Tom turned away as from the searing light flashing across the sky, covering his ears from the assault of large bangs like sonic booms and huge flashes of light high in the sky.

Tom pulled out his cell phone. "Tom! Oh Tom, I'm so glad to hear from you. Are you okay?"

"Yes I'm fine. Claire, are you seeing this?"

"Yes, I certainly am."

"Any idea what it is," asked Tom

"The reports are coming in quickly. The information is incomplete but the indication is that missiles were fired in the East. There was then a retaliatory response. Massive system failures were reported at every major military base in the world. No one seems to be able to explain how, but every nuclear war head on earth was launched." Claire paused, taking a breath. When she began again, her voice was filled with a tangible joy, her smile evident in her voice. "Tom, when the nukes were launched something happened. They were all sent off course. They've been detonated in space. We've called on every expert we've been able to get on the phone. What happened is impossible."

Tom couldn't speak for a moment as he was overwhelmed with emotion—gratitude, relief, a swelling love knowing God had protected him, had protected the world from evil. He closed his eyes and turned his face toward the sky. Claire continued. "Tom there is so much more to the reports that are coming in from all over. The New Kingdom and their leaders have vanished. Their weapons have disappeared."

"Can anyone explain what happened," Tom smiled knowingly.

"No, but I would say it was the hand of God."

"Exactly! Merry Christmas, Claire." said Tom.

"Merry Christmas, you earned it," she replied.

EPILOGUE

Every news station on the television was working frantically to keep up with the inexplicable events. Accounts poured in detailing the swift intensity of the earthquake, the epic lightshow in the sky, searing lights, ear splitting booms, the miraculous disappearance of the New Kingdom extremist and their weapons but nothing that could be proven. All the pictures documenting the events were missing. Countering the spectacular reports was an equal amount of speculation, especially among the scientific community. Modern science can explain everything away.

The gray-haired board member was the president of National Foods, a large grocery store chain. In an article appearing in the *Wall Street Journal*, he indicated that he suspected Mirza was up to something citing that he had too strong an interest in rationing.

Pope Francis III was unanimously confirmed as pope in a special session held immediately after the Christmas Day Mass. In the aftermath of his attempted assassination, and the rapture in reverse, he appeared briefly on the balcony of his residence to a crowd estimated in the millions. "On this Christmas Day we have been given a great present. It is important to realize that a power greater than ours has intervened. Let us use this great gift to live in peace, loving all our brothers and our sisters as ourselves."

A short, anonymous press release was issued to major news stations:

Over two thousand years ago, I sent my son to you to open the gates of heaven. He was, is, and shared with you the Way *and the* Light. *Many did not follow. He has given you a second chance and shall be among you for a while. Follow his way and you may live in peace and prosperity eternally.*

As the news reports came out, despite the pundits and rationalizers, the churches filled to capacity all over the world on Christmas evening.